RUN & HIDE

MYTHS & MONSTERS
BOOK 1

BEATRIX HOLLOW

Copyright © 2021 by Beatrix Hollow

All rights reserved.

No part of this book may be reproduced in any form or by any electronic or mechanical means, including information storage and retrieval systems, without written permission from the author, except for the use of brief quotations in a book review.

❀ Created with Vellum

FOREWORD

Book One in the Myths & Monsters Series

Run & Hide is a monster romance with multiple love interests the female lead will not choose between. There are mature themes including sexual content, significant violence, language, and etc. This is book one of a series and will be slow build, meaning not all love interests are introduced in book one.

In this book, ASL (American Sign Language) is written out as American English for clarity purposes.

Content notes can be found on my website or the goodreads description.

PLAYLIST

Spotify Playlist

Courtesy Call - Thousand Foot Krutch
Beggin' - Måneskin
Monster (Dotexe Remix) - Nightcore
Take Me Home, Country Roads (Metal Version) - Leo
Stalker's Tango - Autoheart
Shut Me Up - Mindless Self Indulgence
Somebody's Watching Me - Hidden Citizens
Thriller - Little V.
Scream - SAINT PHNX
Rock Anthem - Black Violin
I Wanna Be Your Slave - Måneskin
Monsters - Ruelle
Nowhere To Run - Stegosaurus Rex
Killer - The Hoosiers
Slept So Long - Jay Gordon
The Wolf - Siames
All I Ever Wanted - Basshunter

Playlist

Game of Survival - Ruelle
Lay All Your Love on Me - Amberian Dawn
Hunt You Down (feat Ruby Friedman) - The Hit House

1

Ava

The venue was uncomfortable chaos. A thin layer of spilled drinks was half-dried into a tacky sheet on the floor, making my shoes stick with every step.

"Excuse me," I shouted but the words were swallowed whole by louder sounds. I worked my way through the crowd, trying to politely push myself deeper into the sea of fans. I grimaced as glares continually shot my way. Finally, I made it to a couple of fans who wouldn't budge at all, stonewalling me from moving forward. *Great.*

The band Nix was too popular for this indoor venue. It felt claustrophobic under the strobing lights and the pulsing mix of wailing fans and screaming guitars. People pressed together tight enough to make breathing difficult. The mass of sweaty bodies was fueled by equal parts excitement and irritation.

I looked around, trying to find an opening. I couldn't stay back here. I'd promised Caspian I'd be here *before* the band went on but instead, I got waylaid by my mother and aunt trying to give me some kind of strange intervention about my upcoming trip. The idea of me not wanting to go into the family business and temporarily move out of the family house had them acting like I had developed an addiction to hard drugs.

The stage remained an invisible goal behind the swarming crowd. A groan rumbled from my mouth but, of course, couldn't be heard. The music was so loud I felt the bass in my heart, giving me an arrhythmia. High octane rock that skirted between pop and something grungier. There was a dark heart to the band bleeding through—no catchy chorus could drown it out.

I went sideways, bypassing the people who refused to let me by. Then the singer suddenly stopped mid-chorus.

"Ava!"

My eyes rounded as I heard my name echoed up to the ceilings—a breathless voice coming clear through the speakers. The band kept playing but the singer didn't offer any more lyrics. He was too busy *mortifying* me.

"Ava, come on!" Caspian chuckled as he helpfully pointed me out for the searching spotlight. I turned towards the stage. The crowd parted like the Red Sea before Moses, as a hundred leering faces ogled my own.

A mangled smile cut into my face as I began to push through the parted sea. People lifted their cell phones to snap a picture in case I was someone important. I wasn't, but Caspian's band was one breath away from epic stardom. Anyone he called out to by name was going to have a camera flash following shortly after. *Especially* if he paused his entire concert to yell for me.

Or at least, I assumed. I hadn't actually *seen* Caspian in years and despite talking with him every day, he gave very little intel about his fame. All I had to go on was what Google coughed up when I searched his band, Nix. There was a staggering amount more about Caspian himself than the band as a whole. Hundreds of fan pages and art dedicated solely to him, the overly charming front runner.

Caspian began singing again as I got closer, his voice rich and energetic. He was lively and his smile was bright, demanding everyone smile along with him. The crowd leaned in closer, their focus quickly diverting back to him. I relaxed as their interest veered off me.

My eyes lifted to Caspian as I pushed my hair behind my ears. He owned the stage, the crowd, the entire building. We were still teenagers the last I saw him but now he was most *definitely* a man. The youth had left his face, making him look dangerous to anyone prone to heartbreak. He was almost too attractive, *too* sexual, and now he had tattoos covering his arms that hadn't been there before.

His body was as fit as ever, an etched swimmer's build with wide shoulders and lean muscles. Considering he only wore dark jeans and a collection of metal necklaces, everyone could look on in awe at a half-naked body fit for an Olympian. Including me. That body left *no* doubt that he still swam compulsively—he couldn't be comfortable unless he was in the water at least once a day.

He moved on stage like he was in water—fluid, sensual, and hypnotic. His hips rolled, his abs hardened, and his hair kept breaking loose from the bun, long dark waves plastering to his face as his rich voice filled our ears.

This wasn't the boy I'd known throughout high school. This was a rockstar. A man that strangers adored and obsessed over. Everyone wanted Caspian—men, women, the world. They didn't even need more than a snapshot photo to become enamored.

Hands reached out from the crowd, straining, fingers stretching just to feel as if they could touch him if they tried hard enough. The glossy eyes of the entire room were filled with desperation for more of Caspian as if under a spell weaved into his music.

It took till this moment, seeing him on stage with adoration in the eyes of an overwhelming crowd, for me to truly understand how much larger than life he had become.

My ex-stepbrother was a star. Yet, I could still easily remember him following me around at home, teasing me constantly. The dichotomy left me breathless, feeling both comfortable and uncomfortable with the man in front of me.

I stopped ten feet from the stage and Caspian smiled down at me as he sang. There was dark makeup smudged around his eyes. He curled a ringed finger in a come hither, insisting I get even closer. There was nothing to do but what he asked. I'd forgotten the bewitching quality Caspian had. He made everyone want to come in a little closer and soak him in. Made you want to do what he asked. Made you want to please him.

I forgot the crowd was even here screaming, singing, recording, and watching me, as I stepped forward with stunned awe at what he'd become.

When I got to the edge of the stage, Caspian suddenly went to his hands and knees, crawling towards me like a lithe beast—all lean muscle and sensual grace, a wide smile on his face. The crowd screamed in mania. I was shocked. Then he was up on his knees, thighs spread wide right in front of me. Slickened abs and low-slung, tight pants filled my field of vision. He pulled the mic up to his mouth and in this over-packed venue he was suddenly singing only for me, a glimmer of excitement in his eyes.

That's when I realized his lyrics were sexual, a plea for an unnamed woman to give him what he craved.

A ripple of shock rolled over me. Caspian and I weren't

like that. Our previous semi-familial connection had made the possibility inappropriate. I looked around, saw people recording, and felt like I was being caught doing something wrong. As if our parents were still married, we were still in school, and someone had just caught us being a little too close.

I looked back at Caspian with a glare that made his mouth curl into a smirk of entertainment. Then he felt the need to take the teasing further. He leaned in close, his voice quieter, huskier, and his lips pressed into the mic as if it were a lover. His singing became a desperate plea for a woman to take *everything* he had—a thinly veiled innuendo that made the crowd roar in excitement.

His fingers came up, a leather cuff on his wrist, his brown eyes smoldering as he touched my lips. I felt my heart stutter in my chest.

Caspian was on his knees on stage, inching forward, leaning down. Everyone watched as he appeared to be begging *me* to lay myself bare and fuck him. I couldn't look away as his face grew closer. For a moment I became sure he was going to kiss me as he pulled the mic from his face—right in front of the entire packed venue.

My heart thumped so hard in my chest I thought people might see it through my rib cage. The entire room held its collective breath, watching his face inch towards mine.

"Caspian!" Someone yelled, their body brushing mine as they leaned on the stage, invading our space. Caspian was forced to lean back.

The woman tried to climb up but was too drunk or high. Her makeup was running down her face and her eyes couldn't focus. She finally gave up trying to get up. Caspian leaned back and began looking for the closest security.

"I love you," she gasped, her hand driving into her oversized hoodie sweater. A gun came into view, barely clutched in her hand. *One gentle knock and she'd fumble it*, I thought, but it all happened too fast to act.

She pulled the gun up and my heart lurched, a painful pinch in my chest. She made the barrel kiss her, shoving the tip past her teeth, her fingers shaking and eyes never leaving Caspian. No one seemed to notice yet but me. Even Caspian was looking away, motioning over security.

Someone bumped her, her body spun slightly in place.

A bang went off so loud it boomed above the quiet part of the song. My ears rang high-pitched, disorienting me.

Blood sprayed, sprinkling my face. It splashed over Caspian too, as if someone flicked a well-coated paintbrush over us both. I couldn't breathe, couldn't move. The body slapped the edge of the stage and flopped to the ground. An unmoving lump of clothes and limbs that I didn't dare to look at.

Everything halted.

There was a pregnant moment of processing before the screams started—a crescendo of fear grating my ears and nerves.

Caspian looked at the edge of the bloody stage in mild disconnect. The same look someone might have when seeing a long line at the coffee shop. It was the wrong expression with someone's blood and fluid coating his face.

His eyes slid to me and I jerked my gaze away, suddenly scared of what I might not see in his eyes. Normal things like alarm and distress. He hadn't even jerked when the blood slapped his cheek. He hadn't even hesitated to look at whatever carnage the woman had just inflicted on herself.

The swarm of bodies pressed on me and began to drag me back. I reached out to the edge of the stage as a guy kept yelling near my ear, asking over and over what was going on in a panicked shout that put me on edge. Shrill cries and barked shouts were everywhere.

My attempt to grab the stage failed, my fingers slipping from the smooth, wet edge. Blood, I realized. I just swiped my hand through blood. Maybe more than blood.

Suddenly I was surrounded by panicked bodies who felt the need to flee at any cost. The tangy, fermented stench of sweat clogged my nose. Animalistic fear shone in wide, dilated eyes. My gaze darted around as I struggled against the pack and I felt someone's elbow push sharply into my ribs, making me jerk in pain.

This was bad. Panic started to develop under my skin.

A large hand wrapped around my wrist and tugged me back to the stage. I looked up as Caspian encouraged me to get on the stage with him. I crawled up and he quickly wrapped an arm around my shoulders and pressed my head down, into his chest. I clung to his warmth.

A moment later we pushed into a backstage hallway. The sounds were loud behind us, echoing around the walls on either side. Then the door snapped shut and the sounds were muffled. I tugged my head up as Caspian kept walking. He slid his hand down my head until his fingers curled gently around the back of my neck.

Anger made his features look sharp and menacing. He huffed out a frustrated sound and ran his fingers through long strands of his hair, pushing it out of his face. Then he looked down at me and smoothed out his face in an instant, replacing aggravation with concern.

"Are you okay?"

I didn't respond. Half of me still felt like I was in the sea of people, being pushed back and forth like an angry wave about to crash down. Caspian stopped immediately in the middle of the hall, turning towards me, eyes darting around my face and body.

"Are you okay?" He asked again, dark brown eyes dragging me in as he bent closer to my height. I let myself ignore the blood on our faces. I nodded and he nodded back before sighing. His hands rubbed up and down my arms, then he tugged me into him, encasing me in a hug.

My fingers slid over the rippled texture of his abs before my arms wrapped around his naked torso, hugging him back. Finally, I shook off the chaos of the crowd as I soaked in the feeling of him. It had been too long since we were like this--maybe five years now and I'd missed it so much.

An hour and a half later we were finally done with security, cops, and workers. Now the scene almost felt like a dream— a crowd thumping in chaotic energy, a girl shoving a gun in her mouth.

Caspian had made me play Candy Crush on my phone the whole time we dealt with questions and waiting around. Apparently, games helped disrupt potential trauma from being hard-wired in your brain.

"Aren't you going to play too then?" I had asked, looking up at his long body draped on the chair next to me. He'd slid his arm over my shoulders and smiled, small flecks of blood were still on his jaw that he had missed.

"I'll be okay," he'd said.

Now we were in front of a door labeled "band", where a building worker had left us. Instead of going inside the room, Caspian stood facing me, his thumbs rubbing in circles over my wrists.

"I'm sorry it all went to shit," Caspian said in disappointment. Our height difference was dramatic—six foot five to five foot two.

"It's not your fault."

"I wanted the show to be perfect for you." A frown tugged one side of his mouth. God, he was handsome. That had always been undeniable but now with the air of a grown man, it felt overwhelming. I felt stifled by it, my mind struggling to let me move on.

"You still managed to impress me in the time you had. I'm sorry I was late," I sighed. "My mom and aunt were trying to talk me out of my trip. They think the travel photography job is suspicious." His eyes slid to mine, a nervous look coming over him. Just then the door beside us opened and the drummer stood there eyeing us through his crumpled neon green mohawk. He raised a pierced eyebrow then looked at me specifically.

"This fucker tell you this was his last show? Bastard is quitting so he can—"

"Enough," Caspian snapped in a rare display of anger that left me with raised eyebrows. It seemed to shock the drummer too, who stood there dumbfounded for a moment before he gave Caspian a slap on the back and a nervous chuckle.

"I don't understand. You're quitting?" I asked, feeling personally offended by the idea. I'd only just seen him on stage but I knew it would be a huge loss.

"It's just a sabbatical," Caspian mumbled. The drummer laughed.

"Sabbatical?" I asked in confusion.

"Ava, right? See, I think what this guy really wants is to get in nature for a while. *Maybe* go on a nationwide camping trip," the drummer said suggestively. My eyes slid to

Caspian. It felt odd his drummer knew not only who I was, but what I was doing for the next year.

"Cas?" My voice held an edge of discontent. His warm eyes went to mine and he smiled.

"I was going to ask you tonight."

"Ask me what?" I countered. The drummer tugged Caspian into the room suddenly. I stepped in after them to see his other bandmates posted around on sofas, nursing drinks. A guitarist, bassist, and keyboardist--all with smeared black eyeliner, tight pants, and purposely shredded shirts. They eyed me closely with a sharp look of curiosity. I got the feeling they all knew who I was, like the drummer had, and felt suddenly uncomfortable.

"Go ahead then. Let's see what she says," the drummer said. He backed away with a smile, leaving Caspian and me in the center of the room. My eyes moved over the other band members. They didn't look entertained or friendly. It made me realize the drummer's smiles and friendliness were likely sarcasm. That he wasn't happy at all.

"I want to go with you this year," Caspian said and my attention jerked back to him.

"What?" I asked in utter confusion. He looked at me with eyes brimming with excitement. He stepped up into my space and I felt uncomfortable because his charm was making my head swim. Plus, the bodily reaction I was having to him made me feel self-conscious. He grabbed my hands, bringing them up between us.

"Ava," he started, looking like a hopeful puppy. "I'd really love to go with you this year on your trip." I looked around at his bandmates but no one acted like this was a joke. They looked disgruntled and pissed off.

"Aren't you on tour?" I asked.

"Not anymore," Caspian responded. His bandmates

visibly stiffened. The drummer barked out a laugh but said nothing. Caspian distracted me from their reaction by tracing his calloused fingers down the side of my face.

When Caspian looked at me, sometimes it felt like I was the only thing he saw. He was so intense sometimes.

"Please, Ava," his voice sounded vaguely similar to when he had been singing, when he was begging some woman to give in—to fuck him—pleading, near desperation. His eyes held mine and I responded the only way I could to Caspian. He was one of the most important people in my life and if he wanted to come with me then it was an easy answer.

"Of course."

He wrapped me in his arms, his entire body surrounding mine, slick, warm skin clinging to me. I slid my arms up his back.

My eyes moved around the room. His bandmates glared —their hatred was a palpable thing that pressed on the base of my spine.

"We'll never be apart again. I promise, " Caspian murmured but I was too distracted to comment. Death glares were burning into my face.

2

Ava

A week later, Caspian and I pulled up to an abandoned colonial revival mansion in Williamsburg, Virginia—about an hour up the road from my family house in Norfolk.

The mansion was dingy brown brick with rows of dark shuttered windows. There were exactly six chimneys and four thick white columns standing sentry at the front. They felt more like a deterrent to visitors than a welcome.

The entire thing screamed an intimidating presence, looming up into the night sky at a staggering height. Instantly, I wanted nothing to do with the place because I knew why my aunt and mom were here.

This place was haunted.

Our car doors snapped shut and I sighed in annoyance as I looked at the tv crew all set up outside, preparing everyone for filming.

"This was a trap," I complained to Caspian as we walked side by side into the fray of vans, tables, camera gear, lighting poles, and people. Caspian was wearing tight black pants and a black tank top, his defined, tattooed arms on full

Run & Hide

display. I was far too aware of his clothing choices these days.

"Yep," he said. "She really doesn't want you leaving, does she?"

"She can get over it."

"Why is she so opposed to it?" His brown eyes slid to me and I forgot to talk for a moment. Not until he gave me a curious look and I realized I'd been staring.

"Because *I'm* not allowed to be normal. She was so happy I was leaving my office job but was then personally offended by this new job. *Freelance photography is unreliable. Traveling alone is unsafe. Camping? You don't even like camping!*" I said in a nasally voice meant to make fun of my mom's nagging.

"Someone is paying me to travel and camp all over the United States for a year. Taking pictures! This is an amazing job." I looked at Caspian, waiting and hoping for his agreement. This job *was* amazing and I was lucky I'd managed to beat out the competition and win the contract. *Really* lucky. I was hardly qualified, having zero experience with product photography. I had to assume whoever was hiring fell in love with my nature photography portfolio enough to overlook the issue of professional experience.

"Yep, it's pretty cool," he said with a genuine smile as he swaggered beside me, still looking one hundred percent the rockstar despite the lack of eyeliner and a sweaty half-naked body. He had rings on his fingers, a black leather cuff on his wrist, and a teasing, confident smile that only a star could pull off.

It wasn't that I needed my family's permission—I was well past the age of needing that. Or at least I should be. It nagged at me that they were upset and worried though. I wanted them to understand and accept that I wasn't interested in the family business. It was exhausting and stressful dealing with their constant push. I just wanted them to be proud of me like I was of them.

"What's your sister say about it?" Caspian asked.

"*Leave me alone, I'm writing*," I huffed with a smile. "She's finishing her latest novel," I explained.

"Tell her I want a copy." He slung his arm over my shoulder and I stood up a little straighter. Lizzy was a fantastic writer that excelled at science fiction horror. Also, she'd frowned at me when I told her about the job.

Not a single person was excited except Caspian. I reached up and squeezed the hand hanging off my shoulder, trying to show my appreciation for his support. I watched a small smile form on the side of his face in response.

Even a week after the show, I was still a bit surprised he was going with me. However, after the initial shock, I'd really warmed up to the idea. I hadn't realized how worried I'd been about doing it all alone until I wasn't anymore. It was relieving.

I found it odd though, with his career seeming on the verge of explosion. He deflected talk about that, waving it away like it wasn't a topic that needed to be mentioned at all. The tragedy at his concert wasn't a reason because he'd been planning on asking me before that had happened.

What *was* his reason then?

"Five more minutes!" Someone barked out in the crowd of tv workers. There were cameramen, personal assistants, lighting crew, sound crew, and more; all haphazardly arranged in the dead grass of the lawn. Everyone began moving closer to the front of the house, a sense of urgency ramping up.

I spotted my mother and aunt standing at the base of the

large stairs that led up into the dark, old building. The stars of this production.

My aunt was a famed tv ghost hunter. My mom was a world-renowned medium. They were strong, self-made women that I looked up to.

They both had long black hair that reflected a brown tint. Their eyes were a deep ebony. Both had lithe bodies, thin but strong. I was perfectly okay to be more rounded out. A downfall was my thighs currently eating my shorts. I frowned and tugged the fabric back down even though I knew they'd just crawl back up a moment later. I'd have to put this pair out of rotation. It was so hard to find good shorts.

My mom and aunt looked like a couple of witches, decked out in dark clothing, big hats, and gemstone jewelry. My aunt had tattoos all over her arms while my mother was tattoo free. Which meant that despite being identical twins, no one would ever confuse them.

"Guess we have to wait," I huffed since the show was starting but my aunt noticed me just then.

"Ava! Come on, just in time!" she called out, her face remaining serious.

"Why couldn't we talk at home?" I groaned as I stepped up to them. My mom pulled me into a side hug and smiled excitedly. I looked over at Caspian and he blasted me with a wide smile, no help at all. He seemed happy enough to be dragged into this while I was exceptionally frustrated.

"Caspian, is that you!" My mom gasped, moving forward and pulling him into a hug.

"The one and only," he said, flashing a smile before he stepped back to my side.

"What a nice surprise." She seemed genuinely happy, which wasn't surprising considering she'd been his stepmom for four years. She had missed him when he left too.

"Let's put them both in the show," she said with a quick nod as if all was decided.

"What?" My eyes darted around nervously. "Show? No, no, no." My gaze drifted to the ominous house. It felt alive and angry. Its dark windows glared down at us and something shifted in one of the windows. I sucked in a sharp breath.

"Go with the flow, honey," Aunt Maria said, snapping someone over. A crew member came walking over with microphones. Caspian watched apathetically as he was clipped up. I felt my breathing quicken.

This *had* been a trap and I'd fallen for it too easily. I'd been so desperate to talk sense into my family before I left but my mom had been refusing to listen. Then, *all of a sudden,* she was willing to hear me out if I came to today's shooting.

Caspian snatched my mic from the worker's hands.

"I've got this," he said with a toothy smile that looked unfriendly. The crew guy shrugged and walked off, barking it was time to start rolling.

With my mouth hanging open, I shook my head at my mom and aunt. They quickly turned away as if not seeing and began heading up the stairs towards the door.

People swarmed around. The sound of feet hitting the wooden stairs and shuffling up mixed with barked orders and the strain of a showtime countdown.

Caspian was suddenly close. His nearness distracted me momentarily from the sudden swept-up feeling and budding panic.

I looked at his long eyelashes and slightly parted lips as he bent over. He finished clipping the microphone on my shirt and brushed his fingers over my collarbone, his eyes tipping up as he gave a cheeky smirk. He was a constant tease, finding great pleasure in making me uncomfortable.

My cheeks heated since he'd caught me staring at him *and* because his fingers continued their trail over my collarbone. He brushed his thumb down the side of my neck before pulling away with a wink.

Stop, I told myself. My body didn't listen though, my stomach fluttering weightlessly. Caspian was incorrigible sometimes. Even when we were step-siblings he was always doing things like this—flirting relentlessly just to see me blush and get angry with him.

He grabbed my hand and pulled me up the stairs towards the looming house that expelled a sense of foreboding and somberness. The top half of my body bent forward as my feet stumbled to catch up.

"It'll be okay. I'm here," he promised.

And that's how I found myself corralled into a haunted house for a ghost hunting show.

My aunt and mother walked side by side in front of Caspian and me as we wandered deeper into the haunted house. A camera crew followed our progress, pushing lenses in our face and shooting enough light to blind us from actually seeing anything in the foyer. Our noises drifted up to a ceiling far above our heads as the show recording started.

The air smelled moldy and was cooler than outside. Darkness was all around. Underfoot the thin wooden planks of the colonial house creaked with every step. I watched my feet move one in front of the other as we ascended the grand staircase, frustrated I'd somehow been tricked into this.

Would my family never stop? Did they not understand how much I hated this?

Soft fingers slipped under my chin, pushing my face up. My mom smiled at me.

"Eyes up. I don't want you missing anything. Help your aunt find something good here." She turned back forward and kept moving. I shot a glance at Caspian who looked entertained by my disgruntled nature about this whole thing.

It was amazing how five years apart from him felt like nothing now that we were back together. Of course, we talked every single day despite our physical distance. Maybe that was the reason why it felt so natural.

This was the grand finale of the tenth season for my aunt's ghost hunting show. My mother, a world-famous medium, had agreed to be in the episode. Fans were excited, their managers were pleased, and now, somehow, her niece and the lead singer of Nix were here too.

My aunt introduced us and I gave a tight smile at one of the cameras. Caspian, on the other hand, gave a smoldering wink that made even the burly cameraman blush.

I hated ghosts. Just the idea of them freaked me out. Of course, I never admitted this. Instead, I acted like the entire concept of them was ridiculous and beneath me. My aunt and mother always rolled their eyes when I said as much.

The truth was, I was terrified of ghosts. Which meant despite my grumpy face and *better-than-this* attitude, my heart was thumping in my chest a million miles per minute and I had to keep dragging my sweaty palms over my shirt to dry them. I nervously nibbled the inside of my cheek, accidentally gnawing through skin and tasting blood. I hated the flavor. It tasted like something was wrong.

Something *was* wrong.

The air inside this place felt thick and oppressive and the house continued to creak and groan as if complaining of our presence. It wanted us gone. I could feel that tension in the air like a hateful glare on the back of my neck.

I shot a glance over my shoulder at the closed front doors. There was a bad feeling in the pit of my stomach, an anxious sense of dread that begged me to run towards those closed doors and leave. My instincts knew this was a risk we shouldn't take but my feet kept moving.

Because of that, I kept gnawing at my cheek, making the wound worse—making more awful tasting blood fill my mouth, reminding me things were bad. I couldn't stop though, too anxious to control the compulsion. It made me feel mildly nauseated. I pressed my hands to my stomach and cringed, trying to will the feeling away.

Halfway up the grand staircase, a door slammed down one of the dark upstairs hallways. I wasted no time flinging myself at Caspian, clinging to his arm with wide eyes.

"What was that?" I asked in a panic. Both my aunt and mother looked back at me with identical expressions of perplexion and judgement. Caspian was unsurprised by my sudden reaction. He was the only one who knew the truth—that I was terrified of my family's calling to fame. He slid his hand over one of mine and squeezed, gentle at first and then harder. The small ache of his grip finally let my mind stop moving too fast. My body lost some tension and he loosened his hand but didn't remove it.

"Are you... *scared*?" Aunt Maria asked as if the concept was hard to grasp. My eyes zipped between my aunt and mom. I was so not admitting to being afraid of ghosts.

"Of a serial killer, *yes*," I hissed, pleased with my excuse. Honestly, a serial killer would be much more welcome than a ghost. A serial killer could be taken down by all the people standing around. A bullet would lay a man out flat but what defense did we have against an evil house and its parasitic ghosts?

My aunt shrugged and began talking about the history of the building to the cameras while moving towards the sound we heard. My mom raised an eyebrow at me, looking unconvinced.

"Hold on a minute," Mom said, touching my arm. She let the camera crew and members of my aunt's team pass us.

"Why am I here?" I asked as the crew left us behind in the dark. My grip tightened on Caspian as he stood there silently. "You said you'd listen to me."

"You know why," she said and I shook my head and sighed. Hopelessness came over me, dragging down my energy. I felt tired. She would never stop pushing. Never let me be free from this.

"You have the calling, Ava."

"*The calling*, right," I said in annoyance. The famous Luna family calling. As the saying goes, we were the daughters of the witches they couldn't burn. A generational compulsion towards the strange and unusual. An uncanny ability to sense it. And me? I got the special jackpot according to my mother.

"If you keep running, the strange and unusual will catch up with you Ava. *It's* drawn to *you*. You're charmed." She crossed her arms loosely under her chest and gave me a hard look. I didn't like this type of talk. It made me uncomfortable. Made me scratch at my arms and push away the memories of strange situations rising to the surface to defend her argument.

I didn't like ghosts. I didn't like weird, strange, unusual, unexplainable, or paranormal. I liked photography and nature. I wanted to be *normal* and in this weird family, that somehow made me the black sheep. It made me the denier, the odd man out, the rebel who needed to be put in her place.

Caspian cleared his throat and my mother's dark eyes shifted to him.

"I'm going with her this year," he admitted.

"Oh?" Her eyebrows raised and her eyes darted to where I still clutched his arm. I detached myself.

"He is. So your argument that it's unsafe for me to travel alone isn't valid anymore. I'm going. *We're* going," I said motioning at us both, feeling like a team. I walked around her, going up the stairs in search of the camera crew and its lights. I was done talking to her.

At the top of the stairs, it was dark. Somewhere off in the distance, I could hear the soft sound of feet moving over creaking boards. It made it hard to pinpoint where my aunt and everyone else had gone. The smell of mildew grew and particles of dust tickled my nose, making me sneeze.

I heard my mother talking to Caspian behind me, asking him about his music career and how the trip would work out with that. I wandered down the hallway, further from the comfort of their voices. Licking my lips, I nervously peeked into open doorways, trying to avoid the mirrors.

Mirrors were the worst, sometimes showing things you couldn't see with your eyes but could only feel rattling up your spine. Like shadowed men just behind you.

As I traveled down the hall my instincts were louder. Anxiety squirmed inside me, trying to tell me this wasn't good, we should leave. I took deep breaths through my mouth and just wanted to find the crew as fast as possible.

I saw attic stairs ahead that had been pulled down and huffed my way forward, eager to get back with everyone else.

As I approached the bottom of the ladder, I could hear

nothing above. No hushed voices, no footsteps. I felt entirely alone despite knowing others were just around the corner. They were probably standing in silence up there, trying to capture unexplainable noises on their machines. Above was foggy darkness.

My fingers wrapped around the old wood of the ladder and I went up, my hands coating in dust as I gripped the sides. The wood groaned under my shoes and I worried about the safety of the old ladder.

It wasn't until I was at the top, looking around at a dark collection of old furniture stacked around that I realized if other people had used the ladder tonight, it wouldn't be that dusty.

No one was here but me.

I felt a pressured lump in my throat that made it hard to swallow. Questions floated to the surface of my mind, like corpses in a lake. Why was the attic ladder down if no one was up here? Why was it so cold, a slow chill inching up my spine to the base of my skull?

Don't think about it, I told myself.

The room was stagnant and thick with shadows—the vague outlines of a room filled with forgotten things.

I shouldn't be here. Quickly, I turned to go back down when a noise slithered into my ear.

"Wait," it whispered, sounding like a paper-thin little girl—hollow, weightless, and tired. "Don't go." The words were faint but clear. My lips trembled and my eyes watered as I turned to look in the room.

"Is someone in here?" I asked. My eyes traced over dark lines, trying to identify everything so I didn't imagine it as something it wasn't. Dressers, chairs, tables, lamps—there was so much antique junk packed haphazardly that anyone or *anything* could be hiding in the mess.

Someone could be crouched behind the dresser right next to me, just a few feet away. My breath quickened and my muscles locked up as I imagined that was true. That maybe some evil ghost was just on the other side of the furniture, capable of jumping up with whited-out eyes and an open mouth, yellow teeth cracking. They could wrap their hollow arms around me, trap me here with them forever.

Goosebumps raised on my arms and I felt dizzy. I didn't like this, not at all. I couldn't understand how anyone in my family actually enjoyed doing these sorts of things.

Then again, they didn't have to deal with the strange and unusual coming for *them*. They didn't deal with the sense that something was always after them, wanting them, leading them away from the group, and convincing them into dark places.

"Ava?" Caspian called from below. I swallowed and turned back to the ladder, ready to go down. Ready to *run* if I had to.

"I'm coming," I called out and I heard him walking closer as I slipped onto the ladder and started to go down. The sensation of something brushing against my arm, as if reaching out to touch me, made me close my eyes and swallow a whimper.

It was nothing, I told myself, *a phantom sensation my over-excited mind invented*. I kept moving down, faster. One foot down the rung and then another. The wood creaked and bent as I slammed my shoes on it. I couldn't get out fast enough. I winced as a splinter slid under one of my fingers, burying under my skin like a bug in the dirt.

"Don't go," a whispered breeze seemed to say in that little girl's voice. I stilled with my head level with the attic floor. I swept my eyes around, dying of fright that I'd see movement under the legs of the furniture. See something running towards me.

Caspian approached the bottom of the ladder and looked up at me. Wind tickled my ear.

"He's scary," the ghost whimpered. A whispered secret from a dead little girl who should no longer know fear. *Who was scary?*

I got to the bottom of the ladder and rubbed my arms. Caspian cocked his head at my freaked expression and pulled me into him right away, rubbing my back in soothing circles. The lump in my throat finally started to relax away.

"Why were you up there?"

"I thought my aunt and the crew were up there. Come on, I'm not staying in here." I pulled back, begging with my eyes for him to follow me out. Caspian peered up into the attic then looked back down at me.

"Did something happen?"

"Of course not," I said quickly. He looked me in the eyes and I could tell he didn't believe me. "Can we leave?" I pressed, feeling desperate to get out of this house. I shouldn't have let myself get led in here.

"We can do whatever you want," Caspian said, cupping my face and brushing his thumb over my jaw. "I'm sorry I wasn't with you," he whispered as he leaned in to kiss me on the cheek. Except his lips brushed too close to mine, hitting the corner of my mouth, making me suck in a startled breath. He pulled back smiling in pleasure at my reaction then grabbed my hand and led me back down the hall.

My face tingled where he had kissed. I touched my fingertips to the corner of my lips when he wasn't looking and felt uneasy by the strong reaction such a small thing had on me.

I was in trouble with him. Here I was, feeling half

breathless from an innocent peck. Caspian was just so... *alluring* and his eyes were always glimmering with flirtation.

I knew his peck meant nothing but some part of me didn't want to agree. Which made me feel nervous. I didn't want to nurse an unrequited crush.

I tugged my hand from his. He looked at me with a frown then put his hands in his pant pockets.

A slamming noise came from behind us, startling me enough to scream. Caspian grabbed me immediately, pushing me behind him as he jerked around to face the noise.

"What is it?" I asked, peering around him, my body shivering from the sudden jolt of adrenaline. My gaze traveled down the long, dark hallway and I realized what was wrong.

I tilted my gaze to the attic door. It was closed, the ladder suddenly gone despite being down a moment ago.

The sounds of people moving fast down the hallway had me sliding beside Caspian. I didn't want to be found shivering and scared behind him. I wasn't supposed to believe in these things.

"What was that?" Aunt Maria asked, her eyes wide and face open in excitement.

"The attic door closed on its own," Caspian said and my Aunt's face screwed in confusion.

"The attic has been sealed shut for decades. No one has been able to open it," she said. My mom came walking up behind my aunt, her eyes heavy on me and a satisfied look on her face.

"You can't run from it," she said to me.

"Watch me," I ground out in frustration and anger, grabbing Caspian's hand. I stomped to the stairs ready to get out of this damned house and away from my family's never-ending pressure.

Ghosts scared me. The paranormal scared me. Yet time and time again my family tried to force it on me. They didn't get it. They never would.

My mother was one hundred percent right that I had this damn curse more than the rest of them. *A blessing*, she would always say but she didn't *live* with it. With the voices whispering through the night. With the strange things always going on around me.

No one understood the foreboding sensation that it was only a matter of time before some type of monster captured me.

"Ava," Caspian said as I tugged him outside the house, breathing in the fresh air like I'd just come up from the water. I ripped the mic from my shirt and he quickly did the same, leaving them on the porch for someone else to deal with.

"What?" I snapped and he took control, pulling me around the side of the house, away from the curious people left outside during filming. Their eyes followed us intently and I was reminded again how famous Caspian was becoming.

At the side of the house, it was dark and quiet. Goosebumps popped up on my arms as I spied a cellar door and I tried to pull up short but Caspian just held my hand tighter and pulled me a few more feet before we stopped.

He suddenly got in my space, hands going on either side of my head as my back hit the brick. His head dipped down, dark eyes peering into mine. My heart sped up and I uncrossed my arms, pressing my palms to the wall behind me.

"What are you doing?" I asked, sounding breathy. He held my gaze and the seconds stretched, anticipation growing in my gut. Finally, he sighed and pulled me into his arms. I felt myself still trembling from before. I hadn't even realized.

"It's okay, Ava," he said calmly, squeezing me in his arms and I felt my girded tension melt from my body as I clung to Caspian. I was taken back to high school, the reason Caspian knew that I was hiding my fear.

I used to go to Caspian's room on nights I heard voices or woke from haunting nightmares. It was something we never talked about and of course, never told anyone. It was a secret, me crawling into his bed trembling. Him comforting me.

He'd never ask questions, just held me. His big hands would drag from my shoulder blades to the small of my back, his fingers spreading out in warmth there. Then he'd tell me over and over it was okay, he was there, he'd protect me.

Except there was that one night... the night before he left. I'd woken up when he set me back in my bed. I pretended to be asleep, thinking he was just going to walk out in a second.

Instead, he'd gone to his knees and gently grabbed my jaw, angled my sleeping face up. His breath had feathered on my lips and then he had pressed his mouth to mine.

It had felt like I couldn't breathe but forced myself to keep my languid long breaths, acting as if I slept while my heart strained in my chest. My *stepbrother* was kissing me.

He'd forced my mouth open with his, his tongue swiping in, taking a deep kiss. The first kiss I'd ever had like that.

Instead of concern, I felt warmth, comfort, and intimacy. It had been something new, something bigger than when we laid in his bed, him telling me everything was okay. A hug and caress but a hundred times better.

I had felt excited, hopeful in anticipation, and dreamt of

what he'd do next. I had wanted him to crawl into my bed, murmuring everything was okay while he touched me between my legs. I'd never felt something like that for him before.

Nothing else happened though. It hadn't been long at all —quick, eager, warm, then over. His thumb had brushed over my lips, soaking in the wetness from his kiss. Then he'd gotten up and left.

And it never happened again because he left the very next day.

I blew out a breath, wishing that memory hadn't come to me now. It was silly to think about. I felt childish—scared of ghosts and clinging to old memories of Caspian before he was famous.

"I'm pathetic," I mumbled into his chest, inhaling the mild spicy scent of either cologne or aftershave. I felt like I was fourteen again, telling him I had a nightmare and insisting he comfort me like I was a child.

"You're not pathetic," he said, petting my head. I leaned into his body, letting myself soak in the comfort he offered. My body tingled with the awareness of his—of his long, lean body and wide shoulders. I wrapped my arms around his tapered waist and felt my breasts pressed tightly between us.

"Reminds me of before," he said. His arms tightened around me. "I know you were awake that night," he whispered in my ear and I stilled. Had he been thinking of the same thing?

"I don't... I don't know what you mean." My voice was shaky. Why was he bringing this up?

"Do you know how often you came to my bed at night? How many hours I listened and watched as you slept?"

My eyebrows furrowed. "Caspian... I don't—"

"I could tell you woke up that night," he said. I heard the complete confidence in his statement. I sucked in a breath and could suddenly feel every inch of his body on mine like electricity. My nipples grew hard and sensitive, more aware than ever that I was against his body.

He pulled back his face to look down at me. One hand came up to cup my jaw and tug it up so my mouth was facing upwards to him, just like he had that night. A vicious smirk teased the edges of his mouth. I couldn't tell what he was thinking. If this was some joke or... not. My mind swam in confusion, hope, and apprehension.

"Caspian..." My voice was an exhale and he watched my lips form his name.

A bright flash of light blinded me. I blinked, opening my eyes to see Caspian cracking one eye open and looking over at someone standing to my right. A girl stood there, holding a camera, a smile on her face as she looked at the photo on the screen.

"Who the hell are you?" Caspian snapped, still holding my face in place, not moving an inch as he kept me pressed against the wall. She tugged the camera back up and a shiny, black lens looked at us.

"Go ahead, a tabloid will pay more for a kiss shot," she said and Caspian dropped my face and sighed in annoyance. I was confused about what was going on exactly.

"What?" I asked, looking back and forth between them. Caspian pulled me away and brushed past the girl.

"Aw, come on! I need some extra cash!" She called after us but I couldn't concentrate. My mind was still all fogged up from what had just been happening with Caspian.

What *had* been happening?

3

Ava

Two days later we were five hours west, the sun just starting to lighten the sky after a night of driving. Finally, the first day of my trip was here.

Caspian had fallen asleep within the first hour on the road. I looked over at him and shook my head in annoyance to see his peaceful state. He looked like a painting—long eyelashes on his cheeks, a little smirk on his mouth, and his long black locks cascading around him.

Of course, he looked like Dorian Gray despite sleeping with a crooked neck in the car. Did he *have* to look so good? I had to stop ogling him but I hadn't been able to stop since the night at the haunted mansion. Who was I kidding? I hadn't been able to stop since the first moment I'd seen him again.

Caspian had always been attractive but for some reason, it had never affected me like this when we were younger. Probably because that wouldn't have been appropriate.

Now it was overwhelming and made my body tighten in places it shouldn't. I'd argued with myself about which was more cliche, lusting after my former stepbrother, or lusting after a rockstar.

A harsh ringing blasted through the speakers, startling me. Caspian jumped awake, bleary eyes swiveling around in a panic. He jerked over to me and put his arm in front of my chest as if protecting me from an oncoming crash. Quickly, I pressed the answer button on the car's screen before either one of us had to listen to the loud noise again.

"Ava!" My mom's voice came through like a shrill cry. I winced and began mashing the volume button on the steering wheel so we wouldn't go deaf. Caspian collapsed in a sigh, finally accepting we weren't about to crash.

"Hey, we're nearly there," I said, happy to have something to do for the final drag of the ride. My energy reserves were running empty after staying up all night.

"Please tell me you didn't *do* things with your stepbrother while in high school?" She asked in anger. My eyes bulged and I darted my gaze to said previous stepbrother, sitting right next to me. My face flamed as he looked at me with his own wide eyes of shock. Wait, why did he look guilty? He shouldn't look guilty! Also, there was something very attractive about a guilty-looking rock star.

"Mom," I gasped, mortified. "No. Just, oh my god," I whined wishing I could cover my face but I had to make sure I didn't run us off the road.

"Well that isn't what everyone else is saying," she snapped. I groaned. That picture taken of us beside the mansion two days ago was blowing up on social media. I was shocked. Sure, maybe it looked a little suspicious but we weren't actually doing anything so who cared?

Everyone, apparently.

I hadn't known this before but, Caspian was well known to have no known lovers and not date. We didn't talk about those types of things. The one time I mentioned dating life he'd hung up and I was so surprised by his reaction I never broached the topic again.

Apparently, his love life was a huge thing to certain fans. A great mystery that left devotees clinging to every potential scrap of information. So much so that no one was even talking about the girl who killed herself at his concert.

The media had also found out we were ex step siblings. The stupid picture of us was a huge deal. A talk show even argued about it.

And me? I'd been receiving death threats via social media.

My mom decided on a different tactic, to my horror.

"Honey, it's okay to tell me. Caspian was a very attractive boy and—"

"Please, mom. Stop," I ground out, My eyes slid to Caspian who was smiling at me like the cat who got the cream while he pulled his dark hair into a bun.

"I don't *want* to believe it but you cried so much when he left—"

"Mom," I snapped. "Shut up." My teeth ground together and I squeezed the wheel. My eyes slid to Caspian. He had a pained expression on his face. Great, just great. He was uncomfortable but was he really that surprised? One day he was everywhere, the next he was gone. I'd thought we were best friends. Then he just left and never came back.

He cleared his throat while my mom was berating me about my tone. She stopped mid-word.

"Oh," she said, realizing he was in the car with me and heard everything.

"Oh," I said back sarcastically before sighing.

"Hello Caspian," my mother said awkwardly. He started to talk but I spoke louder.

"I'll call later," I rushed out before smashing the end call button. Then I sagged in embarrassment.

My eyes slid to the truck beside me and the truck driver was looking directly at me. His mouth was spread in a jeering smile. I tapped the brake. I'd rather go slow than play sex eyes with him.

He drove away and unfortunately the car behind him sped up to my side. I could see movement from the car and sighed, looking over to see the guitarist and drummer of Caspian's band waving at me.

They *hated* me. Even from here, I could see the sharp, unfriendly angle of their flat smiles and their cool eyes glaring.

They were here to mess things up and get Caspian to come back as soon as possible. I hadn't expected so much drama this year. It was supposed to be photography and camping. You couldn't get more laid back than that. Except now I had the whole world, including my mom, talking about Caspian and me having sex. Then I had his band breathing down my neck in anger for something I couldn't control.

"Maybe we should have just told her," Caspian said and I jerked my head to him.

"Told her what?" I asked, my voice a little too high-pitched. He winked and remained silent.

"Told her what!" I repeated. We hadn't slept together. Well I mean, we hadn't had sex. Technically we had slept together—a lot actually—since I was sneaking into his bed most nights. My face flamed and I hunched down in my chair, barely seeing over the driver's wheel. Caspian just chuckled, a smooth sound that tickled my senses.

I just wanted to get used to being around Caspian again, push all this awkwardness in the past, and get over this stupid crush. Lately, his teasing felt almost cruel. As if he were flaunting his sexual appeal knowing full well what it was doing to me.

"That picture has been so annoying," I grumbled about the snapshot that started all this drama.

"The picture *was* something though," Caspian said, opening his phone. I grimaced. Did he have to admit it so casually? I'd looked at it more than once. It was a bit odd to see, like different people. His long fingers gripping my face, our bodies crushed together, our eyes burning into each other, our mouths cracked open and merely inches apart.

Had we really been that close? Had we really looked like that?

The two people in the picture looked a moment away from sex. The girl looked like she could barely stand—clinging, desperate, wanting. The man looked solely focused, completely consumed.

That wasn't us.

Videos from the concert had surfaced too, him stopping the song to call me forward, him crawling on the stage toward me.

Everyone was completely convinced we were having sex and had been since we were teens, living in the same house as step siblings. That tasty scandal was being eaten up by every hungry mouth wanting a bite of something juicy.

It was also making me even more aware of Caspian. All the while he was completely unaffected. He thought it was funny people said we were sleeping together. *Funny.*

He stretched his arms and his shirt lifted a little, showing off deep, cut hip muscles and a flat lower stomach. Caspian was a rare type of creature. Almost too sensual and yet it didn't seem an effort at all.

"Tell me, step sis," Caspian started while still eyeing his

phone. I rolled my eyes. He was calling me that to be annoying. "How was last night?" He asked with a slight purr to his words.

"I was up all night because of you," I grumbled. He bit his lip, his body racking with laughs. He was acting weird.

"See, nothing strange going on here," he said, lifting his phone. I saw he was recording a video and my mouth dropped open. "Me and my *dear* stepsister are completely platonic."

"Caspian," I said in desperation. "Stop." He hummed and tapped his chin.

"That wasn't what you were saying last night," he said with a chipper smile. "You said, we aren't stopping till morning."

"I— I wasn't..." I fumbled for words. I had said that exact thing but I was talking about *driving*. "This better not be some live feed," I practically growled.

"Do you want to go live? Show the world what's really going on?" He asked with a dangerously sexy smirk. He lowered his phone and leaned in close, his mouth near my ear.

"There's one way to get them to stop asking if we're fucking, Ava." His voice was smooth. I felt my heart rate quicken.

"What's that?" I asked.

"Say we are," he commented. He pulled his phone back up and I watched on the recording screen as he licked up the side of my neck. Goosebumps broke out over my skin, a shiver rolled up my neck, and my nipples hardened to tingling needy points.

"Gross." Which would have been more convincing if I hadn't *moaned* it. I inhaled sharply as he sucked my earlobe into his mouth, rolling it over his tongue. My head swam as I tried to look at the road instead of the phone's screen, recording Caspian and me.

He reached out to grip my thigh. His fingers dug in as he ran his hand a few inches higher, his pinky coming dangerously close to the juncture between my legs. I squeaked in shock. The wheel jerked and I nearly rammed into his bandmates' car. They swerved while honking angrily at me. Great, another reason for them to dislike me.

"You're going to get us killed," I said as he pulled back with a look of satisfaction on his face. He clicked around on his phone.

"You better not post that," I said shakily, trying to recover from what he'd just done. Had that really just happened? I could still feel where his mouth had been on my body. It was making me feel lightheaded. I was wet, I realized, feeling the dampness between my thighs. I wanted to groan in dismay but swallowed it up, trying to act nonchalant while my panties soaked through.

"What's so wrong with everyone thinking we're together," Caspian said with a sigh, looking out the window. "Is it that big of a deal?" He didn't care. Why would he? It was a big deal to me though, but how was I supposed to relay that to him without giving myself away?

Ten minutes later the sun had fully crested the little mountains and we were riding the off-ramp towards New River Gorge National Park in West Virginia.

This was the start of something big, life-altering. Sasquatch Inc. was paying me to travel around the country to different national and state parks for an entire year. They wanted me to take product photos of their outdoor gear while running a travel blog. Mostly they sold coolers, insulated cups, and things like that.

I may not have been some famous ghost chaser or an

acclaimed horror writer but I was chasing my dream of photography for once, leaving behind that horrible desk job that nearly killed me the past two years.

I steered the 4Runner on a one-lane road. Trees were packed tightly on both sides of us. I clicked the window down as exhaustion began to take its toll. The cool, wet air of morning spilled in from the window and breezed over my face.

The sounds of birds were all around, all different little chirps and songs. The canopy of trees parted and suddenly we were right next to the New River itself. Ironic name since it was one of the oldest rivers in the world, having spent millions of years slicing through the Appalachian mountains.

Caspian leaned forward to look at the water, his eyes animated as he swept them over the river. He loved water as much as he loved music. Although for some reason he hated the beach and ocean water. He'd joked that saltwater dried out his hair that I loved so much.

Quickly, I fumbled with my phone as I slowed. I bit back a smile as I found the song I wanted and clicked it on. The twangy tune came on and I sang out loudly with it. Caspian leaned his head back against his chair and smiled as he watched me.

"Almost heaven, West Virginia! Blue Ridge Mountains, Shenandoah River. Life is old here, older than the trees!" I continued belting out the song, disturbing the quiet wildlife. All the doubt and paranoia I let eat at me previous to now were cleansed as I took in deep lungfuls of the forest fresh air and sang. A smile spread over my face.

Caspian gave a quiet laugh, enjoying my show. A confidence I had yet to feel since starting this journey livened my body and I straightened my shoulders. I'd had so many naysayers pushing their opinions on me that it had clogged my mind down.

I'd persisted in this adventure, even if everyone else thought it was stupid or crazy. I'd been told I wouldn't last camping. That the job was suspicious. That I was running away from my calling. That I was a disappointment.

I loved my family, but sometimes I didn't always like them. Which sounded horrible but I pushed the guilt of that thought away to enjoy the view in front of me. This extended break from them couldn't have been at a better time. Hopefully, they'd come to accept my decision. Hopefully, they could be as happy for me and my interests as I was for them.

Finally, we found the campground. It was sparse even though it was still the tail end of summer. Caspian and I eyed the small numbered placards labelling each campsite until we saw number twelve, the one I'd pre-booked online.

New River Gorge National Park was the first stop on our year-long journey and we were scheduled to stay here for a week. I remembered what my boss, Ben, at Sasquatch Inc. had said about frequent social media updates and grabbed my phone after parking. When we stepped out of the car I took a big deep breath of fresh air and smiled.

This was it!

A loud bang came from my car. I shrieked and spun around. The largest bird I'd ever seen up close was perched on the hood of my car, glaring at me as if it wanted to test its claws' sharpness on my skin.

"A vulture," Caspian commented, his eyes taking in the massive bird. He rounded the front of the car and came to stand beside me. His arm slid easily over my shoulders and he tucked me into his side.

Its head was featherless, the red and black skin wrinkled. It spread its wings wide and flapped them once. It was only about five feet away from me with its beady black eyes. Suddenly another swooped in, landing on the very top of my car and then peering down at me. The high-pitched scratch of claws on my SUV's paint made me wince.

Their eyes were fixated only on me, never wavering to Caspian. It felt like an omen—as if they sensed death and came swooping down to find it.

Frustration bubbled up in my mind. I was thinking like my family would. It was just birds, not an omen. I wanted to leave superstition back in Virginia along with haunted houses and all things ghostly that crept up on me in the night.

I swallowed, tugged out my phone, and snapped a picture of the vultures before backing away with Caspian.

I looked back over my shoulder to make sure they hadn't decided they were violent predators instead of scavengers. They blinked at me, looking somehow cruel and judgemental despite having wide glossy eyes as non-expressive as a lizard's. They watched me move, their attention nowhere else.

Goosebumps popped up over the back of my neck and I gave a sudden full-body shudder.

"Scared of some birds?" Caspian chuckled, his laugh smoothing over my skin. We walked around the campsite, surveying our home for the week. There was a wooden picnic table bolted to the ground, a rudimentary fire pit, and a nice stretch of flat ground at the back, next to the trees where we could place tents.

"They just surprised me," I insisted. He looked down at me with an oddly serious expression. My eyes dragged over the hard lines of his face, angular but almost artistic.

"Would hate to see how you react to something bigger

and stranger," he said, voice deeper, eyes sucking me in. I frowned.

"Strange is not why I'm here. I'm here for *normal*."

"Right, no strange. Scout's honor," he joked, giving a two-finger salute, his serious expression vanishing as quickly as it had arrived. It left me feeling off-balance, not understanding his strange shifting tone.

"Now, you take a nap in the car. I'm setting up camp," Caspain said, pressing a quick kiss to my head. I bit my lip and averted my eyes from his, afraid he'd see something in my look that shouldn't be there. I didn't have to worry though because he darted away from me, running at the birds, waving his long arms around while he shouted. They scattered and I gave a huffed laugh.

"Thank you," I sighed, shuffling back towards the car while my eyelids grew heavy. He closed the door behind me and smiled warmly through the window before leaving me alone to fall asleep.

4

Ava was asleep and I was watching her with all my attention. Creepy perhaps, but I couldn't bear to take my eyes away. She was my own Sleeping Beauty. My hand was pressed into the window as I stood there watching her chest move up and down breathing. Her eyes twitched behind the lids and I imagined what she might be dreaming.

I couldn't stop watching and why should I? She wasn't awake to see me. Though honestly, I did it while she was awake too. She brushed it off as my charming weirdness. *Funny.*

The past five years without her had been torture. Especially knowing that she was likely dating. That someone had been inside my Ava. My teeth pressed tight together as I ground my jaw.

There wouldn't be a single day without her from here on out. She was *mine* and I'd work out the memory of anyone who dared to worm their tiny dick between her soft thighs. I'd work the memory out thoroughly.

"What the fuck are you doing?" Brandon called out. My eyes swept over Ava's face one last time before I turned to look at the other occupied campsite. Brandon, the drummer for Nix, and Matthias, the guitarist, were staring at me with strange looks. I smiled, *nothing to see here folks*, and they looked even more uncomfortable.

Couldn't a monster watch his obsession without being judged? Guess not. I sighed and walked across the little street until my shoes were crunching into the earth right beside the guitarist, Matthias.

Matthias leaned over the open instructions, squinting. He was trying to direct which pole went where to Brandon while steadily smacking his skin for mosquitos. We hadn't even been here an hour and Matthias already had inflamed red bumps covering his pale arms and calves. He shifted back, putting a little more distance between us.

"Hey," I said with a smile.

"Hey, Caspian." Matthias had a London accent worn down from years in the states. My own accent was in a similar state--although different in sound since I was previously a Spaniard. My "D" and "T" were a little too smooth.

"You know... I thought I told you not to come," I said calmly.

"Well, you don't own the campground," Matthias said with an amused huff. The man was all honed charm and sharp empathy, reading people better than most. Great for interviews.

Clearly, he hated nature. He'd looked constipated by our setting since stepping out of the car. As if some stray pine cone had woken up on the forest floor and crawled on up his ass. His pale skin held a permanent red flush and his blonde hair was damp with sweat.

He smacked his arm suddenly and gave a slew of

colorful curses as a smear of red blood trailed over his forearm, along with the smashed corpse of a mosquito. I watched as he flicked the dead bug. It launched like a missile, landing on the ground near my feet.

"Who knows, it might be fun camping," he grumbled sarcastically. "Maybe you weren't wrong about needing a short break." His eyes quickly jerked up to my face, taking in my reaction to his comment. I gave him a small smile that he eyed warily.

"This isn't a small break," I said. Brandon came walking up, looking almost as out of place in nature as Matthias. His green mohawk was looking tired and he kept sneering at the trees as if they were shouting jeers at him.

He was pissed off at me and completely unwilling to accept my choice. Matthias was too but he was trying to play good cop. Brandon didn't have the emotional control to be anything but angry and confrontational though.

"You can't just cancel the rest of our tour to chase pussy you jerked off to as a teen," Brandon snapped. "Get the fuck over it. A million groupies are clamoring for your cock at every show." He ended in a sneer. Matthias swallowed, his eyebrows going up in concern.

"Chasing pussy," I said slowly, letting the words roll around my mouth. "Just a wet, warm pussy I want to stick my overeager dick into, huh?" A smooth chuckle rolled from my mouth. I stepped up into Brandon's space and he leaned away, his face pinching in distaste. My eyes must have looked wild. I felt wound tight.

"Okay, let's calm down," Matthias said nervously. Some people could sense I wasn't quite right, something directly under the skin hiding. Matthias was a keener man than most. He could sense the undercurrent of violence lurking in the murky depths, beneath folds of sinewy muscle and smiling charm.

These two were annoying. Ava was everything. She was the reason I was in the band at all. I'd wanted her to see me. I wanted more of her attention. I wanted her to *love* me.

However, the days of us being apart were over now. I was done letting her live without me in her life. I wanted us so thoroughly entwined that she didn't breathe without me being able to count the breaths, didn't sleep without me surrounding her—every fucking inch of her pressing into me—and I wanted so deep inside her that not another being alive could touch the places I'd been.

That's why the tour was canceled.

"You should just leave. This is pointless," I said, my eyes sweeping over Brandon's face in fake pity. I gave him a little smile. Smiles were effective in getting people to do what you wanted, in smoothing out confrontation, and in making me look normal. *Look, I'm a human just like you...* not.

Brandon never seemed particularly swayed by my smiles though. It was a wasted effort. He was one hundred percent punk energy, chaotic and angry. I'd never met someone so annoyingly human.

"You're breaking contract. You're screwing us all over."

"You think I give a single shit about that?" I asked and his eyes rounded in shock.

"Don't you?" Brandon asked. Matthias shifted uncomfortably. I could practically hear him begging us to stop fighting in his mind. Confrontation made him anxious. It must be a *joy* for him to be so close to Brandon.

"The only thing I've ever cared about, and will ever care about, is her." I shrugged.

"You're fucking insane," Brandon snapped out, his face

curling in anger. He looked at me like he'd never seen me before. Matthias' gaze darted back and forth between us.

Brandon surged forward, shoving me. It was not the right choice. I stumbled back a few steps. Tension hardened my muscles, all that pent-up need and agitation from an unclaimed mate was like itching powder on my skin. The compulsion to peel it off and show the monster peeking underneath was tempting.

I turned to look at our vehicle. Ava was still tucked inside. Still asleep. That was good. There was a lot Ava shouldn't see when it came to me.

I pulled back my fist and smashed it into Brandon's cheek. I felt the pain radiate near my knuckles as his head jerked to the side. He bent over, spitting blood on the ground then looked up at me with hate bleeding from his eyes.

This wasn't the first time we'd fought. He was confrontational as fuck and once a fight came calling, I never backed down. Instead, I met it with excitement. Brandon wanted to fight? Fine, we could fight. It would be my pleasure.

I gave him a smile and then punched him again, hard enough his feet flew out from under him and he was chewing on a mouthful of dirt.

He was trying to ruin what Ava and I had. He was trying to keep us apart. The thoughts swirled in my head.

"Caspian, stop!" Matthias barked. Violence was natural to me and causing someone else pain was cathartic. I felt that relief unfurl and calm me. *This was fun.*

I stepped over Brandon, smiling as I thought about what he might look like if I kept pummeling him. He'd groan in pain while writhing on the ground. He'd claw at the pine needles and dirt to get away from me. A shudder rolled over me. He saw it and lifted his arms to cover his head.

This was a side of me Ava could never see. The side that reveled in the flush of pain splayed forcefully across the faces of my enemies.

"Fuck you," Brandon growled behind his arms. He was always snarling but he didn't know how to *bite*.

"What's going on!" I heard Ava ask and my eyes widened, my mouth dropping open in shock. I swung my head around and saw her quickly coming across the street, her long dark hair moving around her as she hurried. The sensation of electricity raced over my body, my stomach dropping.

I tried to think of something to say but my mind was swirling. She couldn't see me like this. *Fuck*!

"Brandon tripped on a pinecone, fell into a tree. Probably shouldn't be chugging beer," I said with an amused smile, smoothing my face into a calm, friendly look. I was anything but calm though. I felt like throwing up as I waited to see if she'd believe me. Matthias stood there silently, shaking his head. He wasn't going to say anything though.

"Fucking sociopath," Brandon grumbled from below me. I gave a good-natured laugh and held my hand out for him. He flinched as if I was going to hit him again and I ground my teeth. Ava might have seen his reaction and wonder what it meant.

Brandon realized the fight was over and slapped my hand away, getting up without my help.

"He fell?" Ava asked, her eyes darting around to each of us apprehensively. She stepped up to Brandon and looked at his face with concern. He looked over her shoulder to me.

Since Ava's back was to me I smiled widely at him, happy he'd be nursing a throbbing face. His lip was split, leaking drops of ruby blood onto his chin. I pressed my hands to Ava's shoulder and pulled her flush against me.

I wanted to touch her all the time, her body flush and twisted with mine. I wanted to rip her shorts off on a stage and make the entire world watch as I pushed in between her thighs, sinking in so deep she writhed and whimpered. Show them all they were right, she was *mine*.

I closed my eyes and took a deep breath. I was still keyed up from the violence and shock of her nearly seeing something she shouldn't.

Ava turned to look at me and I smiled down at her, getting lost in her gaze before I soaked in all her features. Ava had such lovely lips and soft skin. I loved the shape of her face. I loved the little hairs at her temples that never grew out. I loved the angle of her jaw, a little stronger than some women's. It matched her.

She was wearing a crop top, the fabric like a second skin. It dipped into a low v on her chest. The plump swells of her breasts were a beautiful sight. My hands slid over the bare skin near her belly until I was gripping her sides, loving how much skin my fingers could span over in this shirt.

Her expression didn't say she entirely believed the story I just gave. Apprehension and confusion were etched into her face. I'd have to be more careful. I couldn't risk this with her. Ava was strong but she was gentle to some things.

"Come on, you rest while I set up camp," I told her. For a moment, she kept trying to read me but then she let it go, the question leaving her face.

"Right, you owe me that," she said with a small, endearing smile that made me feel like wrapping her in my arms and squeezing her tight as if she were a pinata that would burst with sweetness if I could just squeeze hard enough.

She could ask anything of me. So much more than

putting up a tent. She could ask me to do horrible things and I'd do them without question.

Ava was everything to me. She was my peace, lulling the storm inside me to a gentle ripple. A raging wave became a glassy surface when she was near.

And yet... she was also the thing that threatened to send me spiraling.

The only thing I needed was to have her love me like I loved her. Why was it so *hard* for her?

I put my arm around her shoulders and tugged her towards the street to go back to our side.

"I've got a first aid kit," she said, starting to turn back to the other two. I gripped her harder, not letting her.

"They do too. It's okay," I said. No idea if that was true—nor did I care right now.

"Okay." She looked somewhat defeated. I peered over my shoulder at Brandon and Matthias. Brandon spat a mixture of blood and spit on the ground and glared at me. Matthias stood there looking resigned and tired, dragging his arm across his sweaty forehead. They were unsurprisingly pissed off with me.

I leaned into Ava and pressed a kiss atop her head, inhaling her smell before insisting she lay down in the car again.

Quickly, I grabbed water from the cooler and cracked the lid, handing that to her before closing the door. The car window was down now, I realized. She must have gotten warm, rolled the window down, and then heard the fight.

She smiled at me as she took a small sip of water.

"I'm lucky to have you," she said and I felt warmth in my chest. She reached through the window and grabbed my hand, squeezing it. I wanted to do more for her so that she'd squeeze my hand and compliment me again.

Love me, I insisted in my head.

"I'm the lucky one," I countered. She raised a questioning eyebrow and I swallowed down all the words I could give her. How perfect she was, how beautiful, how kind, how gentle. How she was my everything. How I'd never leave her and would *never* let her go.

How I wanted to climb through this window and show her how much I loved her by how hard I thrust into her body for hours on end. My perfect Ava. Even her flaws were loveable if not frustrating considering the very things she feared were the very things I were.

I leaned on the car, pushing my head through the window so that I was smiling just a few inches from her face. Her eyes widened and I saw her gaze dart to my lips. *Mmm*, I liked that.

She didn't know how much I loved her little reactions. She didn't know a lot.

Love me, Ava.

"It's true. Who else would have invited me on a cross-country camping trip?" I asked, being flippant. She rolled her eyes and gave a small huffed laugh. It made my smile grow wider, watching her reaction up close, memorizing it.

"Doesn't sound like a fair trade. You're perfect and I'm a mess."

"A beautiful mess," I said, gazing up at her. She choked on the water she was sipping and I smirked. "Now sleep," I insisted, pushing away from the car. She nodded, her eyes watering as she coughed.

Our five year break had been the right choice, however difficult it had been. I could see her interest now. She looked at me like a man—not a brother, not a friend. When I flirted she reacted perfectly and I noticed it all—the hardened peaks of her breasts, her dilating eyes, her parting lips, the way her thighs rubbed together in invitation for *me*.

Her body craved mine and she was fully aware of it. *This* was the way my mate was supposed to act. It was a relief after all those years she'd considered me a platonic void of brotherly friendship.

5

9 years ago

My dad was getting married *again*.

I leapt, diving into the river smoothly. A sigh of relief expelled from me as I closed my eyes and glided. This would be the last time in these waters. Tomorrow we left. Away from Spain, away from Europe, away from the waters I'd swam my entire life to end up surrounded by saltwater and strangers.

For hours I stayed underwater, never once needing air.

After I pulled myself out, I looked at the surface of the river. My hand rubbed at my chest, just above my heart. Last year it had begun to ache. The sensation made me cranky and mean.

It was also the reason why I hadn't complained when my dad said he was getting married again. That we were moving nearly four *thousand* miles to someplace called Norfolk, Virginia.

We were creatures with flaws—always driven towards a connection, so much so that it ached.

Dad had already had a mate, my mom. She was gone now and there was no such thing as a new one. You only imprinted once. That didn't stop his craving for connection. He had to live with the constant disturbance in his chest.

I felt bad for him. I felt bad for the women he married too since it was a doomed relationship from the start.

It was all shit. I'd rather live my life with the stupid ache in my chest than the cleaving pain of losing something so great. Of losing the one thing that could bring a nokken peace.

I walked home barefoot and naked, leaving a river dyed red in blood behind me. The mutilated shreds of every fish I could find, bobbing lifelessly on the surface, my teeth and claw marks indented into every one. I'd desecrated my beloved river.

I didn't plan to know what peace tasted like.

"WE'RE HERE," my dad said, the edge of excitement simmering under his smooth voice. My eyes slowly cracked open. It felt like it should be night but the sun was blaring down brutally. I stretched in the rental car's seat. My dad's new fiance had a last-minute emergency. Apparently, the FBI occasionally called her in, desperate enough to use a ghost medium for any help they could get. Which left us grabbing a rental instead of having her pick us up.

I blinked at the house in front of me in confusion.

"This isn't a hotel," I said, looking at the ivy-covered stone mansion sprawling in front of me. We were parked on a cobblestone driveway that looked more like a courtyard. My eyes slid to the perfectly manicured gardens and the stone fountains gushing water.

"Didn't I tell you?" My dad asked, looking at me in confusion. "We're moving in right away." He stepped out of the car.

"Fuck me," I grumbled before stepping out too. Guess a moment to readjust to the states before being jammed into a new family was too much to ask. The house had sharp roofs and multiple chimneys. It looked old and gothic. It fit with my new step mom's thing, I supposed.

"Her daughters should be home and her sister—" he stopped talking and smiled at someone emerging from the house. My head tilted to the side in confusion as I saw my dad's fiance emerge from the house and come walking towards us. My eyes slid to the tattoos covering her body and I grew further confused. His fiance had practically lived with us for two weeks while in Spain for a month. I'd definitely remember all those tattoos.

"Maria," my father said in warmth, reaching out and hugging the woman. She looked startled a moment but pulled back with a smirk as she looked him over. Seemed his fiance had a twin sister.

"Amador, I'm glad you made it alright. And this must be your son," she said, her eyes sliding to me. "You two could be twins," she joked. Wow, how fucking hilarious. I stared at her blankly a moment before turning to look back at the house. It was nice at least.

"Sorry, he's tired from all the traveling," Dad said. I rolled my eyes. They'd learn soon enough that this was me in a good mood.

"Well then, come on, let's get you two settled. My sister should be back tonight but everything is all set up for you two." We moved towards the front door, it was made of thick wood planks with iron detailing. Inside was dark with lots of wood. The rooms had vibrantly painted walls. The hall was forest green, the living room a cabaret red. The furniture was modern but the drapes and carpets looked antique.

"Caspian," Maria said, getting my attention. "My niece, Ava, was in charge of getting your room ready. I hope it's to your liking." I raised an eyebrow but said nothing. She shared a smile with my dad as if they were in on some joke. We walked under a chandelier hanging in the foyer and began going up a wide set of stairs. Then we were standing in front of a door and Maria was slipping an old key in my hand.

"That's the key to your room. It's already unlocked though. Come on, Amador, I'll show you the master." I'd never seen a house where each bedroom had its own special key. My dad patted me on the back and then left me standing there alone, looking at the door of my new room. I pushed inside and looked around in curiosity.

It was big and thankfully, everything inside was modern. The room had been painted in gray-blue. I dropped my bag on the Queen sized bed but then something immediately felt off. I walked across the room with wide, shocked eyes. My gaze swept every picture and piece of art the room had been decorated with.

They were all of the water. Rivers, lakes, underwater images, waves, storms over the sea.

"How?" I asked. There's no way they would know. I knew my father wouldn't share what we were. It wasn't even something considered. That part of us was almost always a secret we lived and died with.

"Hello," a feminine voice came from my doorway. I turned around to see a girl around my age standing in the doorway, one arm held across her stomach. She looked nervous, her eyes aimed at my bed instead of me. Her black hair was swept over her shoulder and she was wearing a school uniform made of a navy blue skirt and a white button-up short sleeve shirt. The buttons strained over her chest as if begging to be opened.

So this is who I wouldn't be touching. A catholic school girl.

"Which one are you?" I asked in apathy. There were two daughters. Ava, the same age as me and who apparently readied this room. Then another named Elizabeth, who was two years older.

"I'm Ava," she said, rubbing her arm. "We can change anything you want with the room..." her eyes tipped up to mine and I staggered back, falling into the desk behind me and nearly falling over. Brown eyes took up my entire vision as my chest blossomed in pain. I grabbed at my shirt over my heart, my mouth popping open to try and breathe but I felt like I was suffocating.

She ran towards me in a panic, yelling out over her shoulder for help. I fell to my knees in front of her, looking up at her in awe. Had I ever seen something so beautiful? I grabbed her hands, sliding my fingers up her wrists, needing to touch her. Her skin felt smooth, warm, electric.

My body was on fire, my heart careening at breakneck speeds in my chest. My eyes swept every part of the girl in front of me and the only thing I could think was just how perfect she was.

"Are you okay?" She asked, her eyes crested in concern. I couldn't speak so I just shook my head no. I was not okay.

I was dying.

I was being reborn.

A mounting explosion I couldn't control built inside me. I wrapped my arms around her waist, burying my face in her soft stomach, and groaned as I came in my pants, removing any potential confusion over what exactly was happening. I was imprinting.

Her hands rested gently on my head, her fingers brushing my hair from my face. I'd have expected her to push me away but she was *comforting* me. I heard footsteps running up and I sagged, feeling depleted.

My hands slipped down her legs, gripping her thighs, and then fell to the floor. I was on my hands and knees at her feet, taking deep breaths, and only wishing I had enough energy to reach up and grab her again, press her to me, hold her.

"Oh Caspian," my dad said in what sounded like pity. My eyes tipped up to see him standing in the doorway. He knew what had happened.

"Are you okay?" Ava bent down in front of me. Her eyes were big, sweeping over my face. I could barely comprehend that she was real and not a fever dream.

"I'm fine," I said, my eyes sweeping over the curve of her cupid's bow at the top of her mouth. I turned towards the doorway to look at my dad and Maria behind him. "I'm more out of it from the trip than I thought and she startled me accidentally." My dad gave me a tentative look.

"You sure?" Maria asked.

"Yes," I said maybe a little too forcefully but I wanted them gone. I glared at my dad. Finally, he nodded and they walked off. He had made a point of opening the door even wider though, a subtle point that I wasn't to do anything.

"I guess you're my new stepsister," I said with a small laugh, eyes sliding up her legs. The skirt was tucked under her knees. I took my time looking her over, trying to see every detail hidden behind her outfit. My obvious checking out had her looking slightly flushed. She nervously pushed her hair behind her ear and stood up.

"Not officially," she said, giving me a little smile. "Are you really okay?" I slowly got back up. All of my muscles were sore and my boxers were damp. Her eyes widened as I stood up fully in front of her, towering over her.

"I'm really okay," I said and I'd never answered that more truthfully. The constant ache was finally gone. Suddenly everything was so clear. I knew exactly what I wanted. I wanted *her*. I'd never realized how empty I was until this moment. How aimless and cold until this girl stood in front of me, filling me up with warmth.

Ava was looking up at me with wide eyes, her mouth cracked open, almost as if in awe. It was a look I'd seen plenty of times. All nokken had a charm that no normal human man did. We were like sirens, beautiful water folk who charmed people into the rivers and lakes. We used music and looks to draw humans in.

For once I felt nothing but pleasure to see someone look at me like she was. She blinked and shook her head, the look leaving her. Then she shot me a friendly smile and started to back away.

"Well, let me know if there's something about the room you'd like to change."

"The art," I blurted, feeling panicked by her retreat. I didn't want her to leave.

"Oh," she deflated, misunderstanding me.

"No, I mean, I love it. What made you choose it?" She turned her head towards a wall, giving me her side profile. She looked like a painting, her jaw a beautiful curve, her neck a perfect line. I wanted to sing to her. She looked over all the water art, a frown gathering on her face.

"I didn't realize I'd only picked out water," she said, sounding confused. Why didn't she step back closer to me? I wanted that. Her eyes darted around the room's art and she began to grow upset.

"Why did I do that?" She mumbled to herself, her hands pressing on her stomach. I didn't know what was making her react that way but I wanted it to stop.

"I'm a swimmer," I said, filling in the silence. She looked at me and a languid sense of contentment blanketed me. I never wanted her to look away.

"Oh, well maybe that's it. I must have heard that from my mom at some point." She smiled and I groaned in pleasure to see the amazing expression on her face. Her eyes widened in shock and I coughed, my eyes bugging. I needed to get in control of myself.

No. I needed my new step sister naked. I took a step towards her but she'd already started to turn and walk for the door. Where was she going? I felt troubled, anxious.

"Well, I'm going to get out of your hair," she said, turning around in the hall outside my room and looking at my hair. "You've got nice hair. I wish mine would behave like that. I'd never cut it." I pushed my fingers into the strands. The top was long, the sides shorter.

She liked my hair.

Ava started to back away with another friendly smile. I had to do something, I couldn't just let her walk away! Fuck, stop acting like an idiot.

I shook myself out and stepped into the hallway, invading her space. Her eyes grew wide and she leaned slightly away, taken aback.

"I was hoping you'd help me," I said, giving her a charming smile. I slid my fingers around her wrist and lifted her hand to my mouth, pressing a kiss to the back. My eyes slid shut as the smell of her skin enveloped me.

"Help you what?" She asked, voice trembling. Her eyes

kept darting down the hall as if she either wanted to run or was afraid someone would see us. I leaned forward, my eyes twinkling in excitement.

"Break in my bed," I whispered. Her eyes bugged and her mouth popped open. She jerked her hand from my grip and the sharp sting of a palm landed on my cheek. My head jerked to the side and I stood completely still in shock as I heard her stomp down the hall.

Finally, I lifted my hand to my cheek, pressing it over the sting she left.

"What the fuck?" I asked out loud. This isn't how it was supposed to go.

6

Ava

Several hours later, I was stumbling out of the vehicle after my nap. My brain felt sluggish and heavy, not letting go of sleep immediately. I blinked rapidly as I spilled out into the sunny campsite.

The splinter from the haunted house pinched painfully in my left ring finger as it bumped the side of the car door. A little piece of wood was lodged inside me, worming deeper into my body every time I tore into my skin seeking it out. I sucked in a breath, eyeing the bandaid over the irritated wound.

My earlier attempts to fish the splinter out with tweezers only accomplished making it worse. The sharp ends of my tweezers had torn the flesh as I'd winced in pain, hurting myself.

At this point, I was scared to mess with it any more. I'd likely create a crater while the old wood slipped further into my body, getting so deep I'd never be able to find it again.

I leaned into the car, grabbing more antibiotic cream and bandaids. It was surprising how innocent the wound looked for how much it hurt. After handling that, I fished out my camera and popped off the lens cover before letting it hang around my neck from its thick strap, ready for action.

The air was cooler than I expected. It was mid-August and still warm, but nowhere near as humid and oppressive as my hometown on the coast. I tugged my phone from my pocket and saw it was already noon.

I scratched my scalp and went over to Caspian, who was finishing putting up my tent. He was hunched over, his wide shoulders pulling his tee-shirt taut across his back. Tattoos covered both of his arms, spilling in black and grays from the sleeves of his shirt and stretching down to his wrists. Both sides were visions of water and the creatures in its depths—some real, some fantastical.

There was another tattoo hiding just inside his hip bone, near his pelvis. Sometimes it would peek out of his low-slung pants. I hadn't asked him what it was though, a little embarrassed to bring up I'd eyed the area a lot. He'd also gotten his left pec tattooed before we left, but it was still covered. When I asked what it was he had winked instead of sharing.

As I approached, he stood up with a proud smile, his eyes looking to me for approval. It was amazing how cute Caspian could still be.

"It looks great," I said, turning and taking in the camp. He'd set up a hammock between two trees, had the cooler sitting next to the picnic table, had the picnic table bursting with a bunch of unpacked things, and two Sasquatch Inc. camping chairs were set up by the fire pit. I pulled up my camera from my neck and snapped a picture of the chairs.

"One tent down. One to go," I said, turning back to him. "Is that the only thing left?" Caspian's eyes widened slightly and he looked off towards the trees. "Cas?" I asked in suspicion.

"Well, you see I forgot to pack my tent."

"You forgot to pack a tent... for camping?" I looked at him in disbelief. His rich brown eyes settled on me.

"Silly me, being so forgetful," he said with a taunting smirk and smoldering eyes. I felt things tighten low in my body and swallowed.

"You loser. What are we supposed to do?" I asked, shoving him playfully. He stumbled slightly and his smirk grew to a full smile.

"It means, dear stepsister—"

"Don't call me that."

"That we're sharing a tent," he finished. I groaned then eyed my tent. It was *technically* a two-person. However, that didn't account for personal space. Two bodies could fit in there for sure, pressed up tight like little sardines holding each other in a tin can.

I couldn't handle that. Not with him.

"Sleep in the SUV. We'll put down the back seats." Caspian's smile turned to a look of offense.

"Seriously?" He asked, eyes boring into mine.

"Yeah?" I said in confusion. He made a frustrated groan towards the sky and stomped off. He moved down the little campground road, heading towards the bathroom building.

Then it was just me and nature. A nice silence intermingled with the sound of birds chirping and leaves rustling. Caspian was acting weird but that was pretty typical. Eccentricity was part of his package.

He didn't really want to be all squished up together in the tent, did he? I'd likely embarrass myself if we were forced to have our bodies pressed tight in a hot tent.

I imagined us in our sleeping bags together in the dark,

his teasing voice making jokes as I felt his large body behind mine.

"*You love your stepbrother, don't you?*" He'd joke, his fingers scratching into my scalp, moving my hair away from my ear. "*Want to show me how much you love me?*" He'd murmur, his breath tracing the lines of my neck.

"What's wrong with me?" I mumbled, swallowing thickly and crossing my arms over my hard nipples. Why did he have to joke about those types of things all the time? He was putting strange thoughts in my head. Especially now, with the whole world thinking we already had sex. That we used to sneak around, living in the same house, fucking when everyone's heads were turned.

I groaned and smacked my heated cheeks, trying to dispel any and all visuals suddenly flashing in my head.

I heard the abrupt beep of a little vehicle and jumped. Turning, I saw a golf cart at the front of our campsite. A woman sat on it and she did not look happy to see me. Had I done something wrong? Was I supposed to check in with her first? There hadn't been instructions or even a building at the front of the campground, so I'd just drove on in.

The woman sat there staring at me, not getting up or waving at me to come hither. She had gray and brown curly hair cut into a mullet. On her head was a pair of sports sunglasses and on her feet were sandals that looked a size or two too small.

On her waistband was a gun.

I heard the screams and felt the panic from the concert. *I love you*, the girl gasped. Teeth and metal touching.

I blinked and took a deep breath, letting the visceral memory die.

I couldn't seem to stop looking at the weapon though. My tongue felt dry and the woman's apathetic expression now felt tainted, as if she was masking anger, her hand itching to snatch the metal from her hip and point the dark tunneled end right at me.

"Well aren't you a pretty little thing," she finally huffed out. "Here," she said, grabbing something from a fanny pack and holding it out. I walked over and took the paper from her hands.

"Put that in the front window of your vehicle. Write in the days you're going to be here, your campsite number, your name," she paused and I looked up to see her hawking a mucousy piece of spit loudly into the dirt. I jerked my gaze back to the little paper and nodded my head.

"How long you here for?" Her tongue came out, swooping across her lips almost nervously, as her eyes darted around.

"A week." My eyes drifted back to the gun. Why did she need to wear it around a campground? Was she that concerned about campers? Or maybe it was something else she was prepared for just in case. Her eyes snapped back to mine after scanning the woods.

"Them two with you?" She asked, jerking her thumb towards Caspian's bandmates.

"Uh, sort of." I frowned and looked over at them. Matthias was asleep in their hammock, his mouth wide open as he snored. Brandon was sitting in a chair with eyes closed and headphones on, his fingers drumming the chair arms.

"Two sites is two payments," she said, her eyes scanning the trees behind me again as if she were looking for something. "I'm the big RV you passed on the way in. You need firewood, then I can sell it to ya. I'll need upfront payment on the campsites."

Run & Hide

Once the last word was from her mouth she pressed on the gas and drove away as fast as the golf cart would go.

"Ma'am! We prepaid online!" I yelled out to her but she just kept going, not responding to me at all.

Caspian walked back around the curve, looking over his shoulder at the rapidly retreating golf cart. The lady seemed in a big hurry but slowed down to eye Caspian plenty before grinding her foot into the gas and disappearing entirely.

My eyes drifted to the campsite across from ours. Brandon was now wandering around with his phone in the air, looking as if he were struggling to find service. His face had an ugly area developing into a nasty bruise. I thought about what I saw earlier.

Falling into a tree made no sense. They'd all been standing at least twenty feet away from any tree. Caspian's knuckles had been red. Brandon had his arms lifted as if to protect himself from an attack. Matthias had been tugging on his hair, a look of panic on his face as he watched the two men.

They'd been fighting. I wasn't stupid.

It was hard to imagine Caspian punching someone in the face but the evidence was all there. How could he do that?

Maybe it had been about me. That thought both upset and angered me. His band was acting as if I was the cause for Caspian's choices. Part of me felt guilty but the other part of me rallied against the idea, logic telling me I had nothing to do with it. I didn't. Caspian had wanted or needed a break for some reason. I was just a convenient option.

Caspian wasn't very chatty as he walked into camp. He sat in his camping chair and watched me as I searched for a spot with phone service.

I climbed on the picnic table and held up the phone in the sky.

"Your tongue is sticking out," Caspian said.

"Leave me alone" I grumbled self consciously as my tongue indeed wiggled out of my mouth as I stretched my phone towards the sky. Finally, I got the vulture pictures from earlier to post to the Instagram I was running. Sasquatch Inc had wanted me to update regularly there.

"It's cute when you do it," Caspian said as I jumped down from the picnic table. I looked over at him and something about his heavy attention and words made me feel like climbing in a hole and squealing.

"Good to know," I said awkwardly, yelling in my mind not to think about the thing I'd thought about before. With us both in the tent and him whispering and teasing.

Nope! Not thinking about it.

"I better take some pictures," I said, scrambling around to get a Sasquatch cooler out and get some good shots of it.

Product photography wasn't something I had a ton of experience with so it took me a long time to figure out good placements and angles. Caspian got his acoustic guitar out at some point. The sound of smooth, languid Spanish songs filled the campsite.

He watched me the entire time, his eyes lazily taking in my movements as he effortlessly played music. It made me feel aware of my body, his gaze almost like light touches caressing my heated skin. It was a familiar awareness though.

When we lived together, we were always around one another. He tended to watch me a lot, no matter what I was doing. At first, I'd griped about it, getting irritated by his attention. He never stopped despite my complaints and eventually, I'd come to accept that was just something he did. He was a people watcher I suppose. Charming people were often like that, fully focused on the person they were around.

Matthias and Brandon stayed on their side of the street, not bothering to even look our way. There was an edge of anger in their movements I could see even from here. Their attitudes had taken a nosedive since the fight earlier. It left me feeling unsettled.

After a few hours and a million photos, I flopped in the other camping chair next to Caspian.

"Now what?" I asked, looking around at nature.

"We could make a fire and eat," Caspian offered. My stomach groaned from the suggestion and I realized I'd been ignoring it all day. I looked over at him with a smile. That was all he needed to set his guitar to the side and begin making a fire. Sometimes I felt spoiled by him. He always jumped to do everything with eagerness, more than happy to be useful for people.

"This is so exciting! Our first fire! Should I help?" I was giddy, bouncing in the chair as I watched him set up the wood in a teepee shape.

"I've got this," he said with a small smile. He had changed into a sleeveless gym shirt at some point. The muscles on his arms flexed as he went about moving pieces of wood. The armholes were so big they showed off the side of his chest and body. The bandaging from his new tattoo was still in place. It was big, covering his entire left pec.

When our parents first married he was skinny and lanky, his hands and feet too big for him. Like one of those massive dogs with oversized paws they needed to grow into. He was tall and filled out now. My eyes kept catching on his defined arms and wondering how he was ever gangly.

My eyes darted away when I realized I was ogling... again.

"Thank you, by the way. I know I've said it before, but I want to say it again." Caspian looked over at me as he bent down, stuffing dry leaves between the firewood. "Not the fire, but that too. I mean coming with me. For being excited for me. Supporting me." I waited for a response but his eyes dipped away from me as he lit the fire. It started to smoke and build. He pushed up from crouching and walked over.

He always moved so fluidly—smooth, powerful, and confident.

He stepped right in front of my chair, looking down with his thick dark eyelashes and smirk. He was almost too close. I tried to pretend his crotch wasn't at head level but it was hard when he was practically shoving it in my face.

He reached out with both hands, holding my face gently... right in front of his pant's zipper. My tongue darted over my lips and I looked up. Did he even realize what he was doing? Was this him teasing me? One corner of his mouth tipped up in a little smirk. He *had* to know my face was two inches from him.

"I'll always support you, Ava. I'm always here for you." He held my gaze. My eyes tried to dip to his crotch and I had to bite my lip to stop myself from looking.

"Thank you," I breathed out before swallowing hard. This was too much, I needed a cold shower. "You're the greatest friend I could hope for."

His smirk dropped, a look of annoyance coming over his face as he pulled back. He walked to his chair and flopped down.

"Yep," he grumbled, picking up and thrusting a long stick into the fire to poke at it aggressively. I frowned. His attitude was throwing me off. His emotions seemed a bit all over the place since we got here.

"Oh, I want a pokey stick! We can use them for smores later!" I said, trying to brighten the sudden strange mood.

I leaned forward to peer at the other campsite, wondering if they might join us eventually. They noticed me looking and eyed me back. Then they leaned closer together and began talking, *still* looking at me.

I bristled and quickly looked away, uncomfortable they were so obviously talking about me.

7

CASPIAN

"Ava, why don't you come sit on my lap?" I asked with a cheeky smirk. The hotdog was halfway to her mouth when it stopped and she gave me a wide-eyed look. I could almost see the words in her head--*is he joking, is he serious*? I patted my knee and smiled wider. Her eyes drank in the expression.

Yes, Ava, be lulled by my face—come in close. Also, be careful because I bite. My tongue rolled over my teeth as I thought about her thighs. I'd love to sink my teeth into those —bury my face in, drag my tongue up, and chomp. Ava had such *delicious* thighs.

"Stop joking around," Ava said with a nervous chuckle.

"I'm not. Come on, right here," I said, brushing my hand over my crotch and gripping myself a moment. Her eyes widened in shock. Oops. "I'm cold," I said with a wink. Her eyes swept around the camp like there might be someone to help guide her on what to do. She munched the rest of the hot dog while eyeing me. I kept patting my knee and smiling.

"I guess..." she finally said, sliding off her chair and

coming over to me. *Fuck yes.* She sat on my knee and I wrapped my arms around her, pulling her in closer, until I could feel the cheeks of her ass pressing heavy on my cock. I loved the pressure. I wish she would grind in, bruise my balls with her weight.

"I don't know how you're cold," she said, sucking in a sharp breath as I squeezed her tightly.

"You smell good," I mumbled against her back, inhaling her.

"I do?" Her breathy voice made me excited. I ran my hands up and down her thighs while my face stayed pressed into her back. Up and down, my fingers inching higher each time. Her legs started to spread wider and I had to inhale a groan that tried to escape.

She leaned back against my chest. I looked over her shoulder at her body draped on mine. She was beautiful in the campfire's light. My face turned into her neck and I closed my eyes, brushing my lips against her neck but not really kissing it. My fingers dragged back up her thighs and her legs spread wider, her breath hitching as my thumbs briefly slid below her shorts.

A little golf cart beeped at the front of our campsite. Ava startled, her legs closing back up. My teeth ground together and I nearly dropped Ava on her ass and chased the motherfucker through the woods. I could imagine him wailing in terror all through the mountains while I flashed my teeth behind him.

Ava peeled herself off my lap. I flung my head back and groaned as she walked over to the man. He was telling her about campfire stories by the time I came over. I put my arm over her shoulder and rubbed her arm.

"Campfire stories?" I asked in annoyance. The ranger

nodded in excitement. He was a middle-aged man with wrinkles around his eyes.

Brandon and Matthias trotted up and listened in. Their moods seemed better now that evening had arrived. Good for them. They could take their good attitudes back to civilization and leave me all alone with Ava.

"I like to tell stories when there's a nice group around," the ranger continued. He had a thick country accent. He looked at us with hopeful eyes. I turned to Ava to see what she wanted to do. It was very unlikely she wanted to join in. Campfire stories sounded suspiciously like scary stories that involved everything she hated.

"Absolutely. We would *all* love to," Brandon interjected quickly. He was smiling at Ava who looked annoyed. My eyebrows pinched.

"Great!" The ranger said with a broad smile, clearly excited. "Head on over then. The fire is already going at campsite number three. Bring your chairs and s'more supplies if you want them." He began driving off. "Hope you like scary stories!" He called out and Ava made a face of disgust that was so cute I couldn't help but laugh. I reached out and pulled her into a hug, kissing the top of her head.

"You can't avoid the strange," I said in entertainment. Brandon gave a mean smirk and trailed back to his camp to collect their chairs with Matthias. I frowned but let it go, going to collect our own chairs and s'more supplies.

"My mom might be pleased to hear the calling is still finding a way into my life even out in the woods," Ava said sarcastically.

"Ah yes, the Luna family calling," I said with affection, grabbing the folded chair from Ava and shoving it under my arm with my own.

"Yes," she huffed. "Just the women though."

"There *are* only women in your family. Sort of freaky." I leaned in with a toothy smile that made her laugh. Ava had such nice laughs but I was ready to hear what other noises I could force out of her. Moans, groans, gasps, whimpers... screams.

We walked down the little street behind Brandon and Matthias, towards campsite three—closer to the front entrance.

"It's *all* freaky. I'm the only normal one," Ava said. I let out a sudden bark of laughter that made her jump and look at me in shock. She eyed me strangely as I tried to calm my dying laugh.

"Sorry, sorry. You're completely right. You're the normal one. Completely unaffected by the draw your family has on strange things." Ava was hilarious sometimes. I gave a wide smile and bumped our shoulders playfully.

"Screw you," she grumbled without any real anger as we arrived at campsite three. Oh Ava, if you only gave me the chance I certainly would screw you. Roughly, passionately, and with just enough restraint that you wouldn't go running away screaming. *Hopefully.*

"Welcome!" The ranger said. The campground manager was here too, eating a s'more in the messiest way possible. Pieces of melted chocolate slipped from her graham crackers and landed on her knee. She wiped at it, smearing it around into a sticky mess as she tongued the s'more's insides while eyeballing me suggestively. I grimaced.

She was strapped up with a gun and kept eyeing the trees like a nervous habit. I looked around too, feeling as if I needed to make sure we were alone as well.

We all settled in. Ava bounced in her chair as she pushed a marshmallow on a stick and got to roasting. I reached out and gripped the edge of her chair, tugging it as close as possible. Brandon was a few feet to her right, slumped in his chair with his arms crossed. Matthias was on the other side of him, mopping his brow with his shirt while glancing at his phone with a frown.

The family we'd seen earlier didn't show up and I realized we would be the only victims. By now the sun couldn't be seen and the sky was starting to turn purple.

"Y'all know about the murders here?" The ranger asked, instantly dispersing my wandering thoughts.

"Here?" Ava asked, pointing down. He nodded, a sly smile curling up his face. She shot me a look and I shook my head and gave a huffed laugh. He was making things up.

"Every year at this *very* campground at least one person goes missing. Sometimes it can be as many as five," the ranger said.

Brandon and Matthias sat up straighter, looking more interested now. My eyes slid to Ava, enjoying the warm golden glow of the fire on her skin. If we pressed our bodies together I bet I'd be able to feel the heat lingering.

She clutched my hand and lowered her marshmallow to nearly touch the red coals. I watched as it flared with a brief flash of flame before dying into an ashy husk. Was she worried? I didn't want her to worry. She should feel safe. I was right here. I threaded our fingers and pulled her arm closer. Then I shot a nasty glare at the ranger who ignored me.

"Bullshit," Brandon said.

"It's true," the campground manager spoke up, aggressively licking chocolate from her arm. "People go missing every year in the summer." Her eyes slid to the forest again, scanning. She really seemed to be looking for something.

"Ever hear of the Mothman monster?" The ranger asked

us. My body tightened in response to his words. Ava noticed and looked at me questioningly.

"Have you?" She asked.

"No," I responded apathetically with a blank face. Everyone was looking at me so I decided to try again. "I haven't," I said with inflection and a small smile. I brought Ava's hand up to my mouth and kissed the back. She sucked in a little breath and averted her eyes quickly in embarrassment. I hoped she looked just as embarrassed when I crawled between her legs and fucked her. I imagined pulling her hands from her face, not letting her hide just how embarrassed she was to have me inside her.

"He's famous," the ranger started. "A legend that came from these very woods. Matter of fact, not far down the road is Point Pleasant. Every year they hold a big festival all about Mothman."

"That sounds cool," Ava said, forcing a little smile.

"It's to inform people about what's out there. The creature with glowing red eyes and wings twenty feet long," the ranger said, throwing his arms out wide. I nearly barked out a laugh but Ava nervously slid her attention to the forest line. She squeezed the blood flow from my hand so I brushed my thumb in circles over her thumb.

"Some say he's the devil. A furred man with taloned feet and the pits of hell burning in his eyes." The ranger's dark eyes were wide. I could see the flames of our campfire reflected in them, emphasizing his point about the monster. At some point, he'd gone from easy going to serious. His eyes dug into us as if begging us to deny his claims.

"People have seen him?" Ava asked.

"Oh yes," the ranger said, nodding. "Lots of people. Most literature likes to think this all started in the sixties but Mothman sightings have been going on since people existed in the area." A monster story, how ironic. If only these humans knew what was sitting around the fire with them. A smile spread over my face.

"Mothman lives in these very woods, hidden closeby and waiting," the ranger continued. "Hungry. Blood is always drenched around his mouth because he is always feeding. Always eating. Sometimes the animals of the woods aren't enough. Sometimes he wants human flesh."

My smile flipped into a frown. It was always the same with these stories. The monster was a human eating beast, practically a rabid animal. My eyes darted to Ava, she was looking at my frown with curiosity.

Brandon and Matthias were listening in while sharing a bag of gummy worms in neon colors. They looked mildly entertained.

"Every summer campers come to these woods. Every summer some go missing. Sure, we say they got lost in the woods or fell in the river but the bodies are never found. There is a cave somewhere out there," he pointed into the shadowy woods. "A cave filled with bones. Bones of settlers and explorers from hundreds of years ago. And at the top, bones of campers freshly picked clean." I rolled my eyes.

"That's metal," Brandon commented with a smile before throwing a gummy worm in his mouth.

The fire made a crack noise and something scurried loudly in the woods nearby. Ava clawed at my shoulder, looking as if she wanted to climb right in my lap. *Please do.* The campground manager gave a throaty laugh at her reaction.

"What was that noise?" Ava asked, almost trembling as she stretched out the neck of my shirt. No one answered and that only seemed to make her more worried.

The ranger leaned in and talked lower as if fearing someone... or some*thing* was listening.

"Mothman is a bad omen," he said. Ava shivered and I squeezed her hand. She hissed in pain and my eyes widened in surprise. When I opened up our hands I saw her splinter bandaged up. Was it still bothering her? Why didn't she tell me? What if it was infected? Maybe we should drive to an emergency clinic tonight, get it checked out just in case.

"Why is he a bad omen?" She asked the ranger.

"He hides deep in the caverns of the old Appalachia. Two great big demon eyes blinking out, seeing everything and feeling when something bad is going to happen. In the late sixties, he stretched out from his hiding place, ran people off the road, chased them down, terrorized them. The entire area grew paranoid and afraid. Neighbors began turning against each other, no one went out after dark."

"He left them alive though?" She asked. I twisted her hand around to get a better look at the bandaged area. I couldn't see any red skin. The urge to peel the bandaid off and look at it was strong but I'd wait until we got back to camp.

"Yes ma'am, he wasn't looking for food. He was warning us."

"Of what?" Matthias asked with a sigh. He seemed to just want the story over with so he could leave. He was constantly scratching at his collection of bug bites and mopping the sweat from his forehead.

"Warning about the bridge collapse," the ranger said, his lips tugging down at the corner. He leaned back, shaking his head. "Silver Bridge was built in the twenties. For forty years it was reliable until one night it wasn't."

"What happened?" Matthias asked, looking more concerned now as he ignored his scratched raw skin. I could even see a little blood on his fingernails from how he'd broken the skin trying to relieve the itch.

"It was rush hour, people traveling from work to see their families. Cars were loaded up on the bridge. It was a disaster. Forty-six people never made it home. Two bodies were never found."

"But what does that have to do with a monster?" I asked, annoyed. They blamed monsters for everything. "It was the bridge."

"I'm not sure anyone blames him." The ranger scratched at his jaw "But no one wants to see him flying in the skies. It means disaster is coming. That people are going to die." I rolled my eyes then looked down at Ava. She was looking at my rude reaction. I swallowed then smiled shyly as if embarrassed by how I just acted.

It had grown fully dark as we folded our chairs up and grabbed the s'more supplies. When we started to walk off I eyed the trees around us. Ava suddenly grabbed my arm, wrapping her fingers around the bicep and squeezing, her eyes darting around everywhere.

8

Ava

"Oh! You all be careful, 'kay?" The ranger called out to us all. "No one has gone missing yet this summer and people always go missing. Summer is almost over." He looked out into the woods. "Mothman must be hungry."

The camp manager watched us go, her eyes steady on us, no longer looking into the woods.

"He didn't say why they call him Mothman," Matthias commented as we walked away.

"Maybe he's a big moth," Brandon joked, throwing his arm around the other man's shoulders and tugging him close.

"A moth wouldn't have taloned feet, glowing eyes, and a bloody mouth," Caspian commented like he was annoyed with the conversation.

An image rose in my mind. Of something dark, shadows wrapped around its body. Two round red eyes. The image was so strong I barely could see the woods around me anymore. Dizziness came over me and mild nausea roiled up in my stomach. The image in my mind shifted, alive. Massive wings spread out, brown and black patterns. The buzzing grew stronger until it felt like my brain was stinging. I winced, pressing my hands to my head.

"Are you okay?" Caspian asked in concern, feeling the sway of my step. I closed my eyes and shook my head. The buzzing slowly drifted away, the images disappearing into blackness. I swallowed, my mouth suddenly dry.

"Maybe it's because he has big wings like a moth," I said, answering Matthias' question.

"Hmm," Matthias said, seeming to genuinely think about it. His arm slipped around Brandon's waist naturally. Caspian looked down at me with a questioning gaze boring into me.

Matthias and Brandon veered into their camp throwing goodnights over their shoulders. Their attitudes seemed markedly better than before. They almost seemed friendly towards me, smiling and waving as they went. I hadn't noticed before but they seemed really close to one another.

"What made you say that about the wings?" Caspian asked as we moved towards the dying fire at our campsite. I headed straight for the cooler, tugging out a beer that I popped open and began to gulp. The cool carbonation was rough on my throat but I let it slide down regardless. Trails of beer leaked out around the sides of my mouth, sliding down to my chin.

I didn't stop until the can was empty, pulling it away from my mouth with a big inhale. I hadn't even tasted it at all.

"I have no idea. It just came to me," I mumbled, half lying. That hadn't been normal imagination. I didn't want to think about what it was. Quickly, I fetched another beer from the cooler and popped it open, tipping it back and swallowing greedily.

I was drinking too fast, it went to my head right away,

Run & Hide

making me sway. I flopped in the camping chair and let out a breath, a smile curling up my face as I felt my concern ebbed away by the alcohol.

"You sure?" Caspian asked, looking concerned as he began nursing the fire back to life. A snorted laugh came from me but I didn't answer him.

My mother's words from the haunted house replayed in my mind: *You can't run from it.*

That night, I went to bed scared.

During the day I could pretend I didn't believe in any of this stuff. I could push away strange feelings and weird experiences. I could roll my eyes and scoff.

But when all was dark and quiet, all I could feel was bone-deep belief and fear. The campfire story had bothered me. The missing campers were enough to worry anyone. The monster was what made my gut squirm though.

Before I'd scrambled into my tent, it felt like someone was watching me. No matter how many beers I chugged I couldn't shake the sensation.

Every time I closed my eyes, I saw two round, glowing red eyes and heard a faint buzzing in my head. The burning image that felt forced into my mind left me feeling jumpy. It was as if something ancient really did live in these woods and had opened its eyes and *saw* me. *Me*, who couldn't escape the strange and unusual. Who ghosts called out to and wanted to touch.

I was a beacon for some reason, drawing out things that shouldn't exist.

"Stupid family curse," I grumbled into my pillow. My head felt like it was bobbing out on the river nearby, swaying with the current. My thoughts were like melted watercolors, blurring. I drank too many beers and now my mind was getting carried away with stories.

Right now in these woods, it felt as if all things occult could suddenly come to life from the whispering shadows and clutch at my mind, demanding a taste of my acrid fear. I squirmed deeper into my sleeping bag, clutching my bat squishmallow to my chest. I brushed its cashmere texture as if it were a pet cat. I didn't care at all if someone thought a stuffed animal was a childish tactic for comfort. It was better than climbing in other people's beds and demanding they let me disturb their sleep.

Except, I was starting to wish Caspian was in the tent with me. Old habits die hard apparently. Even five years of going without him hadn't quenched my thirst for his comfort in the night.

I hadn't really considered camping as an activity likely to freak me out or trigger my strange 'ability'. My family was all *ghosts ghosts ghosts* and those lived in creepy old houses, not dark, creepy woods.

"I'm being so ridiculous," I mumbled, pretending as if I could just shake off the fear. This was ridiculous. I was letting my family's mindset taint my logic. My tongue rolled over my dry lips and I pushed a finger into my splinter slightly, giving myself an endorphin rush with a side order of pain to help clear my mind. Even with several beers drowning in my system the wound gave such a sharp spasm of ache that I sucked in a breath and shuddered.

My bladder felt over-filled from all the beer I'd chugged. I'd been holding it for what felt like forever and felt ready to burst. I bundled up my courage like a shield and wiggled from the sleeping bag. I very slowly unzipped the door. The sound of the zipper was loud enough to briefly silence the cacophony of crickets and other night time creepy crawlies.

When the door flap hung loose, I sat still and listened but the only thing to hear was the ambiance of a summer night in nature. I peeled the flap back slowly and swept my eyes across the dark scene in front of me. The fire was out but the moon was big in the sky. It cast the faintest white glow from above. Just enough to see dark shapes and darker shadows.

I grabbed my flashlight, flicked it on, and swept it around quickly.

Nothing was out of place but the flashlight made long, stretched-out shadows. They felt nefarious. I grumbled while slipping from the tent, shoving my feet in sandals, and quickly moving to the street. My eyes slid to the campsite across from us but it was quiet except for the rattling sound of snores coming from their shared tent.

Once around the bend in the street, the bathroom building's bright yellow light lit up the area. I didn't dare move my flashlight towards the trees. If I didn't *see* anything scary in the woods, it didn't exist. Everyone knew that.

A high-pitched chittering noise started deep in the trees and my feet glued to the spot. My eyes watered as I stared into the darkness without blinking. The noise grew and I tried to place it.

It was an animal. I *knew* that. My heart thumped hard in my chest though.

The trees started to shake as if a strong wind had suddenly grabbed them.

There was no wind though.

The chittering was coming closer and getting louder. Multiple animals were coming towards me, I realized. Which felt unnatural. Animals were supposed to avoid humans. These were not. They were almost *running* towards me like animals fleeing before a raging forest fire.

I felt weak and alone standing in the middle of the street

with no cover. My instincts finally clicked on and a single thought burst into my mind: *run*.

I ran as fast as I could, the noises only growing until they were right to the edge of the forest. I'd disturbed whatever it was, a whole herd of them loudly calling out. The trees shook and a hundred chitters called out around me. I ran sloppy, my body still burning off the alcohol. One sandal tangled with the edge of the concrete sidewalk surrounding the bathroom and I tripped, barely catching myself.

I dove into the bathroom and slammed the door shut. Yellow light saturated painted cinder block walls, washing out all the color the bathroom had to offer. My fingers fumbled with the deadbolt then I backed away from the door. My eyes jerked up to the window high on the wall. There was no screen, just an open hole. My mind provided images of faces lurching into view, smiles too wide and cutting, eyes large and pupils blown out in unnatural excitement.

The noise retreated outside until it was all quiet. Then slowly the sounds of bugs and owls returned, everything returning to normal.

I took deep breaths as I went to relieve myself. Then I washed my hands in the sink, trying to avoid the freshly bandaged splinter on my ring finger. Caspian had insisted on examining it. He had tried to push the splinter out himself but my vision had gone black when he bore down on it. He was concerned, even tried to convince me that we should leave tonight to find a local hospital. Finally, we agreed if it got worse in a couple days we would find a clinic.

The strange thing was, it didn't appear infected at all. Even the red, irritated skin had gone away after I stopped messing with it. My finger looked perfectly fine except just under the surface you could see the tip of the splinter. It

Run & Hide

looked so close, so grabbable but no matter what I did, it refused to be removed.

As I finished up I thought about the noises outside. It was animals, that was all. They were freaked out by me walking by and warning each other. Either that or purposely scaring me.

Everything at this stupid camp was trying to terrorize me for its own sick pleasure—the ranger telling his stupid stories, the animals in the forest. Even the campground manager freaked me out, always scanning the trees for something and acting nervous.

I cursed them all while flipping the deadbolt and pushing open the door. I pulled my shoulders back and tipped my chin up. I wasn't going to let fear get to me out here. This trip was the start of me putting fear behind me, leaving it back home with my family and their stupid ghosts. Even if I accidentally brought a piece of a haunted house with me on the trip. I frowned, looking at my finger again.

Outside the bathroom was basked in yellow light. Down near my sandals, long daddy spiders walked in jerky movements. The small street before me curled into the darkness. My eyes burned into the tree line but there was nothing. No noise, no movement.

My dry tongue ran across my lip and I started to head back, clicking back on the flashlight. I needed to drink an entire bottle of water then fall asleep right away. Drunk and scared in the middle of the woods wasn't a good look on me.

As soon as I made it around the curve the noises started again. Louder. The chitters were all around revealing they had been waiting.

Whatever it was—animals, demons, creatures—it was

after me and the noise was so loud it morphed into screeching.

I took off, my sandals pressing into the street and biting into the top of my feet. Terror sliced through me. My back felt ice cold with a million goosebumps. The trees shook, the screeching surrounding me, echoing and joining together.

What if it really was something truly dangerous—something real, not my imagination running wild? What if it was boars that could gut me with their tusks? I didn't even know if they lived in the area but the image stuck. A whole hoard of bloody snouts, snorting out the stench of rot from their mouths as they trampled me to the ground squealing heinously, greedy mouths snapping open and shut.

It wouldn't take much. They were made for gutting things.

The screeches morphed into the hellish squeals of hogs in my mind. I panted roughly and careened into camp.

The noises abruptly stopped.

The trees didn't shake. The chittering and screeches were gone.

I took deep breaths of air as I leaned against the SUV, considering pulling open the handle and slipping inside to stay with Caspian. My heart began to slow and I took calmer breaths.

A soft brushing noise of movement made my eyes round to saucers. The sound of plastic and metal came from the picnic table, our items being moved around. I heard the crinkle of a chip bag.

I didn't want to look but it felt unsafe not to know what the danger was. Breath came staggering from my mouth before I swallowed. My eyes swept the dark shadows around me as the quiet noises of movement continued.

Don't let fear rule you, I told myself. Slowly and soundless I inched forward, my entire body shaking as I peered around the back of the SUV.

Tiny shining eyes looked over at me and stilled.

Raccoons. Furry bandits shoulder-deep in our food for the week. A whole freaking pack of jerkhole raccoons eating our food after they'd terrorized me on the street. That stupid chitter I'd been hearing in the dark was theirs. Anger bubbled up to eat away the fear. I barrelled forth in a swift rage.

"You little thieves!" I hissed, rushing them. The bastards started gathering my food in their paws, making sure to get as much as possible before running into the forest with it. Everything minus the cooler food was being dragged away by little clawed hands.

As I got to the picnic table I spied the egg carton open and half the eggs were missing. The other half were broken shells and the thick liquid inside had been slurped out. The thought of raw eggs sliding into a hungry, suctioning mouth made me feel nauseated.

"Agh!" I cried out at them. The raccoons were just at the edge of the forest, moving slowly with their hoard of our food. I darted into the trees, letting my anger push away any fear. My stomach still pinched and my heart still raced but I didn't let it reach my mind as I scrambled around with a pack of raccoons, cursing their mothers and fighting them for half-destroyed bags of bread and my boxes of pop tarts.

I lunged at the fat one holding my cherry pop tarts and ended up with a face full of dirt. I looked over and saw a raccoon on its hind legs, waving around my jiffy pop in a taunt.

"You can't even eat that!" I cried in offense. At this point, it felt personal. I scrambled up and ran towards the jiffy pop raccoon. It dropped to all fours, shoved the handle in its mouth, and ran away.

"No!" I swung around and ran after one holding an unopened chip bag. It leapt away and I chased after it. Twigs smacked my face and I had to spit out a leaf.

This went on for a few more minutes, me collecting leaves in my hair and growing more frustrated as the entire collection of raccoons went chittering deeper into the forest, leaving me panting and stomping the ground. They almost sounded like they were laughing at me.

"I hate raccoons now," I huffed. They were no longer cute little mischievous fluffballs. They were agents of chaos and destruction and they were rodents—oversized rats.

My eyes swept the area as I grumbled my hatred. Then it hit me... I was in the dense forest, away from my campsite, in the dark with no trail.

The earlier fear slithered up my spine, making my fingers begin to tremble slightly. For a moment, the only thing I did was stand there in complete silence, feeling as if I'd turned into stone. My ears and eyes strained in the darkness and the strong sensation of being watched pressed on my skin, making my heart thump loud in my ears.

This is how people got lost in the woods. They walked in, thinking they could find their way out but got turned around and never made it back out. I didn't even have the benefit of light.

The shapes and shadows around me all looked horrible. Big shadows could be a person, or worse, Mothman with its blood-drenched mouth and horrifying massive body. *It's hungry*, I thought. So, *so* hungry because no one has gone missing yet this year. It would be the type of hunger that drove something to tear into living things before even ending their life.

My eyes latched on to one particularly big shadow. It was shaped like a monster would be. Taller and wider than me. *Big*. My eyes watered as I refused to blink.

I stood catatonic, my eyes burning into the dark shape, waiting for it to move. I shook my head and took a step back. I was being ridiculous. I just needed to turn around and run back to camp. It should be right behind me. Hopefully right behind me.

Before I urged my body into action, the big shadow shifted.

Flight or fight punched me in the gut and the next thing I knew I was running and screaming so loudly that the entire forest was likely listening to my shrill cries of terror.

I burst through the treeline and nearly crashed into the wooden picnic table. I came to a sharp standstill and panted. Which was enough silence for me to hear something *running* behind me in the woods. Something big and loud, feet stomping at a fast, frantic pace coming at me louder and louder.

Every inch of skin broke out in goosebumps as I barreled to my car, gasping for breath. My muscles burned, my skin felt electrified.

Stomp, stomp, stomp.

It felt as if hands were reaching out for me and every little half-second counted. I could feel a dark shadow at my back. A person, a thing. I didn't know what it was but it was after me and I could hear it panting.

I grabbed the handle of the door and flew inside the car. Caspian grunted loudly as my body suddenly toppled on his. I scrambled around all elbows and knees, making Caspian grunt and groan some more as I abused him in my panicked haste. I reached out and jerked the door shut, locking it immediately. Then I flung myself around the entire car, pushing the locks down on all of the doors.

Without hesitation, I scrambled up to Caspian, burying my face in his chest and clinging to his shirt.

"Ava? What's wrong?" His soothing voice washed over me. His arms wrapped around my body, holding me to him. He could feel me shaking.

"There's nothing out there," I hissed to myself, not sure if that was true at all.

"What's wrong?" Caspian repeated, sounding concerned while he held me tighter. I shook my head and wrapped my arms around him, calming myself down. When the adrenaline finally leaked out and I was left an exhausted puddle, I talked. His hand smoothed down my back just like it used to, eliciting a shiver that had nothing to do with fear.

"Racoons were out there messing with me. They were screeching, trying to scare me for their entertainment," I grumbled in anger.

"For their entertainment?" Caspian asked in amusement.

"Yes," I hissed, finally lifting my head from his chest. It was so dark I couldn't make out much. "And they stole our food."

"Shit," he sighed in irritation.

"I tried to get some back but then I was in the woods and there was a shape—"

"A shape?"

"*Yes*, a shape. A scary shadow shape. I got freaked out and ran. Didn't you hear me screaming?"

"I was dead asleep. Flinging your body on top of mine woke me up though," his voice turned teasing at the end. I rolled my eyes in the dark and began to detach myself from him. Once we were lying side by side I realized I *really* didn't

Run & Hide

want to be alone. But also, the car was really uncomfortable. There was no padding underneath us, and the hardness bit into my bones.

"Aren't you uncomfortable in here?"

"It's okay," he dismissed.

"Can you sleep in the tent with me?" I blurted out. I no longer cared about any weird sexual tension. I wouldn't be able to calm down unless I had him next to me. He shifted around to face me and I could make out the briefest outline of his face.

"Of course," he said with a soft voice. His hand came up and brushed my cheek. I felt myself relax a little more.

Caspian got out of the car and confirmed there was nothing there. Then we packed tight into my tent, two sleeping bags underneath us and sharing a thin quilted blanket. The bare skin of our legs brushed against each other.

Everything was quiet outside. The buzz of wildlife picked back up but I heard no more raccoons—likely they were growing fat bellies on our groceries somewhere under a log.

"Did you think it was Mothman?" Caspian asked. I could feel the heat of his body at my back. I was faced away, eyeing the edge of the tent, and trying to ignore the wetness between my legs.

"I don't want to talk about that." I was angry at myself for letting a stupid story about a monster get to me. I felt Caspian shift around, then one of his arms slid around my waist as his chest pressed to my back. My breathing picked up but I tried to act cool.

"Are you afraid of monsters, Ava?" His voice was quiet and smooth, right next to my ear. I felt chills on my neck.

"No," I said quickly. He hummed and the vibrations traveled over me. I squeezed my eyes shut. Our legs were touching, his shin rubbing against my calf.

"You don't like monsters, Ava, but maybe *they* like you," he whispered as he swiped the hair from my neck. The soft sensation of his lips pressed into the side of my neck and I let out a gasp of shock.

"Stop messing with me." My voice was breathy and I cleared my throat, embarrassed by the way I sounded.

"Do you *really* want me to stop though?" I could hear the smile in his words. He placed another kiss on my neck and I didn't like the overwhelming way it made my body light up. I squirmed, pressing my legs tight together.

"Let me tease you some more, Ava. Okay?" He purred the question in the golden voice that charmed the world. His hand brushed downwards on my body, trailing over my stomach until he found the edge of my shorts. His fingers played with the material's edge, making my heart hammer in my chest.

"Caspian," I said in shock. His lips pressed into my neck again. "What are you doing?" My voice was shaky and my neck tingled where his mouth kept pressing. My head felt light, my thoughts swirling into a mess.

"Teasing you."

"Teasing me," I repeated in an apprehensive whisper, my body a ball of anticipation. He hummed in response, the sound rolling over me.

"Yes. Do you want me to take it further because I can take it much further," he promised, his intimate voice against my neck. His fingers pushed inside my shorts and kept traveling lower until finally, I could feel them between my legs. My breath hitched, my legs opening slightly for him. Was this really happening?

Run & Hide

The tip of one of his fingers pushed through my folds, playing at my entrance. His breath hitched.

"You're so wet," he commented, his voice husky. I felt my face burn in embarrassment. "Wet for your teasing stepbrother," he taunted while pressing his mouth to my ear, the words rough and thick. The tone didn't sound playful at all.

"You aren't my stepbrother anymore." My voice warbled at the end as his fingertip began to languidly circle around my clit. Why wasn't I telling him to stop? Why were my legs opening further, my hips pressing towards his fingers?

"Do you want this?" His question wasn't fair because he swirled his finger around then finally pressed directly where I wanted him. A small sound of relief got caught in my throat.

He continued to rub my clit languidly and a whimper came out before I could stop it. I slammed my hands to my mouth in mortification. Caspian didn't tease me about it though. I could feel his heavy breath on my neck as his fingers picked up pace, making pleasure climb higher.

"Ava," he breathed out. His lips pressed to my neck tenderly again. "Answer me. Do you want me to do this?" His talented fingers stuck to a rhythm, making my muscles tense and my pussy throb in need.

I didn't want him to stop but his fingers slowed when I didn't respond.

"Yes, I want this," I whispered and he groaned. I felt a change in him—from passive to active, from teasing to heated. Tension pulsed off him as he pressed my belly to the ground, rolling half on top of me, partially pinning me as if keeping me from escaping.

He put his mouth on the side of my neck as his fingers continued rolling in a wave of pleasure. I felt teeth on me, sharper than they ought to be. I was too distracted to care. Distracted by how he had me suddenly pinned to the ground while his fingers swirled, plucking pleasure from my body with the same skill he had used playing his guitar earlier.

It hit me that I was going to come. *Caspian* was going to make me come. The thought elicited knee-jerk panic. *This is wrong*, my mind said—an old concept that still lingered. It wasn't wrong, I knew that, but I couldn't stop the ingrained reluctance to accept this as okay.

"Relax, Ava," Caspian whispered in my ear with that wicked voice he enchanted everyone with. It rolled over me like a languid, warm wave and I realized I'd been whimpering and squeezing his forearm. My hips moved back and forth, my ass pushing into his hip.

His fingers plunged lower, caressing my entrance, exploring and teasing the area. Slowly he sank his fingers inside me, not stopping until he was buried to the knuckle. He groaned against my neck. Two long fingers spread me out, so deep inside that it made me squirm and gasp.

The sensation of Caspian inside me was boggling. Years of resistance to the idea was ingrained into me and yet my pussy clenched down on his dancing fingers all the same. It made me shiver with thrill at the slight wrongness of it—the sudden shift from platonic to sexual was almost too abrupt but more than welcome.

"Tighter, Ava. Squeeze me," he demanded, warm breath on my ear, body still pressing into mine from behind, pinning me. I clenched, squeezing my muscles as tight as possible, wanting to please him, impress him. He hummed in deep approval, the sound reverberating in his chest. He pushed his fingers even deeper, the edge of his hand tightly crushed against my body.

"That's good," he purred. "A pussy like this deserves

something special," he remarked, pulling his fingers out before plunging them back in.

"Cas," I moaned as the embarrassing sounds of my wetness filled the tent, turning my face hot. I pushed myself up and down on his hand despite that, following his rhythm, fucking myself on his fingers. My clit rubbed against his thumb, creating a dull pleasure punctuated by his plunging fingers inside me.

He hooked his fingers, playing at a bundle of nerves that made me gasp and my walls tighten.

"Fuck," Caspian murmured in reverence. He was breathing heavily as he pulled his fingers back out and worked my clit faster than before, with almost desperate movements.

Was he turned on? Did he want me?

The building pleasure grew between my legs, stretching deep inside me and rolling up my body to my chest. Caspian's labored breath was right in my ear, hard and fast, making shivers race up my spine. I felt his hips grind into my side, moving against me. Was he hard?

"Oh god," I whimpered a moment before an orgasm crashed into me like an angry wave. My insides strained in tension, pleasure rippling down to my toes and up to my ears.

"Fuck, Ava," Caspian groaned, finally pushing his body on top of mine entirely, making my belly press harder into the ground. His erection pushed against me, trapped between our bodies, rubbing against my ass. His abnormally sharp teeth scratched at my neck. Blanketing bliss rolled over me as I felt a painful pinch where his mouth was.

It hurt. It hurt more than a small bite.

I cried out and tensed, the orgasm blending the sensations of pain and pleasure. Quickly Caspian buried his fingers inside me again, feeling me tighten from his surprising bite. A deep, rumbled groan rolled out of him. The tail end of my pleasure became violent and all-consuming. It brought me higher than I'd ever been before. I stretched my neck for him instead of recoiling like maybe I should.

I moaned as I relaxed. His fingers slipped out of me but then he tightly grabbed between my legs, holding my crotch as if he didn't want to let go. His mouth left my neck and the trickle of warm liquid slipped to my collarbone.

"It's okay," Caspian whispered, his lips pressing to the tender spot on my neck that he'd bitten. It was sore already, throbbing.

His hand slid out from my shorts and he settled beside me again, pulling me back into his chest and wrapping his arms around me tightly.

All the fear from before had bled out of me. I felt content, satisfied, and safe. My eyes felt heavy, my muscles relaxed.

I wasn't sure what to say. Make a joke? Ask why he just did that? He squeezed me to him and it was almost too tight but I was too tired and satisfied to care. My neck hurt, his bite a sharp feeling but none of that felt concerning. It felt good. It felt like he'd wordlessly laid claim and I never realized how much I'd enjoy something like that.

I began to fall asleep. The combination of spent adrenaline, an orgasm, and the tail end of alcohol in my system made me suddenly exhausted. I didn't even want to move my arms.

"You're mine, Ava," Caspian whispered into my ear. I was so tired I didn't open my eyes, just furrowed my brow. The words were far off, slipping into my mind as I fell into the darkness of sleep.

9

Ava

I was dreaming. Shapes and colors were crisp and sensations felt sharp. I could even smell the soft scent of smoldering fires in the distance and feel the cool air of night on my skin. I couldn't recall ever dreaming this lucidly before.

The soft patter of rain dripped on leaves and soaked into the black dirt but no rain touched me, even when I held my hands out and waited.

There were no sounds of animals or bugs. The moon was being choked by clouds in the sky. I didn't feel any fear in the dream, just a detached calm.

I was standing in the exact spot where I thought I'd seen the shadow move. There was an empty space where the shadow had been as if something had been there but was now gone. I turned around to head back to camp but a cave was jutting up from the ground behind me, a gaping entrance beckoning me to come closer. Curiosity and lack of fear made my feet move forward.

I peered into thick darkness. The moon's light couldn't

permeate it. A damp, cool air slithered out and I took a step in, seeing if my eyes might adjust.

Swiftly the darkness was all around me. The prickled sensation of being watched rolled over my back, making my hairs stand on end.

A sense of unease began to develop in my belly and I pressed my hand there, pushing my palm hard against the fluttering anxiety. The darkness in front of me felt vast and I imagined a giant cave, the ceiling a hundred feet above me, and its tunnels going deeper into the earth than any person had been.

Anything could be in a cave like this.

I wanted to leave. The urge hit me in the chest and I jerked around towards the entrance but there was just more blackness. I had gotten turned around, like falling into the water and not knowing which way was up or down.

I felt dizzy, my head bobbing on my shoulders. The anxiety grew, culminating.

Then two glowing red orbs appeared in the darkness. An insidious buzzing noise burrowed into my ears, making me sway on my feet. I knew the red orbs were eyes, a monster looking at me.

The noise grew louder, making me grind my teeth. Nausea roiled up and I began to feel chilled while sweat collected on my forehead and above my lip.

This thing didn't feel like it should be in this world. It felt all wrong and it was looking at *me*. It didn't blink, it didn't move, but its presence pressed on my mind harder as if it was capable of seeing the very fabric of my mind and unraveling it.

I could sense its curiosity weighing on me. Its attention was almost too much to bear.

It shifted closer and I jerked away from it and spotted

the exit. I ran from the cave and through the woods, hoping I was heading back to camp. Instead, the ground suddenly sloped downhill. I felt my feet come shooting out from under me as my butt hit the ground and I slid downhill. The trees ended and the New River was in front of me.

Violin music caught my attention. It was smooth and sensual, drawing me in.

"Caspian," I said to myself. He was here playing his violin. It was the first instrument he ever played and the one he loved the most. My neck throbbed where he had bitten me and I felt myself clench between my thighs.

I stood up and moved towards the sound. Tree roots and a thin shore made me stumble along slowly as I followed the noise. The edges of the dream blurred the closer I got to the music, making me feel as if I were drugged.

"Caspian," I called out, finally seeing him. He was sitting on a rock in the river that was half-submerged in water. His long black hair was hanging down his back in waves past his shoulder blades. He didn't stop playing his violin and didn't acknowledge me at all. I moved closer, listening to his song in the night, both haunting and beautiful.

As I got closer, things seemed to be wrong. His hair was thick strips instead of small strands and glossy with a green shine. His skin had a pale, blue color instead of the normal olive tone. He was only wearing pants, his feet buried in the water to his calves.

The calmness and peace began to leak away. The music sounded harsher now, too fast and jerky. All the notes were sharp. It sounded threatening.

I walked around to see his face, trying to get his attention, but his hair hung thickly in front of his head. I felt nervous and unsure—an anxious feeling building in me. There were no tattoos on his blue skin.

"Caspian?" I asked quietly. Was this *really* him? My eyes trailed to his violin where he pressed the strings and pulled the bow. The music was growing louder into a crescendo, the notes straining over the increasing noise of the river. The water's flow was fast now. It splashed brutally against rocks, spraying up behind Caspian and sprinkling his body.

He refused to look up, to even react. My eyes trailed to his fingers, something was wrong with them. He stretched them out to play a note and I stumbled back, seeing webbing. My heart pounded in my chest.

His hair began to divide and glowing yellow eyes peered out, resembling an alligator's at night—like mirrors, reflecting light. I held my breath as we looked at one another. His stare felt mesmerizing, his music overwhelming. The urge to walk out into the water plucked at my muscles.

The sound of Caspian whispering flew around my head like a haunting of ghosts. The words were all the same, "*come to me*", overlapping and merging. It was as if there were more than one of him, all pleading quietly in my ears —taunting me forward.

His lips never moved.

"Come to me," whispered in my ear. I wanted to even though I was scared and confused. Even though he looked strange. Stranger than I first noticed—sharp long ears poking from his hair, bony fin-like protrusions glued on his forearms.

But it *was* Caspian. I could feel it and I wanted to do what he begged me to. I wanted to be with him.

A high-pitched grating noise shot through my head, making me cry out. It sounded like speakers screeching with bad feedback. I jerked my head to the forest. Two circular, glowing red eyes looked from between thin trees and shadows. The monster's body was shaped like a man's but hidden in shadows.

The dream felt too real—all of it—and suddenly I just *knew* that Mothman was real and that he was coming for me.

Mothman stepped out from shadows and I saw a leather hat on his head, the brim wide and worn, cloaking his face in shadows. A dark brown leather duster coat hung down to hide the tops of his boots, swaddling his body from sight, hiding what differences might lay underneath.

The glowing red eyes never blinked, burning into me, making my eyes widen. I felt unable to look away. The rest of his face was pure blackness. A void of darkness.

Behind me, Caspian's violin screeched, the bow bearing down on strings that threatened to snap. It sounded angry, filled with rage.

It was all too overwhelming, two monsters demanding my attention, angry it was divided. The violin squealed and the white noise from Mothman buzzed in my head at the same time.

I screamed, slamming my hands to my ears, half expecting to feel blood leaking out.

"Ava!" A voice in my ear called to me.

My eyes popped open and the tent's ceiling came into view just barely visible in the darkness. Caspian was pressed up on his elbow, looking at me with wide eyes.

I patted the mattress around me until I felt my phone. It was four in the morning. I swallowed and laid there, blinking at the ceiling of the tent. Caspian must have woken me because I was screaming in my sleep. I shuddered for a brief second, still feeling the cloying dream in my mind.

"Sorr—" Before I could finish apologizing for screaming he pressed his hand to my mouth, not letting me finish.

That's when I heard it. The shuffle and crunch of twigs and leaves outside the tent.

The raccoons were back? A twig broke under the weight of something too big to be a raccoon. Steady, heavy footsteps moved close to the tent, circling around the camp.

The sensation from the dream wouldn't leave me. It felt even stronger now. There was something in the woods that wasn't human or animal and it was close—watching.

It was *here*.

A scratching noise slid slowly across the side of my SUV. My heart pounded in my chest and my inside churned nervous energy. My mind replayed the ranger's details about a blood-soaked mouth and I imagined a pile of rib cages in a cave.

Mothman was in our camp. I felt it in my bones. That wasn't Caspian's bandmates or some other camper. It was something that terrified me. Something that felt unnatural and alien.

The scraping, scratching noise continued dragging across the vehicle as if someone was pacing around it. Did it think we were inside the car? Did it want to eat us?

Caspian moved his hand from my mouth. I reached out and grabbed him, not wanting to lose contact.

This wasn't happening. I was delusional. Half asleep, hungover from beers, and still freaked out by the campfire stories and running around in the woods. My fear and dreams were combining. The scratching noise suddenly stopped and a pregnant silence took over the night.

A knock.

A horrifying, quiet knock on the car that an animal wouldn't make. I pulled the covers over my head and unlocked my phone, trying to send off a text to my mom.

Me: *Something is trying to get us!*

Me: *I'm scared!!*

Both texts failed to send.

Caspian slowly moved to the front of the tent, blocking the entrance.

The knock came again and frightened tears spilled from my eyes. *I was not crying*, I insisted to myself. This was an adrenaline reaction, something biological. *I was not crying.* I wiped at the water leaking from my eyes as I tried to calm down and think logically. Think like a person who grew up in a normal family and didn't jump to wild conclusions.

I popped my head out of the covers.

"Hello?" I whispered as quietly as possible. It had to be his bandmates. Maybe they were trying to scare us.

"Ava," Caspian said quietly in warning but I ignored him. I cleared my raggedy throat and tried again. "Hello?" I said louder.

In response, the knock came again. Goosebumps rose over my arms. Why wouldn't they *say* anything? Something felt off.

I thought of the eyes, the cave, the sensations of wrongness. Mothman, a shadowed monster cloaked like some western gunslinger—hiding how different he really was.

I shook my head. I came out here to get away from these things.

"Who is it?" Caspian barked out.

Silence. We sat there eyeing each other, Caspian's eyes looking inky black in the darkness. His nose twitched as if he smelled something. I took a deep inhale but smelled nothing.

Then the knocking came again.

And again and *again*. Each time it seemed to reach inside my chest and tease more fear from me.

I shivered and more water leaked from my stupid noncrying eyes as I squeezed my arms around myself. Caspian laid back down beside me, holding me tight in his arms.

"It's okay, Ava. I can protect you," he murmured into my ear and he sounded so confident, so nonplussed. His confidence eased me a little. He squeezed me tight, holding me protectively. His hand gripped the base of my neck and his thumb purposely pressed into the bite he'd given me. It throbbed painfully but then I could breathe easier.

The knock came again but this time it was against the picnic table—right next to the tent. A dull thud of knuckles on wood.

"Cas!" I gasped.

"I'm going out." He started to pull his arms from around me.

"No!" I cried, clinging to him. He settled back down right away and whispered to me that everything was okay over and over—just like he used to. His gentle words and the slow way his hand rubbed between my shoulder blades made me breathe easier.

The noise never came back and Caspian's quiet, calm assurances that everything was okay settled me.

Eventually, I fell asleep exhausted.

10

Ava was still in the tent, sleeping in after the scare of last night. I roamed the woods behind our tent, trying to find evidence of what had been sneaking around. I wasn't having any luck though. I sent a look over my shoulder, making sure Ava was still in the tent.

I didn't want her to see something that scared her and there was so much of myself that could. *That* wouldn't be very conducive to my love.

I cracked my neck and rolled my head, stretching as I felt the shift come over me. It was instantaneous, a small ripple over the skin. It felt like stepping in water. My eyes blinked open and I winced from the sun, too bright for these eyes. They were made for darker places.

I shifted my eyes back to human, then swept my gaze around, inhaling through my nose again. The scent from last night wasn't here though. Ava said something had been in the woods—a shadowed shape.

Whatever it was, it wasn't what was at the camp last night.

The thing that had come to terrorize her in her sleep wasn't human. I'd sensed that much. Its smell was peculiar—like nature more than an animal. It smelled like dirt, smoke, and something I couldn't define.

I knew Ava called out to the weird and strange—knew that intimately. I looked down at the thick blue skin of my arms, the razor-sharp claws on my webbed fingers and toes. I used to pretend I was different from all the ghosts that latched on to her. They were needy things that wanted her so badly they didn't care if they scared her.

At some point, I'd realized I was similar. It was about the time I was kicking the shit out of the fourth guy who came sniffing around in high school. I was just as selfish as everything else strange that clung to her.

Still, I was different. I was *better*. I'd care for her, not scare her. I'd protect her, comfort her. I'd be anything she needed and hide who I was.

Anger slashed through me. Some creepy fucker was in these woods, something more like me. A monster. I'd never let it get her.

The loud sound of squealing brakes came from behind me. I shifted back to fully human. It was more an illusion than anything. Hardly something I'd call a true form but it was a functional form, operating as a normal human's.

I turned and went back to camp, furrowing my brows when I spotted a big bus parked on the street.

Fuck, it was the tour bus. I sighed as I walked across the street, making my way into Brandon and Matthias' camp. Brandon looked like he was enjoying himself while watching his morning fire. I'd better say good morning, it was only polite.

My foot connected to the camping chair Brandon was

sitting on, making the legs close up and the entire thing crumple beneath him. He yelped in surprise as he went down into the dirt. A moment later he was jumping up and snarling at me.

"What the fuck," he hissed.

"What is that?" I hitched my thumb behind me, pointing at the bus. The sound of the door opened and I groaned as I heard feet spilling down the stairs and into the campground. Brandon looked on at my displeasure with a wide smile. He slipped his arm around my shoulders and turned me towards the rest of the band.

"Look who decided to show up," he said proudly.

"Why?" I asked. There were two other members of the band—the bass player and the keyboardist. They spilled out of the bus, yawning, stretching, and squinting up at the sun.

"Well, I got to thinking," Brandon said as he waved at his friends.

"Where's Matthias?"

"Matthias is around, don't worry about him. He thought this was a great idea too." A fourth person spilled out of the bus that I didn't recognize. He had a video camera hitched on his shoulder. He swept it around and then settled on Brandon and me. Brandon waved and my body stilled.

"Don't be so tense," Brandon said and I shrugged him off, disliking touching him any longer.

"What is this?" I asked.

"A Nix camping trip! We'll post it to the band's youtube page. Hey, where's Ava?" Brandon asked, his head turning towards our camp. I looked back over at the camera with a frown before I flashed it a smile and waved like I was excited. It finally swept away to take in the rest of the campground.

The other band members came hopping over, looking *actually* excited. Their toothy smiles stretched widely at me.

"Ava is none of your business," I told Brandon as the camera guy set the camera down and started to pull luggage from the bus storage. I flicked my head back to the guys standing around me.

"Hey, Cas," the keyboardist, Grady, said. He had thick, black-rimmed glasses. One of those nerdy punk types that had a sweatband around one wrist at all times.

"Hey," I said with a flat smile of displeasure. This caused them all to laugh.

"I see he hasn't changed at all out in the wild," Grady said.

"Oh, I beg to differ," Brandon said, leaning in close to me. I eyed him, unimpressed. "He's genuinely pleasant when his girl, Ava, is around." I looked around at them as they smiled at me. They were up to something.

"Where is she? We were hoping to meet her again. Last time was weird, we want to make it up to her," Grady said. The bassist, Simon, remained silent. He wasn't a big talker and mostly kept to himself, something I normally appreciated but here he was to make my life difficult.

It almost felt as if they were trying to keep Ava and me apart. Nokken were furious, paranoid bastards when it came to their mate and I seemed to have that trait in spades.

It was the other reason I had needed a break from Ava five years ago. The tension of living with my unclaimed mate for years left me always angry and brimming with violence. Sometimes even lashing out at my own father.

"She's none of your business," I repeated.

"Don't be like that. We just want to get to know her—" Grady was cut off as I lunged forward, grabbing his Weezer shirt. He held up his hands and panic flashed in his eyes. "Nothing weird, she's yours. We all know that," he said quickly. I dropped his shirt and stepped back. They all shifted around quietly, off-put by my sudden outburst.

I rolled my eyes.

"Sorry," I said, smoothing the wrinkles from Grady's shirt. I rested my hand on the side of his neck and smiled widely. Sometimes smiling didn't entirely work. This was one of those times. It seemed to have the opposite effect, making them give me a strange expression. He also didn't seem to like me touching him.

It was so hard to figure these things out sometimes. Touch me, don't touch me. Blah, blah. What the fuck ever. I stepped back into my own space and dropped it.

"What's going on here?" I asked Brandon. For all his annoying shit I could at least rely on him and Matthias not being interested in Ava.

"We just want to get to know Ava, talk to her. It was wrong to blame her for your decision. See, I don't think she's even really aware of... well," he chuckled, "quite a lot." He gave me a toothy smile and self-satisfied eyes. I swept my gaze over the three of them.

What did they plan on telling her exactly? They had no idea I wasn't human, so it wasn't that at least.

"She doesn't know, does she?" Brandon asked.

"Doesn't know what?" I asked. He stepped up in my face.

"What a little fucking sociopath you are," he said in hate. I looked back and forth between his eyes. A smile slid across my face.

"If you go spouting shit to her—" I started but Brandon took a step back, rolling his eyes.

"I probably *should* warn her... " He trailed off. I noted

Matthias coming back from the bathroom, a damp towel folded over his shoulder, and his hair wet.

"See, I get it now," Brandon said.

"Get what, exactly?" My attention focused back on him.

"You're obsessed with her and for whatever reason, you go where she goes from now on. That's what you were getting at before, right? Well, what if she wanted to tour with the band?" He asked.

"*This* is your grand plan?"

Brandon shrugged, nonplussed by my reaction. I thought it over. The idea of touring around with Ava could be great but why would she agree? Our relationship was just now finally starting. Also, I couldn't ask her to quit this travel photography job. It was her first time away from her family. The first time she was putting her foot down about what she wanted. She was so excited about it. I couldn't take that away from her. I wouldn't even ask.

"Nah," I said, scrunching my nose. Brandon's face flashed with an angry expression. I smiled and shrugged at him. That seemed to piss him off more. At least this time I'd intended that reaction.

"See you guys later," I said with a bright smile as I went back to Ava. They watched me go with frowns, Brandon clenching and unclenching his fists.

Quickly I unzipped the tent, feeling frantic to be near her, to touch her. My eyes went half-lidded and I let out a strangled breath as I thought again of last night. Of Ava underneath me, of her body grinding and squirming, my fingers playing with her pussy.

She stirred as I came into the tent. I didn't bother zipping it back up, just kneeled down, my eyes going to my bite on her neck. All that was left was filling her up deep between her legs. Then she'd really be mine, not that there was any question of that.

Nokken were always male and imprinted with human women. It was an instantaneous thing that made my heart seize in my chest when I first saw her. It had been an overwhelming, life-changing experience.

Some nokken went a lifetime without finding their mate. Yet they were driven to constantly seek them out. It made for a bunch of manwhores, pulling women in with their wiles as often as possible, looking for the one who would be special.

Not me though. I'd only been fourteen when I first saw her. My new stepsister, with wide beautiful brown eyes and a curvy body that made me grind my teeth with a ravenous urge I'd never felt before.

There was not a single thing I disliked about her, except that she didn't instantly love me too.

"What time is it?" She murmured sleepily as I settled beside her in the tent. I buried my face into the mating bite and she made a small noise of pain that made my head spin. Pain and pleasure could be so similar, the sounds almost identical and the intensity equal. My poor Ava, did she realize I wanted to hurt her? Just a little though, just enough so that she could have even more pleasure.

"Nearly eleven," I said as she brought her fingers to the bite, delicately exploring it with the tips of her fingers. I didn't want to think about anything outside this tent. Not the thing in the woods that wanted her, my bandmates across the street, nor the big bus and rolling camera.

Only Ava.

"Caspian," she said somewhat in shock, feeling the wound I left her with. A slow smile of satisfaction spread over my face. I dropped it quickly as she turned, giving her an apprehensive look as I waited to see if she was angry.

"Last night..."

"The part with the raccoons, the knocking, or do you mean when you begged me to make you come," I said with a smile. Her eyes widened and she looked away, embarrassed, biting her plump lip, bringing my attention to it. We were so close in this tiny tent, touching all over. My breathing picked up and I couldn't think of anything else except having more of her.

"I didn't beg," she mumbled. "What was last night?" She asked quietly. I dragged my eyes from her ample cleavage to her face.

"What do you mean?"

"Was that... some strange way of teasing me more?"

"No," I said and her eyes darted to mine.

"Then why did you do it?"

"Because I plan to fuck you on this trip," I said, unable to stop myself from saying it. The shock on her face was priceless. She floundered, her face red.

"What?" She asked a few times. "Is that a joke?"

"You tell me," I said, caressing her wrist. She shuddered. I brought her hand down to my pants, pressing her palm hard against my cock. "Am I joking?"

Her throat bobbed as she swallowed.

"Please, stepsister. Help your stepbrother out." I thrust my hips into her palm. Her fingers gripped the outline in curiosity, making me almost jerk in surprise.

"This isn't porn," she grumbled. She hated it when I called us step siblings. I thought it was funny. Her fingers kept gripping me, exploring the size and shape. *Too bad it wasn't the size and shape of what she'd take*, I thought in humor. My mate would never take anything but my true form between her legs.

As she willingly continued to touch me, I felt desperate with need. She was touching me. She wanted me.

"Please, Ava," I asked quietly, the desire for humor drying up. My mouth cracked open, as she slid her palm over my length through my pants. Fuck. I couldn't act cool. I fumbled with the button of my pants, my eyes watching her face, making sure she was okay with this.

I unzipped my pants and pushed them lower on my hips until my cock was naked between us, a welling collection of precum emphasizing how needy I was.

"You okay?" I asked. She nodded and I swallowed, feeling too frantic. I grabbed her wrist and slid my fingers into hers, threading our hands together. Then I pushed into the grip that our combined hands made. I felt hot all over as my cock slid against our palms.

"Fuck," I hissed. She looked shocked but aroused with straining nipples, the brown tint showing through the thin tank top she wore. I jerked the fabric away from her breasts, baring her nipples to me. She sucked in a breath as I leaned forward and ran my tongue over them. She tasted divine-- her skin fresh and the hard points an exciting texture in my mouth.

I pushed into our grip faster, my breath hitching. She was breathing hard and I pulled back from her breasts to see her lips parted.

I couldn't stop myself.

"Ava," I breathed out, removing my hand from hers and cupping her face, bringing her in. She gripped my cock all on her own as my lips pressed into hers. A ripple of pleasure rolled over me. It had been so long since I'd kissed her. Too long. It was fucking pathetic how much this meant to me but I didn't care.

Instead of tensing when I kissed her, she relaxed into it. Her hand slid up my length and back down. A dry hand job, fuck I didn't care because she was touching me. That alone had my balls already drawing up. My tongue pressed between her lips and she made a small noise that had me consuming her mouth in smooth languid desperation. I was always desperate for her. It was as much a part of me as was my blood and bone.

I couldn't come like this though. Not in her hand. I needed between her legs, *deep* inside. So deep she screamed. Oh, how sweet her cries would sound.

My skin was hot, my arms shaking as I kissed her. My instincts were demanding I take my mate. A growl rolled from my mouth as I pushed on top of her, slapping her hand away from my cock.

"What—" She tried asking but I didn't let her talk. Our lips pushed and pulled, my tongue dancing with hers. I pulled back and looked at her, pupils blown, chest heaving. There was apprehension on her face too, a bit of confusion still there.

"You feel so warm," she said and I laughed.

"That's what you have to say?"

"But you are..." she grumbled. My eyes slid to the bite. Pinprick holes spaced close together. That wasn't a human's bite mark. My tongue slid over my lips and I settled my thumb on the mark.

"You didn't even complain," I said, pushing my thumb a little harder on the wound. The skin around her eyes tightened but her shoulders went back, her breasts pushing into me. It made me breathe harder, an eager smile begging to break out on my face. She liked me pressing on her bite.

I leaned forward, burying my face in her black hair and inhaling before pressing my mouth to her ear.

"Do you like a little pain, Ava?" I purred low. She trembled beneath me as I kept pressing on the mark.

"I don't know," she said shakily and I hummed in her ear, making her shudder and squirm underneath me. My cock was still out, still hard and leaking precum from the tip as it sat heavily on her leg.

"Do you? Like pain, I mean," she said gulping.

"A little pain can make the pleasure better. Could make you *tremble*." I stroked her hair and bore down harder on the bite. Her legs spread in an invitation, even as she winced. Her hands went up to grip my shirt tightly. Her body was telling me it was willing.

"What I'd really like is to hear you scream," I said into her ear. She sucked in a sharp breath, her heart hammering in her chest. I pulled back and looked down at her. Ava was biting her lip—anticipating, hoping, wanting.

Fuck, she was ready. I needed to get to the water and fuck her in a way no other thing could.

"Come on," I said in a rush, fumbling around the tent until I found the swimming suits I'd thrown in here earlier this morning.

"What?" She asked in confusion, sitting up.

"The water. I'd like to fuck you there," I said, laying down to slide off my pants and tug up my swim shorts. Her eyes zeroed in on my bobbing erection. When her tongue darted over her lips I nearly changed my mind, wanting her sensuous mouth around me. That wouldn't relieve this need to mate though. The instinct was a painful feeling in my gut, a demanding bastard.

"Wait," she said, her eyes furrowing as I got my shorts all

the way up. She reached out and tugged one side of them down.

Shit.

"Is that my name?" She asked, eyeing the tattoo on my hip. I swallowed, tugging the material back over the tattoo. I started to leave the tent, nerves squirming in my stomach. Was she going to freak out?

"Caspian?"

"Get dressed," I said, standing outside. She huffed in frustration but I heard her changing.

11

Ava

"Ava!" I heard a chorus of male voices call out as Caspian tugged me from the tent. His grip tightened on my hand as I looked up in surprise to see a huge tour bus with Nix written on the side in big letters. The entire band came trotting towards us with excited smiles all aimed at me.

The last time I saw these guys all together, they looked like they couldn't stand me. Now they appeared jubilant and it freaked me out. They all hurried across the street while Caspian groaned.

"Ignore them," he griped, attempting to pull me in the direction of the hiking trail. I didn't budge. I wanted to know what was happening. Brandon led the pack, three men behind him, all equally throwing off their rockstar vibes. Tight pants, tattoos, lots of confidence. Brandon even had neck tattoos, a rose in the center of his throat that sprawled across the side of his neck.

When they finally made it to us, they immediately invaded my space. Brandon wrapped an arm around my shoulder and pulled me into their group where I felt like a bug being pinned down to observe. Being suddenly surrounded by four cocky rockstars in the middle of the forest was making my head spin.

"Uh, hi?" I said and they all laughed like it was the funniest thing ever. Caspian stood there looking angry, *really* angry. It made me feel off-balance since I'd never seen him truly angry before. With no previous experience with his anger, I had no idea what to expect. My mind drifted back to him standing above a frightened Brandon, who was still sporting a nasty bruise on his face that looked even worse today.

"We would love to hang out with you today. Get to know the girl Caspian won't stop talking about," Brandon said.

"What?" I choked out, confused. Caspian talked about me? Caspian was looking right at me now, a blank look on his face as he observed—waiting for a response. My eyes widened. Was he checking my reaction because it was the truth?

What did that mean? Could he possibly like me? Had all the teasing actually been honest flirting? Plus, just a minute ago I realized he had my *name* tattooed on his hip. It was such a wild thing I had no idea what to think of it.

I felt my face blossom in heat at the idea of him pining for me. Of him possibly so interested in me he secretly tattooed my name on him. I mean, what the hell? But also, *oh my God*. Could someone squeal and look confused at the same time?

Some tension leaked from Caspian's body and the tiniest little smirk lifted on the left side of his mouth as he watched my embarrassed reaction.

"Sorry, we were just heading out," Caspian said to the

band, flashing them a friendly smile that didn't match the previous anger I'd witnessed. Brandon started to walk, pulling me along with him as the other band members swaggered beside us. I felt overwhelmed and confused, my thoughts spinning.

Caspian was acting odd, his actions swinging back and forth in opposite directions. It made me question his thoughts and actions. What was the truth? Was he just pretending to be friendly? I'd always imagined him the epitome of charm but had I been wrong? Was that just a surface layer?

I closed my eyes and tried to clear my thoughts but his bandmates were still talking—asking where we were going, insisting they come along.

"The camera is coming too," Brandon said and my eyes flipped up. I looked at the mohawked Brandon in confusion. He had taken to combing it back flat against his head while here, unlike the gelled monstrosity of height he'd had at their show.

"Camera?" I asked. The entire band laughed again and I frowned. Then they were off, leaving us behind as they raced across the street towards their camp to get changed.

"What's going on?" I asked, turning to Caspian. He was watching them with a blank look on his face and I wasn't even sure he heard my question. I reached out for his arm, it was hot to the touch. His eyes snapped to mine when I made contact.

"They want to turn this into a youtube series. *Camping Adventures with Nix* or something," he sighed, running his fingers through the strands of hair that had fallen out of his bun. He reached for me, tugging me into his body, and wrapping his arms around. He squeezed me before grabbing my face and tilting it up to his. My eyes traced his angular features.

"I still plan to fuck you, Ava," he whispered and my eyes widened. How could he talk so boldly like that? *I plan to fuck you, Ava.* Although I guess it wasn't surprising given his overtly sexual character. I thought back to what Brandon had revealed.

"Did you really talk to them about me?" I asked. He smiled widely at my shy expression.

"Do you like me?" He asked, instead of answering my question.

"I, well," I fumbled for words, taken off guard. It was embarrassing to admit I'd been struggling with a crush since the night of his show and that it was only getting much worse. Then again, he had a tattoo of my name on his hip. "I guess I do," I mumbled. He hummed in response.

"You *guess* you do?" He asked with a smile, his thumbs caressing my cheeks as he continued to hold my face. I finally tugged my face from his hands, tired of his teasing. I wish he'd just say he liked me back and end my cringing misery at the moment.

"Yes, I *guess* I do," I sassed. "And what about you Caspian?"

"Well," he said, his tongue swiping over his smiling lips before he leaned over, bringing his face very close to mine—so close it was hard for me to breathe. I was used to our touching but I wasn't used to the thick tension it now caused. Wasn't used to knowing he was a moment away from kissing me. "I *guess* I might have had a slight crush for a while now," he admitted.

"A while?" I whispered as he began to bring his lips to mine. He kissed me, a sweet peck, our lips pressing together softly.

"Yeah, a *while*," he responded with a small chuckle before kissing me again. This time his sweet kiss transformed into something deeper. A groan rumbled from his mouth into mine as his tongue slid between my lips. Caspian's kisses felt just like him, languid, smooth, and intense. I felt swept away by them, overwhelmed.

The heat of his hands made me feel feverish. The bite on my neck throbbed. Caspian moved, wrapping his arms around my body until he was holding me so tightly to him I felt squished. The imprint of an erection dug into my stomach, making me squirm.

My hands traveled up the sides of his body tentatively, touching his body in an exploratory way I never had before. Well, not counting when I had his cock in my hand a few moments ago--rubbing the skin of his shaft up and down his hard length.

"We should leave before they get back, maybe they won't be able to find us," he said, pulling back from the kiss. His forehead pressed into mine as his hands moved over my back, caressing me like he couldn't help himself.

"You two making out all day or are we having a river day?" Brandon barked out, startling me. I tried to jerk back from Caspian but he gripped me hard, not letting me escape.

"Guess we can't leave without them," I said. I felt a bit let down, wanting more alone time with him, wanting to explore this new thing we had. It made me feel fluttery and light as if I could lift right off the ground.

"That's okay. I don't mind them watching as I make you come," he said, making me suck in a breath so fast I began choking on my own saliva. That reaction delighted him. He chuckled, grabbing my hand and threading our fingers together as he tugged me towards the group. He wasn't being serious, was he? My mind offered imagery that made my face burn.

A few minutes later we were all bouncing down the trail that led to the river's edge.

There was supposed to be a good place to swim at the end of this trail. The two new bandmates were carrying a full-sized cooler while Matthias poured beer in their open mouths when requested. I couldn't help getting infected with their sense of fun.

Caspian walked behind me and every time I turned around to look at him he smiled knowingly, his eyes drinking in every inch of my body. Would he really fuck me in front of them?

Thoughts of last night slipped into my head. The *disturbing* parts. Had it been his bandmates playing a prank? That's what Caspian had told me this morning but something in my brain whispered that I knew different.

The paranoid sensation of being watched had me scanning the woods much like the campground manager did. My eyes swept through the trees, looking deep and far, trying to make out shapes in the distance. My eyes latched on to something and I squinted, trying to make out what it was. A buzzing started in my head making my heart rate quicken.

"Hurry up!" Matthias called out ahead of us. "We can see the river!"

"Are you okay?" Caspian asked, coming up behind me. We stopped on the trail as he melded his body to mine, his hand squeezing my shoulder. He looked out into the trees where I'd just been looking.

"Yeah, sorry." I almost told him I was still freaked out about last night but didn't want to bring it up. Caspian squeezed my shoulder again and then we pressed forward, spilling out into a tiny dirt beach with the river spreading out in front of us.

My eyes slid to the cameraman and I tried not to frown. It seemed like he was pointing his lens at Caspian and me a lot more than the others.

The guys started to shed their shirts and wade into the water.

"It's cold!" Matthias cried in shock and Brandon leapt at him, pushing him down in the water and causing him to shriek. It brought a chuckle out of me. My eyes slid to the camera, it was still on Caspian and me. I frowned, feeling uncomfortable by its constant attention. It was as if it was waiting for something.

"I'm surprised you haven't been swimming every day," I teased Caspian. He flashed me a smile, kicked off his shoes, and then ran forward. He lept upwards, climbing a rock that jutted above the water. My eyes widened as he didn't slow down, reaching the edge of the boulder and leaping, chucking himself over the edge.

I gasped in shock, my stomach twisting as he crashed into the water. We didn't know if the water was deep or not! My heart stuttered in my chest as he disappeared into the water. His bandmates looked over in silence, looking shocked themselves.

I ran to the shoreline, my shoes getting wet as I waded in, waiting for him to come back up. *Why wasn't he coming back up?*

Brandon yelled out suddenly in shock but by the time my head whipped around, he was gone, ripples and bubbles where he'd been pulled under the water. My head whipped back and forth, right to left, as I waited for either one of them to come back up. Caspian had been under so long.

Brandon suddenly emerged from the water, sputtering

and inhaling. A moment later Caspian quietly emerged beside him, smiling widely as Brandon swam away from him as fast as he could.

"How did you swim that fast!" Brandon barked with wide eyes. "Jesus, you ass," he snapped, splashing water at Caspian who laughed, diving back down. He popped up right in front of me and began lifting from the water.

"Don't do that again," I snapped, angry at how scared he had made me. "You didn't know if it was safe. What if there was a rock? What if it was shallow?" He came up out of the water, his swimming shorts and shirt clinging to him, totally drenched. I saw the outline of his new tattoo, peaking through but couldn't make out what it was.

"I'm sorry," he said genuinely, looking upset. "I didn't mean to scare you. I knew the water was fine—"

"How?" I asked. There was no way he could have known that.

"I could see it, from the top," he offered and I sighed as he rubbed my arms up and down.

"Okay," I said, still rattled but the tension left my body as he touched me.

"I'm sorry," he responded again, pulling his hands to my face and then leaning in, kissing me in front of everyone. I sucked in a breath and looked over at the camera aimed at us. I squirmed from his grip, thinking about what kind of show he suggested we put on for them.

I went back to the water's edge, kicking my shoes off and pulling off my dress. I slipped my fingers into the fabric of my bikini, adjusting everything. It was hard to find the right two-piece but this one had good support, with thick straps instead of anything too stringy.

Caspian's arms slid around me and he pressed me to

him. His eyes were burning as they traveled over my skin with hunger like I'd never seen on his face before.

"I need to be inside you," he said to me and my eyes widened, looking around but it was hard to tell if anyone heard him. I couldn't get used to how he kept shamelessly saying it like that. It gave my body a visceral reaction every time. He leaned in, kissing my neck below my ear.

"Caspian," I complained and he bit my jaw like an irritated cat. I could feel the others watching us and I could see the cameraman fiddling with something like he was zooming in. Oh hell. Caspian didn't seem to mind, he was pawing me, kissing my neck and jaw, grinding himself against me. I'd never seen him like this. It was making me dizzy and my body felt heavy.

"What's on your neck?" The cameraman asked with a frown, confirming he was indeed zooming in on us. Caspian sighed in annoyance but finally dislodged from me, holding my hand as we moved into deeper water. There was a pull in the water that could sweep us downstream lazily if we wanted to float.

"It's nothing," I responded to the question, covering the bite with my hand. It felt embarrassing for everyone to see it. A display of kinkiness for everyone to peer at closely. I wasn't even sure how I should feel about it entirely. It shocked me how much I didn't mind it, how much I *enjoyed* it. The idea of Caspian biting me again had places low in my body tightening in anticipation. It had been so brutal and raw, a man unable to control just how much he wanted me in every way. Then the way he kept looking at and teasing the area as if the mark was something he was proud I wore.

Brandon came over closer and his eyes widened.

"Fuck, that's a bite mark," he said as he jerked his attention to Caspian. "Did you do that to her?"

"It's fine," I grumbled, trying to talk low enough that the camera wasn't part of the conversation. I imagined this leaking out too, the entire world watching as their rockstar crush desperately pawed at me at the river. I sort of liked that idea though, having everyone see how much he wanted me.

Another bandmate swam up and gandered at the mark before I covered it back up with my hand and sunk lower in the water. It was deep enough in the middle that my feet couldn't touch. Caspian was at my side, his arms wrapping around me underwater.

"Holy shit," the other guy said. His eyes went back and forth between Caspian and me. "That doesn't look human." I felt my heart begin thumping hard in my chest. The memory of teeth too sharp on my neck, the dream of Caspian as some type of fish man. A mermaid? A siren? I didn't know.

Don't think about it.

"Shut up," I snapped out and immediately regretted it but it got them to stop talking. I frowned, feeling guilty for lashing out when they'd been so nice today.

"Are you okay?" Caspian asked and I nodded. He smiled. Underwater he tugged at my hand, pulling it towards his crotch. My eyes widened in shock as I felt his erection but then I bit my lip and moved my hand up and down its length. Caspian's eyes widened slightly like he was surprised I was playing along.

His bandmates were still swimming just beside us. The camera was still watching us like a remorseless stalker. The water was murky though and no one could see. My heart thumped in my chest as I moved my hand inside of his shorts, gripping him. The idea of making him come in front of everyone made me flush with excitement. I wanted to see it—see his face crack in uncontrolled pleasure as I made him finish with my hand.

Caspian hummed in pleasure before laying a kiss on my mouth. I gently squeezed right under the head of his cock, then ran my hand up and down his length while everyone unknowingly watched. His lips hovered above mine, his breath hitching slightly.

"Someone air up the tubes," one of the bandmates said but all my attention was on Caspian in my hand. His lips pressed to mine in between breaths and a small groan whispered up from his throat. I could actually feel him throbbing in my hand. The throbbing was so extreme it was almost as if the shape of him was changing, enlarging.

Caspian grabbed my wrist suddenly and tugged me off him. He cleared his throat and wouldn't look at me, as if embarrassed all of a sudden despite his earlier attitude.

"We should tube with them. It would be fun," he said, dropping my hand and swimming away. I was confused as he broke contact and left me swimming there alone. He'd started that, so why was he acting so strange now? It was just like in the tent. Things just started to get heavy and then he pulled back.

Did he really want this? Was he shy for some reason? Did he prefer going slow? I wouldn't press him. I didn't want to make him uncomfortable. I swam towards the shore where a motley collection of inflatable tubes and floats had been assembled. There were even floats attached to the cooler and someone tied it onto their tube so it could come with us.

"There's a place a few miles down where we can hop back off the river. There's supposed to be a parking lot," Brandon told the cameraman. "Can you meet us there with the bus?"

"Yeah, sure. Can't take the camera on the water anyway," he said, turning off his camera for once and heading back towards the trail. I watched him go, feeling relieved. Yet weirdly anxious as well. I watched the cameraman walk away until I couldn't see him at all.

12

Two hours later and we were hanging around the pickup area *still* waiting for the cameraman to show up with the bus. He was taking his sweet ass time. He should have been at the pickup stop before we even arrived in the floats. Instead, we'd been here an hour, wondering where he was at.

Ava was having a good time though, so I didn't feel too agitated waiting. My bandmates had stayed true to their word, being friendly but not *too* friendly. They'd just roped her into a Marco Polo game and she was wandering around with her eyes closed, arms out, yelling "Marco". A small collection of "Polo" screamed out as the guys shifted around in the water.

"Cas, come help me with this," Brandon said, tugging the cooler towards the shore. They'd decided to skip the ice so we could keep our phones, shoes, and clothes in there along with the beers.

I glided over to him underwater, breathing in the freshwater before popping up and grabbing the other end of the cooler. Brandon eyed me strangely.

"You never take a breath when you come up," he commented. I shrugged in response. There was no reason to explain myself. It wasn't as if a normal person would entertain me being nonhuman and just as I expected, he let it go. Everyone always did.

We lifted the cooler from the water and carried it up the shore into the small gravel parking area where the bus should have already been. When I turned to head back to Ava, Brandon spoke up.

"Ava is cool," he said and I sighed, turning around to face him.

"This plan to ask her to tour with us is stupid. I'm not letting that happen."

"And just why the hell not? We all get what we want, right?" Brandon was already aggravated, his body tensing. I peeled my shirt from my skin and shrugged. I didn't feel like explaining myself.

"Fuck, we just want to keep touring! We're about to hit it big. What were all those years of hard work for when you just quit right when it's starting to happen for us?" He asked.

"My goals were never the same as yours."

"What the hell does that even mean?" He asked, his eyes slipping behind me towards the river. It meant that all I had wanted was Ava to notice me as something other than her old stepbrother and friend, but now things were nearly perfect. I didn't need to keep doing anything else except take care of her. I wasn't going to explain that to him though. It wouldn't sound sane to a human man.

Brandon stepped a little closer to me, a fake smile stretching over his face.

"How about, if you don't agree, I'll seduce her," he threatened. A laugh burst out of me.

"Sure, go for it," I replied. Brandon frowned, clearly

unhappy with my reaction. His eyes slid over my shoulder and he sucked his lip in his mouth. "You're gay, Brandon. I'm well aware you and Matthias are together."

"What do *you* know? Sexuality is fluid and Ava, well, she's a lovely girl, isn't she?" He didn't stand a chance with Ava and if he did... *no*. There was no competition for me because I removed all the contenders. Still, his words screwed into my skull.

"No," I said, shaking my head, not wanting to believe it. Except, I couldn't imagine anyone not being attracted to her. I shouldn't have left her alone with the other band members. I began to turn around and go back but Brandon wasn't finished yet.

"Okay, how about I tell her what you're really like. An asshole, a *sadist*," he said.

"Oh please," I huffed in amusement.

"Everyone will say the same thing. That was a pretty little bite you left on her. You get off hurting her too?" He pushed up into my face with a wicked gleam in his eyes. "She's got a nice body. Big tits and a fat ass. Does she have a tight little pussy too?" I was momentarily shocked at the length he was going to piss me off.

"Shut the fuck up," I warned, barely holding on to my rage. It was just beneath the surface and he kept saying the wrong things.

"Maybe we'll offer the full band experience. The guys and me taking turns—" My fist smashed into his jaw, making pain burst in my hand. I relished it. He fell to the ground, completely caught off guard. A bark of pain burst from his mouth and the sound made my eyes nearly roll in the back of my head.

I wanted more of it.

"Get up," I growled but he was already doing it. Brandon

pulled his hands up like an amateur boxer. He gritted his teeth and threw a punch. It caught me on the shoulder as I slid to the side. I didn't waste time, shooting my own fist at his center. He cried out, clutching his side and I shuddered in delight. *More.*

He was still clutching his stomach when I pushed on his shoulder. He spun slightly and I slammed my fist into his lower back. When my punch pressed into his body and he cried out, louder than before, my muscles tightened as a rush of satisfaction ignited me.

I swept his leg and shoved him. He fell to his knees, wincing.

"Ava is *mine.*"

"Jesus, what the fuck is your problem?" He spat, wincing as he grabbed his lower back.

"Have I not made it abundantly clear what my *problem* is?" I asked. I took a moment to appreciate the look of discomfort on his face. Was that sweat on his forehead? Fuck, that was nice.

"Let me make it more clear then," I said, grabbing a handful of his electric green hair and pulling. He bared his teeth.

"Repeat after me," I said. He shot hate from his eyes and I smiled wider. "Ava is Caspian's."

"What the fuck—" he cut off when I jerked his hair. "Ava is Caspian's," Brandon bit out and I let go of his hair and pushed his head.

"Good boy," I said with a pretentious laugh. I think Brandon was my favorite bandmate, we always had such a good time together. If we kept all this fighting up, I might even consider him my best friend.

"You're a sick fuck," he spat.

"And you're annoying," I hissed my face careening into

his, my real teeth flashed for a moment, sharpened points of terror. His eyes bulged and he fell backwards on his ass. It was only a flash, something he might explain away later but right now he looked terrified. "If you even think about touching her I'll destroy you."

"You're serious," he said, scanning my face. I smiled but then his earlier words replayed in my head and I couldn't stop the rage. I lunged at him, he lifted his arms.

"Stop, please," he mumbled in a pathetic voice. I'd never once heard him sound that way. He started to shiver. What the hell?

"Caspian," a feminine voice uttered and I jerked around in shock to see Ava standing there, trembling as she looked at me with wide eyes.

"No, no, no, no," I said, feeling sick to my stomach. My hands started to shake. Satisfied laughter came from Brandon. Fuck, had they all *planned* this? Had he been goading me? I ran towards Ava and she flinched away. The air was sucked out of my lungs as I saw her reaction.

"It's not what you think. He was threatening you."

"What?" She asked, her voice sharp and strong again. Her eyes zeroed in on Brandon. "What did he say?" I tentatively reached out then sagged in relief when she let me grab her hands and bring them to my mouth. I kissed each finger as I trembled. I almost lost everything and I still felt like I was fighting for it.

"I don't want to tell you. It involved him and the other guys... with you." I really didn't want to tell her but there wasn't much wiggle room out of this. Ava's eyes went to me in confusion and hurt.

"Why would he say that?"

"They want me to come back on tour but I can't Ava. It was a threat for me, what they'd do if I didn't agree to tour. I need to be *here* though. I'm so sorry. I just got so angry. It made me sick what he said."

"I didn't fucking threaten her," Brandon grumbled out from the gravel. I jerked around to face him.

"You didn't imply the whole band would take turns with her?"

"I didn't mean it like that!" I knew he hadn't been insinuating he'd force her but it didn't sound good either way and Ava didn't know them. All she knew is that before today they'd been mean and disliked her. I patted myself on the back for telling her they'd been the ones in our camp last night, trying to scare us. I'd said it so she wouldn't worry but it worked out well in my favor right now.

Her expression morphed into disgust as she looked at Brandon. I closed my eyes, sighing as my shaking subsided. She believed me.

"Bullshit, Brandon wouldn't say that," Matthias said, walking up behind Ava. My muscles tightened in anger and tugged Ava back towards the river. They were ganging up on me. They were trying to ruin what I had with Ava and in no reality would I let that happen.

"Caspian," Ava said, trying to get me to stop but I didn't. I pulled her into the water and tugged her along as I swam the sixty feet to the other side. We got far enough on the shore that I could lay her down, partially submerged. Her head rested above water while her hips stayed underneath. I settled on top of her, taking her face in my hands.

"I'm sorry that happened. This is all my fault." And it was because I couldn't get them to *fucking* leave. I swiped my thumb across her bottom lip. "It's okay," I said, pressing my lips to hers, hoping she kissed me back. When she didn't I pulled back.

"They really hate me?"

"No, of course not. They hate me for leaving. They know you're my weakness," I said and her eyes focused on mine.

"I am?" Her body lost its tension and I felt myself relax in response.

"You saw the tattoo," I said, hoping it was better to bring it up than keep avoiding the topic.

"When did you get that?"

"Right after I moved out." Her eyebrows furrowed at my response.

"Why?"

"I wanted to still feel like you were close," I admitted. She was looking at me with wide eyes. I pressed my palm to her chest and felt her heart fluttering wildly. Did she like the things I was admitting? She didn't look like she *disliked* it.

Her head lifted and her lips found mine. I groaned as she opened my mouth and instigated a deep kiss. My body slipped between her legs. I needed her. The desire and instinct to have her burned under my skin and ached in my stomach.

Just then a sharp pain pierced my temple, a white static in my mind. I pulled from the kiss, wincing in pain.

"Are you okay?" Ava asked, grabbing my face. My eyes lifted to the woods behind her and I looked around. Something shifted in the trees and I took a big inhale, smelling dirt, smoke, and something indescribable.

It was him. Mothman, or whatever the hell, had come to our camp for Ava last night. Now he was here, watching her. Of course he was. He wasn't going to let up.

"I'm perfectly fine," I said, dipping my mouth back to hers. I wanted him to watch. A smile curled my mouth as I ground between Ava's legs, my lower half shifting to true form in the water. She must have sensed my full intention because she pulled back, looking at me nervously.

"Do you have a condom?" She asked. I smiled down at her, brushing her dark hair from her face.

"No, Ava. They don't fit."

Ava

"What?" I asked. I must have misheard.

"Don't worry, I'm clean," he offered before pressing his mouth back to mine. My body hummed in want as he consumed my mouth. I shook my head and broke the kiss.

"Did you get tested?" I wasn't stupid. Caspian was a rockstar and the most attractive man I'd ever seen. He dripped sensuality. To think he didn't get around would be naive.

"No," he said, pressing his lips back to mine. He ground himself between my legs, eliciting a wanting ache that his hardness teased.

"Cas, we can't do this right now." What had I been thinking anyway? I could still hear his bandmates across the river. They were at a distance but in full view. Caspian groaned in displeasure.

"There's no reason for me to get tested," he whispered. "Do you understand?" His eyes held mine as I frowned.

"No, I don't." We looked at each other as my eyebrows furrowed. "You aren't trying to imply... "

"I am," he said.

"Oh, come on, Caspian," I sighed, pushing his chest to

get him off me. He didn't budge. Instead, he pressed his hips harder into me. He felt bigger than he had in my hand earlier.

"Ava, look at me," he said and I found his warm brown eyes.

"I've only ever wanted you since the moment I saw you." There was a raw fragility in his eyes—a fear of rejection. He was serious. This beautiful man who could have the world eating from his palms was serious. I wasn't even sure what to think about that.

"Not with anyone?"

"No, but don't worry," he said smiling, the self-confidence returning to his eyes. He began kissing my neck. "I know how to fuck my mate."

"Your mate—" before I could finish the question his head had darted into the water, going between my legs. I gasped as I felt him peel my swimsuit off. I couldn't see him at all, his entire body submerged. I could feel warm lips touch my folds in a kiss. His tongue swiped out, slowly parting me open with his mouth. It was tender and passionate. My back arched, my breath coming fast. His tongue slid up and began circling my clit, making me groan.

My head popped up and I looked across the river. His bandmates were looking over in curiosity, their gazes sweeping around, looking for Caspian. They were looking right at me, completely unaware he was between my legs, licking and kissing. It made me feel electric to be so close to discovery. For them to be watching me unfurl under their curious looks. Pleasure rolled over me and I moaned again, my head tipping back.

Wait. Caspian needed to breathe! How long had he been under? *Too long*, my brain whispered. I shook that thought away and tugged him up. He popped up willingly, pulling himself up my body until his mouth was on mine and he was grinding between my legs. I shuddered as I realized he'd taken off his swim trunks.

He dragged his naked length up and down. Something was going on but I didn't know what. He didn't feel normal. He felt... bumpy and sometimes when he ground just right it felt like there was a small suction that pressed on then popped back off as he moved.

Was he using some toy? But how could he? One hand was on my face, the other was tearing my bathing suit top down, revealing my breasts. His mouth went to my chest, his tongue rolling over my nipples before he sucked one into his mouth, caressing it with his tongue. A small suction pulled at my clit and I groaned, my hips undulating against him. I didn't know what it was but it felt good.

"Caspian," I said, gripping his shirt. "Take it off." Immediately he did what I asked, tugging his shirt off and throwing it to shore. He looked like a Grecian god. Poseidon perhaps, with his tall, strong body, wet and stretched above me in the water.

My eyes caught on the new tattoo on his chest right before he laid himself back on top of me. He had taken his hair down earlier today. His long black hair was plastered to his face and neck, dripping droplets.

My eyebrows furrowed as I processed what I'd seen on his chest—his new tattoo. Had that been my face?

Something moved between my legs. No, not something, Caspian's cock. It moved almost like an appendage, dragging through the outer lips of my pussy. The tip was tapered, poking tentatively into my entrance.

What was happening?

"Caspian?" I asked, my voice a strange combination of confusion and desire.

"Shh, it's okay Ava," he said, peppering my lips with kisses. "It's okay," he groaned as I felt the strange tip of his cock wiggle further inside me. "Fuck," he sighed before again telling me it was okay. Then his hips pushed forward and I was being filled up... and filled up.

"Caspian!" I gasped as he went in deeper.

"You've got such a perfect pussy, Ava. It's okay. You can take all of it. I know you can," he said. Could I? Because I felt the urge to retreat back as his tip squirmed around inside me. Deep, so very deep. One of his hands went to my hip, gripping it tightly and slightly pushing it down, holding me in place so he could fill me all the way up.

One side of his shaft was textured. It dragged across the bottom of my entrance, a bumpy texture that felt good. I groaned, my body relaxing as he began to pull back out. Then I gasped as he rocked into me again, nearly too far back.

Caspian suddenly winced and stopped moving. His head jerked up towards the woods as if he were looking at something. He ground his teeth as if in anger.

"What's wrong?" I asked, worried. He started to move again, dragging out of me with that jagged texture, it brushed over my taint and I shuddered, gripping Caspian's back.

"Nothing at all." His attention went back to me. "You're so perfect, Ava. Fuck I wish you could know how good you feel." His pupils were blown, bigger than I'd seen anyone's, like he was drugged out of his mind. It made me shudder but then he was deep inside me again, making me think of nothing but what was happening between my legs. How deep he went, how he moved inside me—an almost squirming sensation that couldn't be possible. It felt odd, but it also felt incredible, teasing my insides into further pleasure. Because of that, I didn't question it. I was chasing the sensations.

He didn't look away from me now. He rocked in and out of me like a wave, a look of awe and wonder on his face.

"Ava," he murmured as if in reverence as he rolled in and out. Over and over. *Ava, Ava, Ava*, on his lips like a repeating chorus. I felt the tip of him wiggle inside me, brushing a bundle of nerves that made me gasp and tighten. Caspian sucked in a sharp breath when I did. Then he did it again and again making me feel like a tightly wound ball that was a moment away from exploding. Instead of exploding though, I just kept getting wound tighter and tighter, release never quite coming. Instead of a wave, it was a surge, swelling up inside me so large I was almost scared to feel it crash down on me.

"You're doing so good, Ava," Caspian groaned, pressing his mouth to mine. He dragged his lips over my cheekbones and jaw, he kissed my nose and eyelids and temple. I liked that I was making him happy, that he thought I was good.

I moaned, writhing beneath him, needing some type of release as he thrust and squirmed inside me. How was he moving inside me like that? I shook my head, ignoring the thought—ignoring it all as Caspian rubbed in and out of me. He moved a hand between our bodies, his fingers pressing on my clit.

"I'm going to need you to come, Ava," he said. The way he said it was odd, like he actually *needed* me to come. My breath hitched as he moved in and out and his fingers worked me higher. His tip brushed and teased the bundle of nerves inside me and I finally, *finally*, crested brutally, my fingers digging into Caspian's back.

"That's it," Caspian rasped, shoving himself hard inside me. "That's it, Ava," he encouraged, his voice rough and throaty. He went deeper than before, the tapered tip of him shooting out straight and bumping so far back I saw stars because it *hurt*.

Caspian groaned, his forehead dropping to mine. A deep pain ached inside me but the orgasm was still rolling on, his fingers still grinding into my clit.

The dueling sensations overwhelmed me, making me whimper and tense up. Tensing up made the pain deep inside me increase.

I cried out.

"Fuck, I *love* that sound. It'll be okay. Ava." Caspian cut off with a groan and I could feel him throbbing inside me. He wasn't thrusting. Instead, he was anchored in that spot too deep. Warmth spread inside and with it, the pain was swept away into a euphoria. I couldn't speak, my mouth straining open on mute cries. Even my uterus throbbed, tensing and relaxing as bliss like I'd never known pummelled my body into pieces.

"It'll be okay. Ava, you feel so good. So, so good," he groaned. I could physically feel him filling me with his cum. Somewhere deep inside me was stretching to accommodate the flood he was gushing into me. I felt full, so very full it was nearly uncomfortable but I felt so good too. I could barely think at all, just lay there, feeling Caspian fill me to the point of bulging. I whimpered as I writhed beneath him.

"Shh," Caspian purred, his voice decadent. "You did perfect, Ava. You took all of it. Such a good girl," he complimented as he pulled out. A sharp pain shot off inside for a brief moment when he pulled back. I winced and he seemed pleased to see it, a languid smile of satisfaction on his face, his pupils still blown.

He kissed the bite mark, sucking on it. It throbbed but the memory of an orgasm accompanied the pain, making me want more. He pulled back, his tongue swiping over his lips then he looked down at my body. His large hand spread out over my belly. I felt so full.

"Look," he said and I looked down to see my stomach bowing out more than normal as if I'd just stuffed myself at a buffet. Caspian ran his hand back and forth. I was about to tell him to stop but he pressed his hand down gently.

Warm liquid gushed out between my legs, making me gasp. That was his *cum*, so much inside that I'd been bloated. That I could physically see how my body had expanded to accommodate it.

Caspian's blown-out eyes flicked up to mine as he gave a nefarious smile. Did his teeth look sharper? Chills raced over my arms.

You can't run from it, whispered in my head and finally, I realized my mom had been right.

13

Ava

"Ava! Stop, please! Let me explain," Caspian called out behind me, sounding frantic. I was shivering in my bathing suit, holding my phone in one hand and my bathing suit cover in the other.

"Leave me alone," I begged. I needed a moment, just one minute to get my head on straight and pretend my fucking cervix wasn't sore. The bus still hadn't come but I didn't care. I was going to walk back. I couldn't be near Caspian right now and I just wanted to be alone.

He grabbed on to me, flipping me around, forcing me against his chest, pressing my face against him. I felt him shivering as he held me and I wished from the bottom of my heart I could comfort him. I sagged into his hug, trying to see if I could let this go.

Then I realized my face was smashed against the tattoo of my likeness on his chest.

I jerked back, stepping away from him. He stood there with wide, open eyes. He looked lost and scared. It disturbed me to see such a strong, big man have that expression. All I had to do was hug him, do for him what he did for me and tell him it was okay.

But Caspian had secrets and they were beginning to terrify me.

"I'll explain," he said. We were standing at the start of the trail back to camp. His bandmates were grumpily sitting back in the gravel parking lot, finishing off the beers and bitching about the cameraman not being there. I didn't want to be around them either. I couldn't tell what was going on between them and me.

"Please don't," I whispered to Caspian. I begged him with my eyes. I didn't want to know anything. I wanted to find a way back to my peace of mind. Where things were possibly normal and not even more strange and frightening than I ever realized.

Caspian nodded, not looking offended at all that I didn't want to hear.

"Of course," he said. "Let's walk back together. I won't talk. I promise." God, he was trying so hard to make it right and I wanted it to be. I shook my head and he looked to be struggling to think.

"I don't want you out there alone. It's starting to get dark," he blurted.

"Then just wait a few freaking minutes to follow after me! I need space!" I snapped because he just wouldn't let up. I needed to breathe and he was stifling me!

I stomped onto the trail, tugging on the flimsy dress I'd brought. The path was dimmer, the trees strangling the dying day's light. I looked at my phone. It finally revealed it had spotty service and that it was eight—*much* later than I thought.

There was a text from my mom and I remembered the freaked out texts I'd sent her last night. Thinking about last night was not what I wanted to do while considering I might be in the forest alone at night again.

Mom: Are you okay?

My texts had finally been sent to her some time today. I shot off a quick text telling her raccoons were evil and I was fine but it didn't send.

"Ugh," I groaned, gripping my phone. It was taking much longer than I wanted to get back and every minute became filled with more anxiety as the woods grew darker. The trail didn't stay in direct sight of the river. Instead, it slid through the trees, making it a less concise path than I'd expected. I kept waiting to come to the original place we'd stopped at with the inner tubes, but it wasn't coming up. The trail kept snaking around trees, showing me brief flashes of the river.

Then, all of a sudden, I realized I couldn't tell what was what anymore. That the shapes around me were indecipherable in the darkness and the sounds had slowly changed from the comforting chirp of birds to the haunting hoots of owls. I looked up. The tiny black bodies of bats were chaotically flying near the tops of the trees, the sky still a dim shade of blue that let me make them out.

"It's okay," I said, taking a deep breath. I'd be back soon and Caspian was somewhere behind me in case anything happened.

There were too many roots that I'd started tripping over so I relented using the flashlight on my phone. It only lit up a small area in front of me. Enough I wouldn't catch my toes on knobby roots but didn't let me see much more than that.

The sound of running water grew stronger and I sighed in relief when finally I made it to the original place we'd stopped. The river's water appeared black in the night as it sloshed over submerged boulders.

I'd heard that people could get sucked underneath those boulders when the water was rough enough. They called them undercut rocks when water eroded away the bottom, creating a little pocket underneath. Combined with the rough pull of rapids, a person could get dragged under and never come back out, pummelled endlessly into the gap until they suffocated.

Sometimes the bodies never turned back up.

The first time I heard of them I thought it sounded like a horrible death—blinded, suffocated, and trapped in a small, foreign place that offered nothing but brutality.

The sound of branches cracking had me shifting my eyes off the trail.

"Caspian?" I called but there was no response. I started walking again but faster. My shoulders hunched and my head tipped forward as I watched my flashlight illuminate the trail only a few inches in front of me. I watched my shoes take one step in front of the other.

Another snap, closer... *louder*. The sound rattled up my spine and shivered up my neck, burying in my head—a pinprick of cold fear that couldn't be removed.

"Caspian?" I called out, stopping and looking behind me. There was no one there. Goosebumps popped out all over my arms as I heard no response.

I took off running like an idiot in the night, flailing over roots and rocks. A moment later I paid the price, stumbling into something big and careening down, my palms smacking into hard-packed dirt and rocks. My splintered finger knocked a root and I screamed out, rolling on my side as I clutched the hand to my chest.

I had to breathe through my mouth and wait for the intense pain to subside. There was something big in the path that my legs were still draped over. My palms and knees burned—they likely got skinned—but other than that I was fine.

I fumbled around for my phone. A noise of movement came from the forest as I searched it out frantically, my heart rate going fast.

Finally, my fingers bumped my phone. I lifted it up, first looking at my splinter. At some point, the band-aid must have slipped off in the river. It looked exactly the same as before. Perfectly healthy, the skin healing, but just under the surface, the old wood sat. Why wouldn't it come out? It was as if he was clinging to me.

I scrambled up to my feet, brushing myself off before I aimed the flashlight at what I'd tripped over.

My body stilled. It felt like I'd been dunked in ice water. Adrenaline flooded my system making me shake in anxiety.

The cameraman was in the dirt.

"Hey," I said to him, my lip trembling. My eyes scanned around but I couldn't see anything. It was all dark. Goosebumps popped over my flesh and yet again, I sensed eyes on me. I swallowed as I looked back at the cameraman. He hadn't moved at all. Not now and not when I'd barrelled into him, falling on top of him. He hadn't flinched, jerked, shifted, and his chest wasn't expanding for breath.

"Please" I whispered, not able to finish the thought aloud. *Please don't be dead.*

We were only twenty feet on the trail past where I'd last seen him walk away. *Twenty feet*. We'd pumped up our floats and laughed while he was laying right here. It made the muscles in my stomach tense in discomfort by the idea that he was close enough for us to help yet we hadn't because we just didn't know. Had he tried to call out and we were joking around too loud for us to hear?

I bent down, sucking in sharp breaths. I reached out

trembling fingers to press into his neck. My hand jerked back in shock as I felt cold flesh. I fell on my butt and kicked out, trying to get distance. My foot connected with the body and it jerked.

My kick caused it to shift. Wide eyes and an open mouth aimed my way—dead and unseeing. My mind careened away from the sight, tried to go somewhere happier. Caspian and me in the tent, his kisses on my neck.

I felt faint and swayed as I scrambled to my feet. My thoughts swirled like I was drunk even though I hadn't had anything to drink. I hopped over the body and took off back where I'd just come, trying to keep my eyes on the ground so I didn't hit anything. My heart thumped in my chest as I breathed in and out my mouth. Where was Caspian?

I tried to ignore the fear creeping in and concentrate on not tripping. I tried to imagine the edge of the trail growing closer and closer, Caspian waiting for me, all the bandmates sitting around. I tried to pretend I was safe.

But there was a noise... something was behind me.

Something was *running*.

A scream bloomed from my mouth, shattering the illusion that all would be okay as the discordant noise shot into the woods. Suddenly I wasn't just jogging back to the guys, I was running for my life.

My lungs burned, a metallic taste slid over my tongue. My thighs strained, my shins gave sharp shots of pain each time my heel hit the ground. I ached deep between my legs and could feel Caspian's cum still leaking out of me and collecting in my bathing suit.

Nothing about this felt comfortable, nothing felt right, and no matter how hard I pushed, how much I tried to suck in more air. No matter how much that metallic taste coated my tongue. I couldn't get away from whatever was behind me.

I could sense the moment I'd lost the chase, the moment whatever was behind me had the ability to reach out and touch me. The sensation felt like hopelessness and frantic terror melting together into a sickening gooey substance.

I screamed but it cut off, my lungs out of air as someone grabbed me. I inhaled, ready to scream again but a rough, calloused hand slapped over my mouth, muffling the noise. A tremor went through my entire body so violently I felt I might be sick.

Fear was white-hot and blinding, making me dizzy and for a moment I felt as if this couldn't be real. That reality couldn't be trusted because this couldn't happen to me. Not that I knew what was happening. All I knew was I felt limp and dizzy, my mind detaching from my body as I was dragged off the trail. There was one arm around my waist and one hand over my mouth.

There was a dead body on the trail just behind us.

The crunch of brush under our feet, the chittering of those damn raccoons, and the vibrant chorus of a million grasshoppers filtered back into my ears as I shook off detachment and came back to myself, kicking and screaming.

I thrashed as tears slipped from my eyes but there wasn't much I could do. He just kept pulling me deeper into the woods, holding me against his body as he went. Not once did he talk or make any noise. I watched in a panic as the trail grew further away. I screamed through his palm, crying.

Thick leather swayed around, rubbing against my arms and legs. I tried to stretch my feet so I could touch the ground but I couldn't reach. This man was a giant, probably taller than even Caspian. I began clawing at his arms that were covered in his leather duster. His grip tightened and I felt sharp points pinprick where his dark fingers dug in.

In the next second, he'd flipped me around and pushed my back against a tree. He pressed his body against mine and the smell of dirt and smoke engulfed me. His hand still covered my mouth and I had to take deep, long breaths through my nose to try and get all the air I needed. I tried to look up at his face but he forced my cheek into the bark, keeping me from looking at him. The rough texture of the tree scraped at my skin.

We didn't move for what felt like ages. He was tense, quiet. It was as if he was waiting for something to happen, listening out for someone to come. Were more people coming for me?

Then he suddenly pulled back so abruptly that I gasped, my body falling forward. I couldn't right myself in time and fell to my knees in the brush. My already skinned knees gave a sharp bite of pain. I jerked up, fumbling backwards on my ass, my eyes darting back and forth but I couldn't see where he was. Was he gone?

Movement caught my eyes, someone darting behind trees.

No, he wasn't gone. I flipped around on my hands and knees trying to claw my way towards the trail and up onto my feet but then a sharp static noise filled my head. I cried out, clutching my ears.

The noise subsided and I sucked in a sharp breath, my eyes widening. I knew that noise. Understanding came over me. Goosebumps popped over my skin and my lip trembled as I heard boots crushing twigs and leaves behind me.

The monster was here. Mothman had found me.

I jerked around and there he stood, wrapped in his leather duster and boots looking like an old western gunslinger. His dark leather hat was tipped down, hiding his face but as I looked at him he raised his head slowly.

Two red glowing eyes burned into my soul and the white noise filled my head, overflowing. Nausea squirmed like I had bugs in my gut and I gagged. My head swam, the world spinning.

Then everything went black.

14

MOTHMAN

Fuck, she passed out. I grunted in annoyance as I stomped towards her, bending down and rolling her so that her face wasn't in the dirt. Her breasts were barely contained by the clothing she had on. Her legs were entirely bare.

I swept my hand down her cheek, feeling how soft she was. My eyes dipped back to her chest and I reached towards her ample breasts, excited to see how they felt gripped in my hand. I hadn't had a woman in... well, trying to figure it out was depressing.

An explosion of pain rattled my cheek and suddenly I was face down in the dirt, pulling myself up on my hands while I shook my head out, trying to get rid of the ringing. My head craned to the side and anger washed over me as her fuck boy stood there in front of her like her white knight. White knight my ass. I was the one who just saved her, not that she knew that.

"What did you fucking do to her?" He snarled and I sighed, getting up on my feet and taking the time to brush off my clothes. "Answer me you creepy fuck!" He shouted.

Well, if he insisted. I spoke into his head and he clutched the sides of his skull and screamed. A muted laugh rolled over me as he fell to his knees, snarling.

Before he got back up he slid over to the girl, bending over her.

"Ava. Ava, are you okay?" He swept the hair from her face and she sighed in content but didn't wake up. So, Ava was her name... He shot a glare over his shoulder at me and I squinted, trying to get a good look at his eyes. They looked different now.

I jerked back in shock as he leapt at me. His body rippled and his appearance changed before he crashed into me, taking me down. I gripped his shoulders, trying to hold him back as he attempted to bite my face off. His mouth was filled with needlepoint teeth.

Well, fuck me. One of his hands swiped out and he slashed at my face. I hissed in pain as I felt claws damage me. I jerked my knee up and he grunted as I smashed his balls. Then I kicked him off me as he was momentarily weakened.

"Fuck!" He spat out, gripping himself between the legs as I scrambled up and pulled out my gun. I kicked dirt at his face for good measure and he sucked in a breath, slamming his eyes shut.

He'd need to learn that I played dirty. One didn't survive all this time in the human world without being a sly sonofabitch. By the time he looked back up, I had the long barrel of a .44 magnum aimed at his temple. *Feeling lucky, punk?*

"What kind of monster needs a gun?" He said in disgust, eyes red in irritation. I snorted in amusement then talked to him again, making him yell and grab his head as he fell to the ground.

"Fuck you!" He snarled. Ah, he must have actually

understood me that time. The sound of a broken twig had us both snapping our gazes to the girl, Ava, who was staring at us. Her eyes looked glassy and unfocused as if she wasn't really awake.

Needle-teeth jerked his face away from her, hiding himself behind his hair. Didn't matter, she'd already passed out again. I sighed and he looked back around tentatively then frowned at her slumped body.

"Do you ever talk?" He huffed out then held his hand up swiftly. "Nevermind." I stood there, holding my gun towards his head. He sat there, glaring at me. A moment later his skin rippled and he looked human again. I tilted my head to the side. When did monsters start coming in pretty boy models?

Whatever the case, I didn't like shapeshifting monsters. They were always the most conniving type of beasts. There was something vulpine about their fake human face that made me feel icky.

"Let me guess, you like Ava," he said.

I shrugged.

"Bullshit," he snorted, shaking his head. Well, he had me there. The girl practically glowed. She'd called out to me, though I wasn't sure how. Her mind had drawn me in over miles, pulling me in as if she'd hooked her finger into my cheek and tugged.

The next thing I knew I had been standing in that nearby campground. The damned campground, where the hunters plucked their victims from. And there she had been, her skin appearing golden with a subdued glow. My eyes could see things other creatures couldn't. What I'd seen from her was something beautiful. She was like a lily in bloom, stamen weighted down heavy with ample pollen.

The antennae on my head twitched under my hat as I thought about it. She was special.

Not to mention, I hadn't had pussy in centuries. Right now her tits were still spilling from her top and her ass was barely contained. I wanted her bouncing up and down in my lap as soon as possible. I could imagine her tits heaving up and down and me burying my face in them while I gripped her round ass, helping her up and down. *Giddy up, girly.*

"She attracts things. Ghosts, monsters..." he trailed off and I flipped my duster open and shoved the gun back in its holster.

"Run along, boy," I signed with my hands. He just looked at me in confusion. I started to talk to him again in my voice.

"Stop! Shit!" He yelled out, wincing.

"What are you? Mothman?" He asked and I shrugged but then nodded. I'd gone by more than one name. The humans used to call me the God of the Appalachia. They used to worship me, erecting totems that had decayed away with time. Humans were like that too, coming and going. Living and dying. Rising and falling.

It was no business of mine to be part of their lives. So why did I feel like I *needed* to be part of hers?

"No wings," he commented and I snorted in amusement. I watched him swallow and eye Ava. He was agitated and wanted her away from me. That much I could tell. Too bad I wasn't giving her up. Even if I didn't understand why I wasn't giving her up.

"You scare her," he said in accusation. Was that supposed to turn me away? I huffed, unimpressed. I'd known a few women that could be convinced to let go of their fear with the right motivation. And I had the right type of motivation. I smiled and he blanched. Most people screamed when I smiled so I guess he had that going for him.

I made a shooing motion and he looked offended, jumping up to his feet.

"I'm not letting you have her. She's mine," he snarled. Looked like he needed a reminder who wore the big boy pants around here. I did. Because I had a fucking .44 magnum that could splinter his skull like it was soft, decayed wood.

"It's Mark!" Someone yelled from the trail, startling the shit out of me. Fuck, I hadn't noticed anyone else. I pressed my hand to my chest as my heart thumped out of my ribcage. Needle-teeth started to laugh at my reaction, the little shit.

"Oh my god, I think he's dead!" The voice came again. I grunted in agitation.

"Caspian! Ava!" Voices called out. I eyed the two people I was with. So his name was Caspian.

"Bye-bye," he said in satisfaction and I huffed. He was right. I wasn't about to get in a fight with a whole group of humans, plus whatever disgusting shapeshifting creature he was. It was tedious fishing my bullets back out of people's skulls. All that walnut cracking took significant effort. Also, I didn't feel like hefting dead men into the water all night.

"I'll be back for her," I signed but he didn't understand so I told him with my voice, happy to make sure he got the memo as he hissed in pain.

"No, you won't. She's mine," he snarled—a broken record. I blinked at him and didn't bother explaining—trying to say that much might make his brain bleed. He'd have to stay oblivious to the fact that they were being hunted.

Of course, I could have written him a note but I didn't

like his freaky fake face. Plus, I was still harboring jealousy that he got to have sex with Ava earlier while I was left with a bicentennial celebration of blue balls. My gaze shot to her and I sighed in appreciation. She was my flame.

Caspian turned towards the trail, cupping his hands to his mouth.

"We're here!" He called out and I took that as my cue to leave, moving fast enough that by the time he turned around, I was gone. It's not like I wanted to stick around for a thank you. The idiot had no idea I'd just rescued her from the hunters. The hunters likely saw me do it too. Which I knew was going to bite me in the ass.

15

Ava

My boss at Sasquatch Inc, Ben, was on the other side of the phone. The morning sun filtered through the trees. The air was still cool as I sat on our picnic table, the only place reliably getting service in our camp.

"I *need* to leave New River Gorge," I emphasized to him. I wanted to leave this forest. The rolling blue mountains no longer awed me, they terrified me. They made me feel small, like a bug underneath a fast-approaching shoe. Any moment the only thing left of me would be the sick crunch as I was squished.

The Appalachian mountains were one of the oldest and, by area, one of the biggest mountain ranges in the whole world. How many deep caverns held never seen creatures? How many people worshipped old gods and believed in magic in these very trees?

I'd thought the woods were an escape from the strange and unusual but now I wondered if I'd willingly walked into something worse. An entire ancient forest of creatures peered out at me from between the trees.

"That's fine," Ben said in my ear and my body sagged in

relief. I hadn't realized how tense I was until suddenly I could breathe again. "Can I ask why?" He continued. I nearly snorted but remembered he was technically my boss and held it in. Then the words stuck in my mouth because I wasn't sure *which* words to share with him.

"Someone died," I finally said.

"Family?" He asked, sounding concerned.

"No, no. Someone here at the camp. I just..." I trailed off, not knowing how to describe how I was feeling. I looked over at Caspian. Thankfully, he'd kept his distance this morning. Right now he was at the empty campsite right next to ours, sitting atop the picnic table with his violin. His warm brown eyes were on me though, always on me, always watching. He was playing his instrument perfectly, the bow pulling beautiful notes. The song sounded like a ballad as if it were telling a story with highs and lows.

"It's okay," Ben filled in my silence. "Can you stay today and get the pictures we need? Head out tomorrow?" I jerked my gaze from Caspian's.

"Yes." I agreed but wasn't happy. I wanted to leave immediately. Get away from this place. Suddenly it felt like the mountains and trees were looming in close to strangle me. As if they never wanted me to leave. As if they'd been waiting for me to step foot here my entire life.

I had to get out.

"Ava, I was wondering..." Ben trailed off.

"Yes?"

"Have you seen anything weird there?" He asked and I stilled. Why would he ask that?

"Weird?" I asked tentatively. He gave a self-deprecating snort.

"Sorry, it's a personal interest I have. That's why I named the company Sasquatch Inc."

"You like Bigfoot?"

"All cryptids. You know, monsters." Whatever else he said was drowned out by the rushing sound in my ears.

"I've got to go," I interrupted him.

"Oh..."

"Sorry... I didn't mean to cut you off. I've just got a lot of pictures to take. Then I'll need to pack up camp," I said, forcing out a chipper sound.

"Of course. Of course. Just let me know, okay?"

"Hmm?" I asked, my eyes sweeping the trees then landing back on Caspian, still watching me. I swallowed and looked into the forest again.

"If you come across any Mothman stories, of course! He's famous where you are."

Ava pulled the phone from her ear and tossed it in her lap before rubbing her forehead anxiously. The song I was playing became faster as my eyes dragged down her body. Could she still feel the places I'd been yesterday? When she walked, did it ache? I loved seeing the way she pressed her thighs together because she could still feel me inside her.

The violin screeched as I lost focus, causing her to look in my direction. I had no idea what she remembered from last night. I'd brought her back to camp and she had slept fitfully, whimpering and moving all night in my arms. In the morning she had woken up gasping, her eyes wide.

"The cameraman..." had been the first words from her mouth.

"The rangers took care of it. Officials came last night and took the body." She'd looked up at me with wide eyes, sleep still clouding them. Then they had cleared and she scooted away.

"Oh," was all she had said before slipping out the tent, leaving me there with cresting anxiety that things weren't okay.

I stopped playing my violin and tried to swallow down the anxiety that still plagued me. Even if she hadn't seen me last night in the woods. Even if she couldn't remember that motherfucker that grabbed her. She still had figured out that I wasn't what I pretended to be.

She'd trembled after we had sex yesterday. I didn't like the fear I'd seen in her eyes. Panic had slithered into my gut. The idea that I could lose her was a thought I couldn't handle.

"Caspian," she called. I jerked up, clutching my violin's neck, and quickly went to our camp.

"Yes?" I asked in earnest.

"I asked my boss if I could move on to the next forest tomorrow." Her eyes held mine. "Will you... are you still going with me?" She asked tentatively and my eyes widened.

"Of course," I said, going to my knees in front of her. I set my violin and bow down before I placed my hands on her legs. "You want me to go?" I held my breath as I waited for her response. She didn't back away from my touch so I squeezed her legs gently, latching on to her. Her expression was filled with conflicting emotions as she looked at my hands on her.

"I need you," she admitted quietly. I sucked in a breath.

"Oh," is all I said as I exploded inside. *She needed me.*

"I sort of hate admitting it. I could travel around by myself but I don't want to. I want you with me. I don't think I'd continue the contract if I had to be alone." She slipped her hair behind her ear, looking self-conscious.

"You don't need to do anything on your own. I'm here. I'll always be here, Ava." Her eyes slid to me, a look of concern in them. I got up from the ground and pulled her off the picnic table. She made a noise of surprise as I tugged her into my chest and held her. *She needed me.*

"I'll always be here," I repeated quietly, running my hand down her back.

"I think I understand that now," she whispered. I wasn't sure what she meant and I needed to ease the anxiety I felt. Reaching up, I cupped her face, tilting it up. I swept my fingers over her temple, dragged them over her eyelids, traced her nose, and then let my fingertips linger on her lips.

When she gave no sign of reluctance I pressed my mouth to hers, sweeping my tongue in and gripping her to me tightly. She tentatively kissed me back--hesitant and stiff. That was okay, she needed time.

I wanted her to love me though. Could she? *Did* she? I pulled back and thought of asking.

"Caspian, I think at some point we need to talk," she said, looking away from me. My heart thumped in my chest and I swallowed. She played nervously with the sleeve of my shirt.

"Of course—"

"Not today though," she finished, pulling out of my arms. Ava walked away to the car. I didn't know what to think about where we stood. Still, I felt better than before. We were leaving together. *She needed me.*

I looked off into the woods and I smiled, walking to the edge.

"We're leaving fucker, you don't get her."

Sharp static entered my head, letting me know the Mothman monster was close enough to hear me. I grit my teeth in annoyance. Instead of imparting me words, he filled my head with a rolling, deep laugh that sounded like a demonic beast hacking.

16

Ava

Caspian's bandmates invaded our camp in the evening and built a bonfire that crawled up towards the treetops. The size of the flames made me nervous and the heat was harsh on my forearms. I kept expecting the campground manager to come by with a warning, or even the ranger to slap us with a fine and stern look of judgment.

Instead, no one bothered us. The family that had been camping here had left sometime this morning, in a hurry after they saw a body bag carted away. That left us the only ones here.

The flames licked the sky as the guys drowned themselves in drinks. It was as if we were entirely alone in our corridor of the forest.

That wasn't entirely true though, was it?

One more night, then I could be gone. All the pictures were taken and most of the gear was packed.

"They said he tripped and his head hit an exposed root. Bad luck," the keyboardist, Grady, said, pushing his thick-rimmed glasses back up his nose.

"Bullshit," Brandon spat out before cracking open

another beer and chugging it. He chucked it towards the trash bag and it landed in the dirt ten feet away. He was sitting in a camping chair with a laptop on his knees.

Matthias plopped down in the chair next to mine and smiled. I wanted to remain angry at them, but tragedy had a way of muting that. Plus, I think we all felt a little unsafe and were swarming together for safety. I certainly didn't want them to leave.

The bass player was hooking up speakers around our camp and Matthias had his guitar laying across his lap. Clearly, they were getting ready to play.

"Well, what do *you* think happened?" Grady asked Brandon.

"The ranger told us that people disappear every year. There's someone out there killing people," Brandon said. I bristled, wrapping my arms around myself, and tried to rub away goosebumps that had no business being there with the scalding fire so close.

"Fuck off. No one killed Mark. What freaks me out is how close it happened to us. He died with us standing right there," Grady commented. I started to get up from my chair, not wanting to hear them talk about it.

"You know he won't go back to the band unless you come with him," Matthias said. I settled back in my chair and looked at him with furrowed brows.

"What?" I asked in confusion.

"Caspian quit for you." His blue eyes slid to me. Matthias didn't look angry or teasing. Though he did look uncomfortable with scratched raw bug bites all over his arms. Plus, his skin was pink all over, having spent too much time in the sun yesterday.

Matthias came across as the friendly peacekeeper type. Yesterday he'd seemed genuinely friendly at the river. I could easily imagine being his friend but the rocky start we had thus far worked against that.

"I didn't ask him to quit," I responded.

"I didn't think so. It's the truth though. Caspian is obsessed with you." He sighed and ran his hand over his forehead, brushing up sweat that had been threatening to roll in his eyes. As soon as he was done wiping it away, more swelled up.

"So, what? You want me to convince him to go back or something? I don't control him."

"You could come too. Go on tour with us," he sounded hopeful as he said it. The conversation was making me confused. Too many possibilities were running around in my head like rats in a maze. Did Caspian really quit because of me? Was he obsessed with me? Would I be willing to quit the job that I was so excited about? And why should I?

"Thanks," I mumbled to Matthias, genuine but not enthusiastic. He nodded and I noticed Brandon eyeing us, his eyes sweeping over Matthias before swooping back to his computer.

I pushed up from my chair and walked to Caspian. He was sitting on the picnic table, his converse shoes on the bench. His eyes glowed with the reflection of the fire as I walked up.

I was starting to feel bad for how I'd reacted yesterday. I couldn't get out of my mind how lost he looked when I pushed him away. No matter what was going on, what secret he might be hiding, he was still Caspian.

He saved me last night. I didn't know how. I just knew that one moment Mothman was looming over me in hunger and the next I was in Caspian's arms, safe in the tent.

I wasn't ready to hear about what secret he might have, but that didn't mean I had to push him away. I didn't *want* to push him away. I wanted him teasing me, holding me, and admitting he liked me again.

When I sat beside him he looked over but didn't reach out to twist his fingers with mine, didn't squeeze my thigh. He looked tentative and hopeful, waiting for me to make the first move. I reached out and threaded our fingers together.

"I'm sorry," I said. He looked confused.

"Why would you be sorry?"

"I pushed you away yesterday after we…" I trailed off and pressed my thighs together. "It was wrong." He sighed, unclasping our hands and wrapping his arm around me, pulling me into his body. His other hand came up and traced my jaw while his eyes roamed my face.

"You were scared." I opened my mouth to deny it but the words didn't come. Even now, I was still scared of the entire truth. It's why I was hiding from it.

"I'm not scared of *you* though. I'm just not ready for the truth," I said. He had been watching his bandmates untangle cords and connect all the equipment, but while I talked he slowly turned his eyes on me. They flashed for a moment, like a lens capturing light and shooting it back out.

"I know you wouldn't hurt me," I mumbled as he continued to stare at me. A smirk spread over his face, taking my breath away.

"But I do want to hurt you," he whispered and my heart flipped in my chest.

"That's different." I turned away in embarrassment because I was still trying to wrap my head around the fact that Caspian and I had sex. It felt surreal. The strange details of it didn't help.

Caspian grabbed my jaw and pressed his mouth to mine. Sharp teeth clamped on my bottom lip, proving his point of wanting to hurt me. I felt him press his fingers into the bite mark on my neck too, making it throb. It reminded me of the pleasure that accompanied his pain. Of the intense euphoria that had overcome me. I wanted it again.

I gasped and I felt him shudder against me in delight from my reaction.

"Are you still sore inside?" He asked, dragging his tongue over my lip, soothing the bite he'd just abused it with. I squirmed, feeling a slight ache deep inside me.

"A little." Our bodies pressed tightly together as he kissed me again, groaning as he held me to him. The sudden sound of music blasted from the speakers around camp. I heard Matthias start playing his electric guitar while Grady complained he was too drunk to go grab his keyboard.

Caspian ignored it all. His mouth consumed mine, his body seeming to heat under my touch, his hands sliding all over me. The ache deep inside teased me, making me remember the feel of his body on mine, in mine.

I pulled back. His face tried to follow, the flash of sharp teeth startling me. My eyes widened but I swallowed and pretended I hadn't seen anything. I pressed a hand to his chest, holding him back.

"How do you really feel about me?" I asked. He'd only admitted to having a crush for a while but I knew there was more going on. He had my name tattooed on his hip, my face on his chest. Matthias said he'd quit the band for me.

Also, it seemed Caspian might be... *something*. Something that felt a strange draw to me. Normally I was terrified by the idea of the supernatural wanting me. I didn't feel terrified by the idea of Caspian wanting me. However, it made me wonder how he felt about me. If it was just some strange fascination that was only skin deep.

"I don't know how to tell you," he said, his eyebrows furrowing.

"I want to know though." He shook his head at my comment.

"I *want* to tell you but I don't know how to describe how much I love you."

"You love me?" I asked with a strangled voice.

"From the moment I saw you." His eyes pleaded for me to understand. He grabbed my hand, pressing it to his chest. His heart was beating so fast. "Ava, you mean everything to me."

"Caspian, let's play," Matthias called out to him but Caspian acted as if he hadn't heard it, his eyes still on mine, his hand still pressing mine to his chest. *He loved me*. I was speechless, struck dumb by his words. He seemed to be waiting for me to say something back but I had no idea what to say.

I felt shocked that this beautiful man, this rock star, was looking at me as if I'd hung the moon and stars. As if there was nothing else in the world but me. Things started to fall in place. I understood finally that it wasn't his personality that had made him treat me with such attention and warmth. It was his love.

"Come on," Brandon griped. As I continued to say nothing, Caspian just smiled sadly, dragging his thumb over my lip before getting up and walking to his bandmates.

What just happened? What was that sad smile for?

Brandon clicked on his laptop and one of their songs began playing, but only with the drums and keyboard. Matthias and the bass player started to play their parts live. I still had no idea what the bass player's name was. He was exceptionally quiet and I wasn't sure I ever heard him say more than "yeah" and "nah".

Caspian walked over, grabbed a mic that Brandon held out to him, and then Caspian sang.

Goosebumps popped up on my arms. There was something about his voice and I wasn't the only one affected. We all were, everyone's eyes slowly going to him and sticking like fly's descending to a sticky, sweet trap.

Caspian's eyes flashed to me as his lyrics trailed off into the woods, his voice amplified by the microphone they'd hooked up. I couldn't drag my eyes away as his voice wrapped around my head, demanding I listen and begging me to come closer. Just like that dream.

He was singing about a desperate love that consumed him and then begging—begging her to love him... begging *me*.

I couldn't sit there any longer. His attention and emotions felt hotter than the flames lapping out towards the sky, singeing the low-hanging leaves. I was overwhelmed, there was too much to process.

He loved me. He'd always loved me. And now what? I was responsible for him continuing his career? That wasn't fair.

I got up and passed them all as I headed to the bathroom. I needed fresh air because it was too thick here. As I reached the building though, Caspian was behind me. He gripped my arm and spun me around.

"Cas—" I was cut off as he pressed me against the outside wall and kissed me desperately. I moaned, my hands going to his face as he hitched me up. My legs wrapped around his hips and he ground into me, groaning into my mouth.

His hands went to my shorts, his fingers inching into the fabric at my thighs so that he could brush between my legs. I was wet, his fingers slid over my pussy and he sucked in a sharp breath as if shocked by just how slick I was.

"You get so wet for me," he said in pleasure, unwrapping my legs. As soon as my shoes hit the ground he was ripping my shorts and panties down, lifting each foot to pull them off me completely. I held on to his shoulders until he stood back up, his mouth finding mine again. I heard him unzipping his pants and pressed my eyes closed even tighter, worried about what I might see if I looked.

I could almost keep denying it if I didn't see it with my own eyes.

His fingers dug into my ass, lifting me back up. My legs wrapped around his hips and I felt him between my legs. The tapered tip of his cock began rubbing my clit in a way no normal cock could, sliding back and forth while applying pressure.

I moaned against his mouth, my hands gripping his shoulders too tight. I felt the tip of his cock move away from my clit, sliding over my folds in a caress. I couldn't help but squirm from the strangeness of it and the concern that maybe I shouldn't be doing this. Maybe what we were doing wasn't natural—my body not entirely made to be compatible with his.

"It's okay," he murmured into my ear, his breath tickling. The tip of him slowly slid into my entrance, warm and slick. It plunged, going deep, rippling in movement as it went like a wave, undulating inside me. My eyes popped open as I gasped. The forest was in front of me. The outdoor light for the bathroom was right above our heads, illuminating us.

My mouth cracked open as the strange movements of Caspian's cock made my muscles relax around him. It was as if he were massaging me open.

"Just like last time. Okay, Ava?" Caspian said in a rough

voice, his mouth dragging from my ear to my jaw. I tensed, remembering the pain but nodded as I felt him rock his hips forward, filling me up. "I know you're scared. I'm so proud of how brave you're being," he purred into my ear as I felt him go deep—enough to make me try to squirm away in panic, a knee-jerk reaction I couldn't help.

His fingers dug into my ass, holding me in place, not letting me get away. There was nowhere to go now, he had me pinned to the wall, held steady by his rough grip.

He filled me, groaning. He was wider at his base than the tip, stretching me at my entrance.

"Caspian!" I gasped, my nails digging into his shoulders. He pulled back out slowly, his cock moving in a massaging ripple as he went. It made me shudder—the sensation strange but pleasurable.

I groaned, holding on to him tightly. When his tip slid back out, it flicked my clit, making me melt into Caspian's hold. My body went slack as he fucked me with whatever he had below his belt--half tentacle, half cock.

He slid back in. Over and over, going so deep I tried to squirm away each time but he didn't let me. I winced, but then it was pulling out, flicking my clit, and caressing my pussy's lips before pushing back in. I felt teased and tense, always being played between the pleasure and the discomfort. I shook in his arms, breathing heavily. He groaned, his movements faltering.

"I *need* you to come, Ava. Be a good girl and come for me." He said it just like last time as if he really needed this to happen for some reason.

"What?" I asked between heavy breaths, feeling his strange cock press inside me against a place that made me shudder. He rubbed into it, making the sensation overwhelm me.

Caspian pulled out and ground his length against me. I felt the circular bumps on the bottom of his shaft rub over my clit, suctioning slightly before popping back off. I cried out and began rubbing against him, *needing* more. I didn't care if it was strange.

"Just like that, good girl. Just like that," he repeated, groaning into my ear. "I need you to come, Ava, It loosens you up so I can fit in your *deepest* part," he rasped, encouraging me to rub against the strange texture of his cock until I cried out, unraveling. The orgasm only just started to roll over me when he pushed back inside me, roughly filling me without restraint.

"Now *scream* for me," he growled in my ear, his voice excited in a way I'd never heard before. Pain pierced me as I felt him touch something inside me, breach it, go past it. The orgasm betrayed me, rolling on as the pain sharply bit into me, making me scream.

My voice carried into the forest and Caspian shuddered in deep pleasure, his cock suddenly throbbing inside me as he growled out a dramatic release. The pain was replaced with that same euphoria as yesterday. I felt my insides loosen around him as he filled me. My groan of pleasure was throaty, my mind lost to the pleasure.

He kept filling me until I felt full, my inside feeling stretched. My body had to expand to take every drop he was forcing in it and it felt so incredible--exhilarating. I wanted him to fill me until I burst in ecstasy—full of Caspian.

"You did so good," he rasped, kissing the corners of my mouth, humming in satisfaction. A small ache pinched inside me as he started to pull himself out. "Fuck, Ava, you feel so perfect." This time when he pulled out it was like a stopper being tugged. Warm liquid gushed out of me, coating my thighs and dripping to the ground below me. It was too much to be normal.

I shuddered in sensitivity as I felt his cock languidly slide across my pussy, caressing my folds lovingly. It slid over my clit for a moment and I jerked slightly, making Caspian hum in approval.

"I love you, Ava," Caspian said, peppering me with kisses, his hands squeezing my ass. "You did such a good job. I was all the way inside you. You felt it, right? How deep you let me in." His mouth sucked at the bite mark and I groaned, my pussy fluttering as if it wanted to do it all over again.

"I felt it," I responded, my voice raspy and weak. One of his hands began stroking my belly as if enjoying how it still felt momentarily swollen from his release. His cock moved through my folds as he slipped his hand down, pressing two fingers into my entrance. The sound was embarrassing, a wet squelch of his cum inside me.

When his cock tip played around his own fingers and then glided upwards to flick my clit I gasped. *It's weird*, my mind said, *strange and wrong*. Yet my mind also accepted it was good—*so, so good*.

A yell pierced the night. A terrible noise filled with sheer terror, coming from the direction of our camp. I stilled, goosebumps lifting all over my entire body.

Something big moved in the forest right in front of me. A big beast running in the opposite direction, crashing through the forest. My entire body tensed.

Had Mothman been here? Had he *watched*?

17

The scream sounded terrible, like someone staring down a horror so extreme that their mind cracked open and broke.

"What was that?" Ava whispered, her fingers digging into me. My mind fired off fast, my instincts were always simple: love, mate, and protect. I set Ava down before quickly picking up her clothes and shoes. I pulled her to the bathroom door, shoving her clothes in her arms before thrusting her into the bathroom.

"Lock the door," I told her. She turned to look at me with confusion, her mouth opening to talk. My eyes slid down to her bare lower half. Her thick thighs were completely coated in my cum. I could see more sliding out from inside her. It was the best thing I'd ever seen.

Before she could talk, I stepped into her body and slammed my lips to hers. Something was wrong and I had to protect her.

What if this is the last time I kissed her? I jerked back from her mouth, terrified by that intrusive thought.

"I don't want to stay here," she said.

"Something is coming for you."

"Something has always been coming for me," she said with wide eyes, her lip beginning to tremble. She was scared but so brave. Haunted her whole life but not letting the weight of it crush her. Brave to let me have her when I could see the fear in her eyes of what I was and of what I did to her body.

"*I* was always coming for you, Ava. I'll save you from the rest of them."

"The rest of them?"

"Mothman," I said. "You saw him, right?" She looked at me in confusion.

"Caspian, I'm not sure he caused that scream. I… heard him in the woods, taking off after the scream. He was watching us," she said with wide, concerned eyes. I knew he was there and I was happy to once again show him how Ava was mine. However, she was right. If Mothman hadn't caused that yell, what had?

"Stay here," I said, backing away and pulling the door closed. "Lock it," I said through the door. I heard the bolt slide in and gave the door a tug to confirm.

"I love you," I told her and then turned and ran towards camp, weaving my way into the woods so I wouldn't be seen. The music was still blasting, making it hard to hear what else was going on.

There were people at our campsite, a collection of strangers decked out in torn-up jeans, stretched-out tee shirts, and camo. They had my bandmates on their knees. Brandon was looking at Matthias, saying something to him calmly that I couldn't hear. Matthias couldn't be calmed down though, his nerves shattered by the thing he kept looking over at.

The bass player, Simon, is what he was looking at. His

blood was soaking into the earth around his body. Simon's mouth kept gaping open but he couldn't get a breath. He was on his side on the ground. Blood slid from his mouth and the entire front of his shirt was completely drenched in blood that looked black in the night. There was a modern arrow jutting from his chest. His face was gaping with raw shock.

Simon's mouth opened almost too wide, his lips stretching, panic culminating in his eyes. Then it washed away. His eyes lost focus and his body stuck in the same position, not even sagging, just *done* moving. Forever.

Matthias was shaking, his eyes wide and shooting everywhere. He began gasping and clawing at his shirt when the bass player stopped moving. Simon's eyes didn't close, they just kept looking at one spot on the ground, never leaving it again.

The loud music cut off as one of the attackers finally destroyed the laptop, slamming it shut then chucking it in the fire.

"Look at me, Matthias. Look at me. *Please*," I heard Brandon now, his words calmly begging. Matthias shook his head, trying to keep his attention on Brandon but unable to. Grady was quiet but crying, his eyes darting around in his own half-panic. Brandon was only calm because he was more concerned for his panic-stricken boyfriend than anything else.

"Where is she?" A man asked and I looked through the trees to see a big guy. He was probably about as tall as me, six and a half feet. He was thick too—well-fed but strong. His arms didn't have any cut to them but you could tell muscle was under there. Lots of it.

"She wasn't here when we showed up, Loren," a smaller guy decked out in all camo said. Loren was their leader it seemed. He reached up and adjusted the brim of his ball cap, hard eyes sweeping around the camp. I processed their words. *She...* Ava. He wanted Ava.

But why? He was a man, not a monster. Just a fucking man. Anger swept over me and I started to move from the trees. I'd kill him before he ever laid eyes on her.

A hand gripped my shoulder and tugged me back. I jerked around, shifting my face to its true form so that when I hissed, my needle-sharp teeth were barred. A hand shot out, a fist bombarding my jaw. My head snapped to the side. He took a big handful of my hair at the base of my skull, pulling it tight and jerking my face in the direction of camp.

"*Shut the fuck up*," a demonic voice sliced into my head, making my vision go black and sweat pop up on my forehead. I had to slam my mouth shut and grit my teeth to keep from crying out in pain. Mothman pointed past my body, jerking his finger at all the guns on people's backs.

"You've made your point," I hissed under my breath and he dropped my head. Why had he stopped me though? Why not let me go out there and die? I looked at him, crouched down with me in the woods. He was cloaked in dark leather —a long duster with a high collar, boots, and a wide-brimmed hat that turned his face into pure shadow.

Yesterday, I saw a mouth. He'd smiled and it was chilling. Out of the blackness, lots of little teeth blinked out of a mouth that was too wide. It reminded me of the Cheshire Cat in *Alice in Wonderland*. A strange, evil-looking smile that was too manic to be pleasing.

He wasn't made of shadows. I knew that the moment my claws had hit his face, the brief sensation of fur on my hands as I connected with flesh.

"Tell me where she is?" The leader asked again, eyes sweeping my bandmates who were on their knees. His voice was deep and powerful but not raised--a dark, storm rolling in over the water. A steady, calm threat pressing forward.

"Who?" Grady asked with wide eyes.

"The girl with your group. Black hair..."

"What? *Ava?*" Grady asked, eyes turning into saucers. He shook his head rapidly, his mouth sealing up. The leader made no response, just flipped open something on his belt I hadn't noticed. It was a leather knife holder. He slid the knife from the pouch and stepped up behind the person closest to him. Which just happened to be Matthias.

Brandon's eyes bugged, panic taking over his face. For once I was gripped with empathy for my drummer and it made me feel horrified because I knew what was about to happen. I could feel it like an ailment in my gut and there wasn't a damn thing I could do about it.

The leader reached out and grabbed Matthias, pressing the guitarist's head to his own body in a tight hold. Matthias cried out and Brandon began screaming. The sound grated on my ears like it wished to harm me.

I didn't see the violence of it, the leader's back was turned to me. It looked so normal from that angle, a man just doing a job. The weapon came away, held aloft at his side, coated thickly in blood. I saw the look on Brandon's face as he watched though and it made me feel sick, my stomach bloated with awful empathy.

Brandon flung himself forward as the leader dropped Matthias' body. He stretched his arms out to catch his lover but didn't make it in time. The body fell to the ground in a heap, dirt shifted into a tiny puff up around him. The ground became stained with dark blood at an alarmingly fast rate.

Brandon wailed and the agony of it made me jerk my

face away, unable to look any longer. The reality of Ava's possible death felt closer now, inching forward in my mind.

She could die. Die just like Matthias. A split second of quiet movement followed by the putrid sounds of loss erupting from within me. I promised myself I'd kill the man who just murdered Matthias. I'd gut him like a pathetic, squirming fish.

Mothman shoved a leather-bound journal into my trembling hands and I looked down at it. He sighed and flipped it open to the first page. Scrawled on the paper was psychotic handwriting that was hard to make out.

"The hunters want to use you all as bait to catch their prey."

"What prey?" I asked through gritted teeth. He pointed at his chest.

"Why do they want Ava then?" I asked. He gave a shrug. "Bullshit." He snatched the journal from my hand and pulled a pen from a pocket in his duster. He scribbled something out while I looked back at the camp. The leader, Loren, had moved on to Grady now, tugging him up to his feet and gripping him in a chokehold. The knife, still coated in Matthias' blood, was poised above his chest, the tip denting the fabric of his shirt.

The journal was shoved back in my hands.

"They must have seen something."

"Oh, they must have seen something. Thanks, really fucking helpful," I said throwing the journal away. He flung his hands out in a "what the fuck" look then crawled over to his journal, grabbing it off the ground. When he lifted it up and began dusting off the page I saw a drawing.

My eyes rounded and I snatched the journal from his hands. He'd drawn a naked picture of a woman. The face was crude, mostly glossed over. The breasts had remarkable shading, revealing where he'd rather spend his attention.

The girl had long hair with bangs, shaded dark. She had curvy hips that flared wide and thick thighs spread wide open to reveal an intricately drawn pussy with delicate, flower petal like labia.

"Is this Ava?" I hissed, slamming my finger into the drawing and smudging the pencil lines. He sighed while snatching a metal cigarette case from his jacket. He slid a hand-rolled cigarette into the black depths of his face. Then he struck a match on his boot and lit the end, puffing a few times to bring the end to a red glow of life. The edges of black fur and a long thin mouth lit up on his face.

Who the fuck was this guy?

18

MOTHMAN

"Is this Ava?" Caspian snarled. His finger pressed to my drawing and smudged the perfectly drawn pussy.

What a shame.

Dealing with this guy made me need a cigarette. I took it upon myself to get one immediately, desperately needing a hit of potent tobacco before I dealt with any more of his shit.

After puffing out a thick cloud in his face, I flipped the page for him, where an even better drawing existed. This one involved me with Ava. It was a close-up of her shocked but delighted face as I presented my cock for her to feast on.

Flip. On this page was her attempting to work my fat monster cock into her mouth. She was drooling comically as she tried to swallow down the bumpy textured shaft. Ava was so cute in her determination.

Flip. Oh, this was a favorite—her mouth open wide, her eyes bugging as I "accidentally" began sliding in the wrong hole from behind. I'd even written a dialogue box with her yelling *"wrong hole!"* because what was porn without a little humor?

Flip— Caspian tackled me to the ground, slashing his claws at my face. I bit into the cigarette as I threw my arms up, trying to protect my head from his attack. A felt a sharp pain in my arm and yelped.

He fucking bit me! I grunted and rolled. He fell into the dirt beside me but kept trying to claw and bite me like a damn cat. I looked no better, batting at his hands and face like I was trying to play-fight a kitten.

I pressed my voice into his mind, trying to remind him about the hunters but he was too far into some rage with me to even flinch when I talked. *Shit*. What was I going to do if he couldn't deal with the hunters? I hated those humans and in no way, shape, or form did I want them gandering at me. Whenever one of them accidentally spotted me it just riled them up for another decade of debacle.

Guess it was time to play dirty with Caspian. I tried to kick out at his balls but we were too close together, side by side in the dirt like a couple of old ladies slapping at each other from their beds. His face lurched forward, teeth snapping. I smacked him across the cheek then reached down. I'd grab a ball or two and squeeze those motherfuckers until he squeaked.

I grabbed a big handful between his legs and started to squeeze—too hard apparently because he barfed all over my face. What the fuck?

He shoved me away desperately and I was more than happy to squirm in the opposite direction. Hot chunks of whatever the fuck were on me. Jesus, was that hot dog? I started to gag while he groaned in pain. We were pathetic.

"Don't fucking touch me," he hissed as he laid in the dirt, glaring at me from ten feet away. I slid my hand down my face and duster, trying to get his gross sickness off me. I threw my hands out dramatically, emphasizing my angry confusion.

"Oh, *you're* pissed! You just tried to... Fuck, what were you trying to do!" His face went from anger to disgust. Lord give me strength, this dumbass thought I was trying to give him an old fashioned tug job in the middle of a fight.

A feminine scream rattled around the woods.

We stilled then scrambled back to our previous places, leering into camp just in time to see Loren shoving Ava around. Caspian immediately tried to burst into the party and I was forced to hold him back. Which just led to us wrestling again.

"You're an annoying little SHIT!" I yelled in his head. His mouth popped open to yell out in pain and I slammed my hand over it, muffling the sound. Then he chomped into my hand. I kicked him in the gut and then it got really ugly—fists flying, claws racing at my head and gut.

I couldn't even threaten him with the gun because he'd know I'm full of shit. Couldn't shoot a gun when trying to hide from a party of hillbilly hunters, couldn't fly or someone would see, and couldn't scream in his head without risking him squealing like a hormonal banshee.

That left me kicking dirt in his eyes and trying to go hand-to-hand combat with something that looked more like a predator than I did. I had a few sharp teeth but nothing like the horror show in his mouth and my claws were strong, but his were sharper.

Great, I'm about to get the shit beat out of me by a pretty boy with disgusting gills slapped on the side of his neck. He slashed and pounded until he got me good in the head. Fireworks exploded as I slumped to the ground. He jumped up and ran off, chasing after the group that had stumbled out of camp with Ava.

I rolled over on my hands and knees, my head swimming.

What an asshole.

It took a few minutes before I stumbled up, my head finally just a small ache. I walked into their camp and eyed the corpses in distaste. The hunters were a sick bunch. Every summer they stole people, trying to lure me out like I was some monster who starved for human flesh. I was a fucking vegetarian.

Loren was the Grand Poobah of crazy though. A smart sonofabitch and evil too. The hunters didn't hurt humans before him. He'd changed it all, snatching campers for bait and gutting them when they proved useless. He'd field dress them like a deer and then he'd grind them up with the pig sausage in the fall.

A bonafide cannibal. Their god didn't make many like Loren and everyone should be thankful for that. One was enough.

Today though, he'd die.

I'd been hiding from humans in these mountains for hundreds of years. Before that, they'd worshipped me. I felt nostalgic and somber for a moment. This was the end of the line for Loren's lot. I didn't like being the cause of it, even if they were sick and twisted. It didn't feel like my place considering I wasn't human.

I swallowed nervously, hoping Ava would make it out of this alive and okay. I couldn't let her die. This thing with her was serious. I didn't just want to fuck the girl. I wanted to carve our names in a tree and ask her to go steady. I wanted to be close enough that if she was already on the toilet when I had to go, she'd open her legs wide and let us piss in the bowl together. That was the type of relationship to aspire to.

In their cooler, I found bottles of water. I popped one

open and washed off the retch from my face and coat. I rubbed the water into the fur on my neck, making sure no leftovers were hiding in it. Finally, I shook myself off and headed out, stomping after her idiot boy toy.

19

I paced back and forth in the bathroom, sometimes shooting glances at myself in the dirty mirror above the sink. I looked scared. My arms were wrapped tightly around myself, my nails scratching at my skin as if there was an itch I couldn't get rid of.

Where was Caspian? What was taking so long? Why did I keep hearing screams?

Who, what, where, when, why. Shit! I was getting more nervous by the moment.

A voice brought me out of my thoughts. It came from right outside the bathroom door. A woman's voice, low and shaky.

"Help," she gasped. Shivers went over my arms as I heard the voice etched in terror, sounding close to tears.

"Please help me," she whined in desperation and I recognized the voice. It was the camp manager. The door to the bathroom rattled as she tried to frantically tug it open. I stepped in front of the door with wide eyes, watching it rattle in place.

"Hello?" I asked in my own shaky voice. The door

stopped moving and I heard her shoes shifting on the concrete outside the door.

"Please open the door," she begged. "Please, they're going to get me."

"Who?" I asked, resting one hand on the handle. I hovered my other hand over the lock. Some part of me wanted nothing to do with her. It was an instinctual need to protect myself and not accept additional danger. I swallowed, trying to shake off the feeling of apprehension. Didn't she have a key to get in though? Maybe she didn't have time to grab it?

"Please," she whined, not answering my question. I imagined her hurt, trembling, and scared, standing outside the door begging for my help. I flipped the lock to let her in but before I could tug the door open it was shoved into me. The edge caught my lip, grinding it sharply into my teeth. The door pushed and I lost my footing. My tailbone smacked the hard tile ground, sending a sharp rattle up my spine.

"She's here," she bellowed out, sounding pleased and confident. All the terror and shakiness from her voice was gone. Chills ran over the back of my neck. The air felt thick with anticipation of violence.

Suddenly, it felt dire that I got out of this bathroom and ran. Something very, very bad was going to happen if I didn't. The campground manager stood before me, blocking the entrance. I could jump up and barrel into her and run into the woods.

I never got the chance. A man stepped into the bathroom's doorway and the campground manager melted away. He was huge, as tall as Caspian but twice as wide with a ball cap hiding his eyes but not the grimy smile stretched across his mouth.

I screamed.

The blood from my split lip was already sticky on my chin. The man reached in and gripped my ankle, tugging me towards him as I clawed at the ground for purchase.

Somehow, somewhere, I'd made a horrible mistake. That knowledge hit me like a swooping gust of wind stealing my breath and crushing my body. I shouldn't have stayed in the bathroom. I shouldn't have left the campsite. I shouldn't have ever come to these fucking woods in the first place and should have listened to my family. Whichever mistake it was, was the type of mistake that could cost me *everything.*

I jerked around and kicked out. My foot connected with the man's wrist. My thoughts were scrambling, a wiggling mass of snakes all twisted together. He grunted when my shoe slid on his arm but gripped my ankle tighter, sliding me closer so that he could wrench me up on my feet.

For a moment we were nearly flush and my body convulsed in disgust and shock but then he shoved me away. I fumbled forward, my body connecting with someone else's. I recoiled, jerking back. All of my movements were jerky, too much adrenaline poisoning my system. I felt like I was choking on it.

The smaller guy attempted to grab me but I fell to the ground and tried to scramble away on my hands and knees.

"Get her!" The big man barked and the scrawny guy leapt on my back. "That's right, just wrestle her to the ground like a hog." The guy on my back was young and not that big but his thin arms had strength and he flattened himself on top of me like he'd been doing this for years.

He rode me to the ground and laid me out as I snarled and gasped. He jerked my arms back and my shoulders tightened. The rough, scratchy sensation of rope tightened on my wrists. Panic reared inside me. I squirmed on the ground, screaming, tears mingling with dirt, brittle pine needles sticking to my bloody chin. The rope cinched in place and I was lifted off my back.

"She's gonna be a handful," the big guy said with a snort of amusement, smacking the smaller guy on the shoulder in praise for a job well done.

A moment later we were back at camp, the big guy shoving me forward the entire way, my feet stumbling to get under me so I wouldn't be sprawled out on the dirt. My mind kept screaming *"run"* as my body shook from unspent adrenaline. I couldn't run though, I was having trouble just staying upright before the next shove hit my back.

An entire group of people stood in our camp—dirty faces and clothes, leering, heavy gazes. The bonfire behind them had died down but still cast their faces in shadows as it crackled behind their backs. My eyes raced over them in a blur as my heart plopped and pounded erratically in my chest.

The big man stepped around me, spitting something from his mouth to the ground beside us. Dark brown gunk soaked into the dirt. He seemed the leader, the rest completely quiet and looking at him for what to do next. He was wearing a pair of jeans, work boots, and a faded gray tee-shirt stretched over his beer gut and thick arms. Despite the story his belly told, his shoulders were the widest I'd ever seen and his thick arms were firm.

I slid my focus around the camp and my gaze stalled on the bass player, slumped and unmoving, blood soaking into the dirt. I reared back, gasping but that had me hitting the leader in the stomach. He shoved me off him. I stumbled forward and fell into the dirt. The copper tang of blood filled my nostrils as I landed in front of the wide, unmoving eyes of the bass player.

Simon, I remembered suddenly. His name was Simon.

It was a subtle but jarring thing seeing a murdered face up close. The type of quiet experience that might silently worm in my mind to haunt me for years. Tears pressed from my eyes, blurring my sight before someone tugged me up. Laughter rolled around the group, a putrid sound of rotten men.

"We've been watching," the leader said behind me. "Watching for a *long* time and we know what's out here. You do too, right?" I didn't respond. I felt shocked, my eyes dragging over to see blonde hair in the dirt. A loud sob broke from my mouth, choking me for a moment. Matthias was laying in the dirt, his face an expression of serene apathy. The bug bites were still on his arms but of course, that didn't matter anymore.

"Mothman is in these mountains and we're gonna catch him tonight," the big guy continued, pointing around at his group. Hoots and hollers let out in the group, excitement for blood sport. My eyes swept the crowd for any sign of civility and found none.

"He likes hiding but he came out for *you*," the big guy said, poking me in the back. I jerked away from him, giving him my front as I shifted continuously, eyeing the people behind me.

"Mothman!" He barked out abruptly in excitement, making me flinch. His face was wide and happy, a smile stretching wide as he retrieved a tin from his pants. He pinched stringy, brown goo out and hooked it into his cheek.

"He likes you," the leader said, his mouth spreading into a wide smile. The brown syrup from his chewing tobacco was smeared over his gums and teeth.

"There is no Mothman," I said, my voice scratchy.

"No ma'am," he said with a chuckle. "Mothman is one hundred percent real and we're catching that motherfucker tonight!" His voice grew louder until it ended in a roar. The group began howling like dogs, jerking their arms in the air towards the moon. His tongue rolled around his dirty mouth and then he spat brown liquid on the ground.

"Now that we have the perfect bait we'll get him," he said, leaning forward to speak just to me as the others continued to holler in excitement. My eyes slid away from his and in the trees, I saw something. The flash of reflective eyes.

Caspian! They blinked out and I swallowed, scanning the woods for any further sign of him. Another part of me hoped I didn't see him again, that he was running through the woods to find the ranger station. To find phone service. To get any help he could get.

"Let's go," the leader grunted out and I realized Brandon and Grady were here too, being shoved around the same as me. Their arms were bound and Brandon had a blank look that reminded me too much of Matthias' lifeless face.

"Loren," one of the men called to the big guy before passing him a glass jug. The big man, their leader Loren, reached out and took it from him. I could smell the scent of alcohol from here. He took a thick swig then eyed me with a smile.

"Open up, precious," he said with a smirk. He snatched my jaw hard, forcing my mouth open so he could shove the jug in and turn it upside down. Liquid fire ran down my throat and still felt hot and burning by the time it made its way to my belly.

He tugged the jug back and I spewed out what was left in my mouth before hacking. He took another swig then gave a bemused laugh. He was celebrating, in high spirits, stomping past the men he'd murdered without giving them a second thought. My throat felt ragged from screaming and from the burning sensation of something closer to gasoline than liquor.

"Let's get out of here before that other guy shows up. The long-haired one," Loren said, eyes swiveling around to the woods.

20

Ava

We were slicing through the forest on the very same trail from yesterday. I realized these men probably killed the cameraman. That they might have been waiting around for the rest of us. I realized Mothman might have saved me last night.

At this point, I had to hope Caspian had managed to get the rangers and that they were about to fumble through the woods, foiling whatever plan these people had.

Saved by monsters. I never expected my life to lead here. I couldn't wait to tell my family. I could already imagine the smug look on my mom's face. Although I hoped she'd look surprised at least, to find out monsters were in the world. I let those thoughts keep me hopeful as if it was so simple. Deal with this and later go home to my family. Tell my mom she was right, there was no running. I didn't care about being wrong right now. I just wanted to be okay.

Loren had tied a long rope to my wrists and held it like a leash. He walked behind me with a swagger and sharp eyes scanning the woods. There was something keener about him than the others. He was smart. Smart, big, strong, and didn't blink at murder. A man that seemed motivated by greed and pride if I had to guess. So motivated, in fact, that he had peeled the morals from his body like dead, sunburnt skin.

I decided to test out the restraints again. I faked left but then jerked right, flinging myself forward with force. The rope tightened but held, Loren gripping it into a fist as he spat out his chew and tugged me backwards. My feet slipped from under me and my body slammed to the ground.

"Get up," he said with a sneer. I did, scrambling with my hands tied because the alternative was someone touching me to help me up and I didn't want one sweaty hand on me.

I rolled onto my knees and pressed up. My breasts were practically spilling out of my gaping tanktop and I looked up to see one of the men eyeing my chest. His eyes snaked up to mine and his lips broke open, his teeth winking at me menacingly.

I got up and we kept walking. The sound of water grew louder. Through the trees on our left, I could see the New River. My eyes trailed down the stream but I couldn't see anything ahead. Even with the moon out, the mountains hugged the river, casting darkness everywhere.

A loud crack sounded on the opposite side of us, like something hard smacking a tree. The group jerked to a halt, eyes narrowing.

All of a sudden the sound of footsteps, fast and hard on the dirt came from behind us—from the water's edge. There was a blur of motion as things started happening. Caspian was jumping through the air, fist pulled back. He crashed into a stout guy, his fist slamming into the man's eye socket. The guy was pushed to the ground with the force of Caspian crashing into him and the punch laid him out cold. His eyes rolled back in his head as his body went slack.

Caspian crouched, kicking out at another guy. His shoes hit the man's knee. I heard a crack, then a wail of pain. Brandon and Grady were quickly thrown to the ground, shoes pressing into their backs to keep them from joining in their friend's fight.

Finally, I snapped out of my surprise and turned around, facing Loren, pulling my head back and aiming to crash our skulls together. His eyes swiveled to me and his lip curled up in distaste. He jerked out of my way and my momentum took me forward. He stepped to the side and gave me a shove, sending me sprawling into the dirt.

"Get him!" Loren barked out. Dirt was in my eyes and I couldn't see what was going on with Caspian but I heard a struggle. I writhed around, trying to get up as fast as I could because I needed to help Caspian.

My vision started to clear and I saw a man had Caspian by the water's edge. Caspian's face looked mottled as if he'd taken a few punches to the face. He was on his back, the man over top of him, holding him down. Caspian spat blood in the man's face, a gleam of pure rage in his eyes.

"You motherfucker," the man hissed, then he shoved Caspian by the shoulders, submerging his head in the river.

"No!" I cried, finally up and moving towards them. Thick arms came around my middle and then I was flung to the ground again. The air puffed out from my mouth and Loren pressed his boot on my upper back. Half my face smashed in the dirt and I could barely see what was happening. I could see Caspian's legs kicking, his hips bucking. I could see the man's hand in the water, holding Caspian's head down.

The sounds were the worst. The bubbles from under the

water of him struggling to breathe. I was screaming, dirt mixing with tears as I felt desperate to stop this. This couldn't happen. It couldn't.

The bubbles ended and his feet stopped kicking. I saw Caspian's arms go from hitting and clawing at the man to flopping on the river's tiny shore.

A ragged sound clawed up my throat, scratching it. Squirming hopelessness, a cleaving of emotions that was already threatening to rip me in half. This couldn't happen. I'd thought... I wasn't sure what I thought but I'd thought Caspian could survive *that*.

I hadn't told him I loved him. That's what he had wanted to hear before, wasn't it? I was just too surprised at the moment to say it back but it was the truth.

The man kept holding him under, making sure the job was done. He didn't see what I saw. Caspian's fingers were curling into the dirt in anger. It left deep gashes because there were claws on the ends of each appendage. I pulled in a breath, hope returning to me.

The man gave a bark of shock as the arms snapped back up from the ground, grabbing on to his shoulders. Caspian's feet shoved at the shore, sending them deeper into the river. The man struggled, trying to throw punches in the water.

They kept moving deeper in, Caspian's body disappearing entirely. The rest of the group were shouting in confusion, yelling for their guy to keep holding Caspian under. The man suddenly cried out in pain, his eyes flashing with panic.

Clawed, pale blue hands reached up from the water, gripping his face, digging sharp tips into his cheeks until he shrilled, his tongue vibrating in his wide-open mouth. The wounds blossomed in red, then thick rivulets ran down his face like tears. Slowly he was pulled under, hooked into the beast's claws. His eyes flashed in pure terror until the moment they disappeared, the water swallowing him whole.

Silence engulfed us. Everybody left standing there in confusion and surprise, with no idea what was going on. The water bubbled and a big gush of red exploded upwards from its depths. The river swept the color away slowly.

"What's happening!" Someone shouted, running towards the water, his boots splashing into the river as he tried to get to his friend. He waded out further until a shape floated to the surface, a whole body bobbing up, the throat ripped out in a frenzy of ragged bite marks.

The man in the water turned back to the shore frantically. His legs moved slowly, the water impeding his progress. His friends yelled at him to hurry. Everyone was confused, not knowing what to do as the situation turned inside out and upside down.

A head poked out of the water, black hair sticking to it. Two reflective eyes shone with the light of the moon. It was like the oxygen was sucked out of the air, everyone's words vacuumed up. Their minds were stalling. I could see it in their eyes, wide and brimming with concentration. Their instincts were screaming to stand still and quiet, to never look away from the predator or attract its attention.

The man in the water fell down and tried to crawl to shore desperately. The creature reached out its clawed hands, fins on its forearms, gripped the man tightly and then began to tug him backwards, back into the water. The man screamed as everyone stood with mouths hanging up, shock seizing everyone's muscles as they looked at the creature.

The man's body slowly submerged as he thrashed and wailed. Terror scratched up his throat until it was just gurgling in the water.

Run & Hide

"Fuck!" Loren bellowed and everyone finally snapped out of their daze. Their leader's whip-crack voice was just the starter they needed for their shock and fear to grind into action.

"Get to the bridge. Don't shoot it," he spat the last command like he did chew, ugly and impolite.

Loren gripped my arm and tugged me too sharply from the ground. My shoulder screamed, the muscle straining. I yelled but everyone was yelling. Everyone was moving.

They were running.

Running away from Caspian.

21

I dragged the man down before pulling him close. My arms tightly entwined around his body in a murderous embrace. Plump panicked eyes darted erratically, frantically searching for some way to cheat death. I slid my hand around his throat and felt the weak fluttering of his pulse against my fingertips.

I'd never felt anger like I did now. A consuming rage boiled under my skin, burning out my ability to think straight. Those motherfuckers had her. There was a pungent sour taste on my tongue that couldn't be washed out. Even my hands were trembling.

I curled my fingers into the man's neck and my thin talons sank into his flesh with the resistance of warm cheesecake. A pale, gooey cheese that pissed out its red raspberry filling. He jerked and bubbles of air exploded from his mouth, trailing up towards the surface.

He inhaled in panic. I could almost hear the sloshing sound of water suctioned into his lungs. He coughed, hacked, writhed, and inhaled more water as he thrashed in my hold. He was anchored in my grip though, his ending already written. I looked on in delight to see him struggle.

Even with water splashing into his lungs, it was still me he was most panicked about. Some reptilian part of his brain was screaming he had to run from the beast that had come to eat him. That if he could just get away from the monster, then he could survive anything else. I smiled wide. Sharp, thin teeth were packed tightly in my mouth. My tongue ran over the brutal tips, showing off.

His eyes bulged again, his pupils enlarging. He gave one last good attempt to kick me off while he drowned but the effort was wasted—a quick burn of oxygen that tapped an exhausted blood supply as life faded. Red rivers floated from the wounds on his neck like smoke tendrils in the air. His body began to jerk unnaturally and then abruptly stilled, his arms floating out to the sides, his eyes lifelessly locked onto my teeth in terror.

His death could only give me a fleeting sense of satisfaction. I liked killing him but there was no time to linger on that fact when Ava still needed me.

I'd done what I could to be the man Ava could want. But a man, I was not. I presented to her a facade so that I could offer her comfort instead of fear.

She was my soul, my heart, my purpose. My calm water.

Now I would rip the blinds from her eyes and show her the beast that lurked behind them. There was no going back after this.

I swam to the edge of the river, my body slowly emerging from dark water as I grew closer to the shore. My watergrass hair was a mess, hanging down into my face and haphazard atop my head. My skin was pale, blue-tinted and thick, made to withstand colder temperatures.

My hands and feet were webbed and tipped with talons.

Gills prominently decorated both sides of my neck. My teeth were razor-sharp, made for ripping into a raw fish diet. My mouth could open wide, the jaw unhinging so I could swallow things whole.

Ava would look at me in terror. The bony protruding fins on my forearms and spine, the thick pupils, and the enlarged eyes were all inhuman. Yes, Ava would be scared but those men would be too. They'd bleat like goats.

I'd save Ava by whatever means I had. Even if it murdered the chance to have her love me.

I moved through the trees, animals scampered away in fear. The group had taken off, wild with fright from something they never expected. What a joke. These people were supposed to be hunting a monster. Seems they'd never expected one quite like me to come knocking.

Something caught my eye, an old axe leaning against the tree off the trail. Considering how often these men must have paraded around these woods it wasn't surprising. The wooden handle had thin cracked lines through it. When my fingers wrapped around the wood it still felt sturdy. I tugged it up, bringing it along.

Ava

Loren's thick fingers bruised my arm. Every time I lost my footing it pulled at the strained muscle in my shoulder.

"What the fuck was that," someone panted as the group moved at a clipped pace. Brandon, who was still being pulled along, looked at me with freaked-out eyes. There was a questioning look, him wondering if I had known. I swallowed and looked back down at my feet, trying not to trip as we went uphill. Grady was still with us too, grimacing and quiet. His movements were sluggish, his eyes somewhat vacant.

"It was a beast just like the one we hunt. It wants her too," Loren said, giving my arm a squeeze. "We'll get it *and* Mothman," he huffed in disbelief and delight. We moved uphill, towards the New River Gorge Bridge looming darkly above us.

It had been the longest steel, arched bridge in the world for decades on end until recently. It stretched out over the river, the moon glinting off the metal. It disappeared into darkness, going beyond where I could see. A great big beast of modern metal.

We moved onto the wide paved road of the bridge. My feet glued to the spot as I saw a group of trucks parked against the side. I just knew it was these men's vehicles. You weren't supposed to get in the vehicle of kidnappers. It dramatically lowered your chances of ever making it home alive.

Loren jerked my arm and I cried out in pain as my shoulder was strained once more. I felt him tense, my loud sounds not sitting well with him. Despite his calm facade, he was on edge from the river. I could see that now. He didn't look as confident as before.

He let go of me, pulled the rifle from around his back, and aimed it at the back of Grady's head. Grady had no idea. He was walking towards the trucks just like his captor encouraged him. The gun fired off and I tried to scream but my ragged throat only coughed out a pathetic rasp. I heard Grady's body thump as it fell down. His glasses skittered to the very edge of the bridge before falling off, sailing down towards the river.

"The hell!" The man who had been standing near Grady said, looking pissed off while he rubbed his ear.

Loren turned his gun towards Brandon, whose eyes widened.

"Wait!" He yelled out.

"Are you human?" Loren asked.

"Yes!" Brandon gasped, his eyes spinning around the group.

"And your buddy down there," Loren said, jerking his gun in the direction of the water. "What is he?"

"I don't know. God, I don't know," Brandon said, his voice a fast-paced lurch. I didn't want to watch. My nerves were frayed, expecting to hear another gunshot any second.

"I swear!" He blurted out frantically. "I didn't know. I thought he was just an asshole not the fucking Swamp Thing." Movement in the forest behind us had every person spinning around. Loren swung his gun around on his back, putting it out of commission.

"Tranqs," he barked out and the men nodded.

My eyes searched the trees. My breath came too fast, shallow little gulps that barely kept me going. I was afraid. Afraid for Caspian. Afraid *of* Caspian.

Something emerged from the trees, stepping out onto the bridge. He materialized out of the shadows, the moon's light revealing his body. My eyes widened at the sight in front of me.

His skin, his eyes, his feet and hands. It was the thing I'd seen in the dream. The version of Caspian that wasn't human. He had the same size, the same shape, the same two legs but all the details were off as if he wore a horror costume.

The men's breath intermingled, fast and loud. They pulled their guns up.

"Wait," Loren drew the word out as if calming a riled animal. "We don't know what we're dealing with. No mistakes. Only take a shot you know you can get and keep shooting until it's down." He thrust me towards another man. There were only four men now and two captives that needed to be held. Which left only Loren and a second man with free hands to aim.

The monster had stopped when Loren talked. It tilted its chin up and thick, wet hair parted slightly to reveal a face I knew well. Caspian's eyes reflected the meager light as if he had mirrors in them. They shone, two little circular yellow orbs.

His face was etched in rage, his body practically vibrating. His lips pulled back from thin, sharp teeth. They reminded me of those creatures that lived in the Mariana Trench with terrifying mouths filled with unbelievable teeth.

A deep, trembling growl radiated up from his gut, a trilling bass that rolled all the way up to his mouth. It was inhuman. I could feel the hair lifting from the back of my neck as the sound expelled out of him.

He wore no shirt or shoes and it felt somehow wrong he wore Caspian's pants. My mind couldn't fully grasp that this was truly Caspian and not some monster that had stolen his body and warped it into something else.

Loren and the other free-handed man shifted back slowly, while Brandon and his handler moved to the side. The man holding me seemed glued to the spot in shock though. Caspian suddenly surged towards us, running full speed while pulling an axe two-handed behind his head.

A tranq dart sailed at him but missed. He moved closer,

right towards me. My heart seemed to vibrate and my breathing stalled out. I couldn't do anything, my body wouldn't move. *It* was coming for me and the pleasing features of Caspian's face were so tainted by rage it hardly looked like him at all.

The muscles in Caspian's arms and shoulders flexed before he swung the axe down with a grunt of effort, putting everything he had into it. The axe fell swiftly then jerked to a stop halfway into the head of the man who had been holding me. The man's grip slipped away from my bicep, his arms hanging dull at his sides.

Caspian grit his teeth in a snarl, put one bare foot on the man's chest, and then wretched the axe back out. His abs flexed as he did it. A sickening slurp accompanied the action. A queasy sensation thrummed through my body, making my fingers numb and my stomach roll.

The man fell on his back and blinked vacantly at the sky, seemingly incapable of doing anything until he gasped suddenly then died.

Caspian stood in front of me breathing hard, axe hanging at his side. A sprinkling of blood had gotten on his face. My eyes felt dry because I wasn't blinking. My body was locked up in shock—ramrod straight. He looked at me, saw my reaction, then took two steps towards me and fell to his knees at my feet, dropping the axe. The rage bled out of his face.

My eyes went to his hands, needle-sharp talons tipped his fingers, webbing between each digit. My eyes slid up to Caspian's face and his pupils were large and black, no light to make them shine and barely a sliver of the brown color lining the outer rim.

Caspian reached around me and I felt him untie my wrists and the rope fell down.

"I tried to be the perfect man for you," his voice wavered. He reached up and I stilled as those vicious-looking claws came towards my face. He pressed his thumb to my trembling lip. His eyebrows pinched in concern.

"You're terrified," he started, his voice cracking. Tears slid out of his eyes, which were slightly larger than normal, almost alien-looking. Caspian clutched both my arms in his hands and started to cry, his body trembling.

Movement caught my eye and I looked up to see Loren walking a wide circle around me, his tranquilizer gun aimed at Caspian's middle.

"Caspian," I said, my voice a whisper. He looked up at me with those alien-big eyes, holding the tiniest bit of hope. "Caspian," I said again, my eyes darting towards Loren. A hummed growl reverberated out of him as he saw the man slinking. The tears dried and his muscles flexed as he stood up tall. He moved in front of me, giving me his wide back—blocking me, protecting me.

Along his spine was a long dorsal fin, the bony protrusions between the webbing ended on sharp spikes. I heard the thwap of the dart being shot and saw Caspian's body jerk as it hit him.

"Caspian!" I tried to reach out and grip him, make sure he was okay, but he darted forward, barrelling towards Loren. He moved fast and the second tranquilizer dart missed him.

"Shoot him! Use the rifle!" Loren barked now that his own life was on the line.

"No!" I screamed.

Goosebumps suddenly popped on my arms, like a chilling breeze of air had suddenly blasted off the mountain. Static hummed uncomfortably in my head. Most of us suddenly stopped and turned towards the sky, mouths agape.

Two red eyes burned into us from above. Two huge moth wings, black and brown, stretched and pumped. Mothman floated above us like a god with his wide arms outstretched. His leather duster flapped wildly but his hat stayed steady. Dizzy pressure filled our minds.

As Loren struggled with Caspian, the other two men dropped to their knees and raised their hands towards the sky in awe.

"My God," one mumbled over and over.

"An angel!"

Brandon looked terrified and fell to his knees too, his head craning to look up. Loren tried to hold Caspian off as he looked on with wide eyes at the creature he'd really wanted. The one he was willing to do anything to catch. Captain Ahab and his white whale finally face to face.

"It's Mothman!" Loren barked but no one listened. "It's not an angel. It's a beast!" He growled. Caspian lunged at Loren, tackling him to the ground. Loren gripped Caspian by the shoulders above him, holding him off as Caspian tried to lunge and snap at his neck with those amazingly horrible teeth. Loren's face was a mix of anger and hope. Anger that he was so close to his goal and might be thwarted, but infused with hope that his dream might now come to life.

One of the men cried out in pain and blood started to trickle from his ears.

"It's talking inside my head!" He wailed in agony and delight. Loren punched Caspian and then kicked him off. I didn't know where to look.

"The angel is talking to me!" The man cried out again, so happy and in so much pain. Blood began to leak from his eyes as Mothman finally touched down, his leather boots smacking the bridge. His wings folded close to his body, disappearing inside the back of his leather duster.

"What is he saying?" The other man asked with wide eyes.

"He said..." he cut off as blood gushed thickly from his ears. He groaned in agony, his voice began to slur, the words a sloppy mess as they crawled from his mouth, "we're a bunch of hillbilly fuckwits." Mothman confidently strode forward, pulled a long-barrelled revolver up, and shot off a bullet into the bleeding man's head. It split into the man's face, bursting the back of his head like a water balloon—a rapid gush of liquid barfed out the broken back of his head, spraying out behind him for me to see.

My throat strained and ached as I tried to scream. Only a rasp hitched out from my mouth.

"W- what?" The live man asked in confusion, sounding like a confused, hurt child. His angel had called him a fuckwit. His angel just burst a man's head open. Mothman swiveled his gun to him and did him the same service he'd done the other. This time, I managed to slam my eyes shut.

I heard movement behind me and jerked around. Loren was clutching the tranquilizer gun and three thick metal darts were buried in Caspian's gut. Caspian laid on his back, giving that inhuman gurgled growl, his eyes pure rage. He was drugged to nearly complete paralysis.

Loren raced towards me, I turned to run but his thick arm came around my shoulder, pulling me into him. The sour smell of fermenting sweat leaked from his body. Caspian's eyes widened but he couldn't move, his body locked up.

My eyes pinged to Mothman. Across his leather coat, I noticed a fresh collection of claw and teeth marks that looked very similar to Caspian's.

A trail of smoke lifted from under Mothman's hat, twirling up towards the sky. He lifted a hand and pinched a cigarette from his mouth, flicking it on the ground and stomping it out with his boot. My eyes lingered on his hand. His skin was black and shiny, reminding me of wet dirt. His fingernails were more like little claws, thick, sharp, and black.

Two round red, glowing orbs peered out from under a leather hat and seemed to settle on me. I could see nothing discernable about his face, just shadowed blackness. He looked no different from when I saw him in the woods. When I thought he'd come to kill me. He hadn't though. He'd saved me from the same fate as the cameraman. From the same fate as Caspian's bandmates.

Brandon was lying on his belly on the ground, his forehead pressed to the bridge's pavement, not moving a muscle. Mothman ignored him.

"Take it easy. No one wants me hurting the girl," Loren said with a calm voice. I felt the tip of a knife grinding teasingly at the bottom of my ribs. It made my muscles flinch. I whimpered as acidic fear flashed inside me. The knife bit into my clothes, pinching my skin with sharpness.

"He doesn't care about me," I said, struggling to no effect.

"No, I think he cares quite a bit," Loren said, walking me backwards. We had to veer towards the very edge of the bridge to avoid Caspian who bared his teeth at Loren and tried to swipe his arms towards us. His arms twitched and then lazily slung up before dropping back to the ground. He panted from the effort and aimed his gaze at Mothman.

"Save her," Caspian wheezed from between needle teeth. Mothman groaned in annoyance. He pulled his gun back up, aiming it towards us. Loren quickly ducked down behind me, trying to shield as much of himself as possible. He also dug his knife in harder, breaking through the fabric of my shirt and slowly spearing into my skin. I could feel the tip slowly sinking into my body, sliding in painfully, and teasing towards my lung. I cried out in pain and Mothman stilled his approach and lowered his gun to his side.

Loren chuckled. I looked over my side, at the edge of the bridge. Loren had walked us backwards when Mothman approached. Now we were right at the edge. My shoe was just a couple inches from the dark valley gaping below us. I could hear the river's sounds but couldn't see it.

"I've been hunting you for three decades. My father hunted you, and my grandfather before him," Loren said. "It's me who gets you though. Me who's taken down the God of the Appalachia." He barked out a manic laugh.

Mothman looked off over the river and sighed. I could hear Loren licking his lips behind me, sliding up a little to straighten his back. A mistake.

Mothman's gun snapped up in an instant and fired. I felt Loren jerk and I sucked in a breath. His grip slid off me as he bounced from the bullet's impact. Then he pushed me.

My stomach lurched up into my throat, feeling weightless as I teetered momentarily then fell from the edge of the bridge. My arms flung out, trying to grapple something but nothing was there to grab.

Air rushed all around, loud in my ears, making my hair whip around my face. I blinked up at the bridge, watching it grow more distant.

I imagined how painful it was going to be to hit the water. I wondered if there were rocks below me. I wondered if I wouldn't die right away but would instead get swept under those undercut rocks to drown in the dark water, my bones already all broken.

A wail of agony came from above—Caspian sounding as if he were being flayed alive.

A black creature shot up from the bridge, faster than anything I'd ever seen. Two great big wings tucked in close to his body as he started to dive.

Hope blossomed in my chest and I inhaled, my hands reaching towards the monster. He descended like a predator bird swooping in for its prey. His speed was impeccable. The sound of the river was growing louder, making every microsecond fill with more anxiety.

Mothman's arms slid around my body, pulling me into his chest—leather and smoke, his arms solid. He spun and swooped. I pressed into his body and wrapped my arms and legs around him.

His back faced the water, flying upside down. A hand came up and pet my head gently, dragging fingers almost shyly down my hair.

"You saved me," I said, pressing my face into his chest as he held me to him, flying. I was flying.

22

My breathing was sedated, calm. My eyes slowly followed Mothman flying away, out into the forest, swooping up and away with Ava clutched in his claws. Just a dark stain in the sky. Fucking bastard.

Someone was slowly writhing towards me, their body moving more like a worm than a man. I couldn't move much at all anymore as the person came closer. They hissed out as their face scratched into the pavement.

"Fuck, fuck, fuck," Brandon spat out, spittle flinging from his lips as he slid over to me. I sighed and looked up at the sky, watching Mothman circle around something in the distance. Brandon finished his way over and managed to maneuver up on his knees to look down at me. I shifted, going back to a man instead of a monster. A curtain rising back up to show the human he knew.

"What the fuck," Brandon huffed out like me shifting was a personal annoyance. He turned to look at the dead bodies, maybe checking they weren't about to leap up at him. The leader was face down, blood pooled under him.

The hunters were dealt with but now I had to go get Ava back from that other monster.

Except not right now. Right now, I needed to sleep. My eyes started to slide closed.

"Don't go to sleep!" Brandon growled out at me. His lip curled up in distaste as he looked over my body. He hobbled around so his back faced me then wiggled his fingers at me. "Untie my wrists before you pass out."

I blinked slowly then dragged my tongue over my lips. Finally, I flexed my fingers, making sure I could still move them.

"Closer," I whispered slowly. Brandon grumbled but managed to get the rope next to my hand. It took a while, pinching and pulling without any strength. I only had to get one loop loose enough for him to manage the rest. It wasn't a complicated knot.

He turned back around, rubbing his wrists and looking me over as if my chest were about to burst open and an Alien was going to shoot out at his face.

"What the fuck are you?" He asked. I didn't answer. I was tired, so tired. My eyes drifted shut.

I didn't sleep long. The tranquilizer shots were weak even by human standards. I think they had loaded up with darts intended for small animals, like raccoons. Maybe the stronger stuff was harder to get their hands on.

My eyes cracked open. I was in the passenger seat of a truck. Brandon sat next to me on the driver's side, gripping the wheel. We were still parked on the bridge and it was still night. The truck wasn't turned on.

Brandon looked like he'd aged. His eyes seemed sunken slightly into his head, his skin paler than I'd ever seen it.

My body was slumped, spread out across the bench seat. I pushed up but Brandon didn't look at me. His knuckles were white, gripping the wheel too tight. How long had he sat there like that?

"They're gone. Matthias—" he cut off, his voice choking as he said the name.

"How long was I out?" I asked. Brandon swallowed and seemed to come back to himself some.

"An hour, I think. I'm not sure. It took forever to drag your massive ass over. I tried looking for the keys in the... well no one out there had the keys I don't think. It was hard to search the bodies too much." His voice faded out then he peeled his fingers from the steering wheel and sagged in the seat. He dragged his hands down his face and wiped at some tears that had crawled from his eyes.

His face was red and puffy, the eyes bloodshot. Clearly, he had been crying. My teeth pressed together tightly in discomfort. His pain weighed on me. It was thick in the car. I didn't know what to do though. I wasn't the type to offer comfort to anyone but Ava.

My eyes slid to the scene outside the windshield. Grady was out there, along with the dead hunters. I noticed a puddle of blood with no body and lunged forward in the truck.

"Where's the leader?"

"What?" Brandon asked frantically, leaning forward. "He was there. He was dead! I looked in his pockets for the keys. He... *Fuck!*" Brandon snarled. He punched the steering wheel and a short honk blasted.

"We need to go," I said, reaching for the handle and opening up the door. I slipped out of the car. My leg muscles were loose and shaky. I swayed and my knees kept giving away as I took steps. I looked drunk but could at least stand up and move.

Brandon came up beside me, his head jerking back and forth, looking out for anything.

"Where did he go? He was right there. Did he fall off?" He finally asked, sounding hopeful as he craned his neck to peer over the edge of the bridge. I shook my head as we moved slowly towards the woods.

"No. A corpse doesn't heft itself off the bridge. Neither does a living man. He's alive," I said. Brandon slid his gaze to me and it stuck there as we moved off the bridge. I went the opposite direction of the trail, pushing into the forest towards where I'd seen Mothman flying.

"Where are we going?" Brandon asked, following without hesitation.

"Ava." Instead of arguing or asking for more details he just nodded. After a couple minutes of walking his energy began to deplete and the haunted look came back to his eyes. I didn't like it—knowing what the cause was. I wasn't going to hug him or say it was okay or anything but I could give him something to concentrate on that wasn't Matthias and the rest of the band.

"It's Mothman that has her," I said. His eyes widened as his attention snapped to me. I kept pushing through the forest. Something in my gut told me I was getting closer to her, going the right way. "He stole her from me," I said in anger.

"Fuck..." Brandon mumbled looking disturbed and confused. "He plans to uh... eat—"

"No," I snapped. I was still tired, my muscles burned from our walk. Off the trail was harder work. We stepped over fallen logs, shuffled through plants, and thorny vines snagged on us.

"I don't think he eats people. He doesn't look the type," I said in amusement, thinking back to when I beat him in a fight. Without his gun, he was just a furry fucker with wings. Brandon grimaced at the tone of my voice. His eyes sliding back to me in between watching his progress in the forest. I sighed.

"I don't eat people either."

"Of course not," he snapped in agitation but swallowed thickly afterwards. The sound of twigs snapped under our feet as we walked.

Loren was alive and out there. He wasn't going to just let this go. He very well could be following us. Actually, I expected he was. I didn't have the energy to deal with him though. If he was just going to slink around I'd let him for now.

Brandon and I had a little ways to go and I needed to reserve my energy, build it back up. My body was still sluggish, wavering around the woods. I had to reach out and use nearby branches as support to help my wobbly legs.

"I'm starving," I grumbled, thinking food might help me shake off the drugs faster. Brandon stiffened and I recalled what we just talked about. I laughed at him and after a moment he started to laugh too. We kept laughing until tears began rolling down his face and he had to suck back in his noises or else he'd start sobbing.

23

Ava

The air this high above the mountains was surprisingly frigid compared to the warmth at the ground level. I was a shivering mess, burrowing into the monster to steal body heat. Mothman's arms wrapped tighter around me when he felt me shaking. His hand gently pressed the back of my head, holding my face to his chest. I felt simultaneously cared for and concerned—unsure if this was comfort or restraint.

We didn't fly for too long but it felt like ages. All I could do was cling to Mothman while thinking about my numb nose and fingers. His wings were big, dark things that stretched behind him, making stars blink out of existence. The edges were tattered, lifetimes of wear to the scales. The wings were fuzzy, little soft hairs covering every part. Near the bottom, the design looked like two dark, red eyes—similar to his own eyes but larger and more menacing.

We began to swoop down and my stomach felt weightless, curling upwards in my gut. I clawed at Mothman's leather duster, my teeth chattering in my mouth as we descended. His hand trailed down my head and threaded through my hair several times. He was petting me, I realized.

His boots smacked onto a wooden porch. The old planks creaked in time to his shifting weight. I wasn't ready to process that I was with the monster in the woods. That he'd just taken me somewhere I didn't know. That Caspian was still on the bridge, along with Brandon.

Clawed fingers stroked my hair. Fear slunk up the back of my arms and tickled my neck. Now that the other dangers were gone, it came into clear focus that I was with something I had no clue about. I didn't know if it talked. I didn't know if it ate humans. I didn't know much of anything.

It had saved me more than once but there were too many unknown factors for me to feel entirely comfortable. I pushed away from him suddenly, backing up. My shoulders hit a door that swung open, creaking on its hinges.

I jerked my head around and realized I'd backed up into a small cabin. There was a battery-powered lantern hanging up on a shelf that illuminated the small but comfortable surroundings. It was furnished with dated, torn furniture—broken legs, ripped fabrics, stains. Most looked as if it had been fished from a trash heap. There was an ancient TV and a bookshelf filled with older movies. I could pick out the cover of westerns from the selection on the shelves.

When Mothman moved to come inside, he had to duck half a foot down just to fit through the doorway. He had to be seven feet tall. Caspian had been the tallest person I'd ever known and this creature was significantly taller than him. I backed up, his height and overall presence overwhelming me. My hip hit the edge of a table. A metal tea kettle fell over and cool water splashed over my clothes. The water did nothing to help the chill still seeped into my bones. It felt like it would take ages to ever feel warm again.

Mothman's strange eyes aimed at the kettle before his head shifted back up to look at me. I must have looked terrified. I felt terrified, clutching on to the edge of the table and shivering, my eyes wide. I wanted to run but I didn't know if there was anywhere to go.

He held up his hands as if trying to calm a frightened animal. I'd never seen skin so dark and each long, thin finger ended with a thick sharpened talon. He began to move his hands, making strong motions. He pointed at me then made a circle with two fingers before straightening them out quickly. He did it a few times with me watching wide-eyed and clueless.

"Is that... ASL?" I asked, looking quickly at the tv for a brief second. It was a ridiculous thought, but comforting to imagine he was trying to communicate. He nodded his head and made the motions again.

"I don't know sign language." My voice wavered as I talked. I wasn't even sure if he understood me but it felt better to at least pretend. His shoulders sagged and he stepped towards me. I gasped in shock and he froze up, his round eyes shooting to me as if *I'd* surprised *him*.

I edged around to the other side of the table, knocking into a chair as I went. He lifted his hands up and kept walking into the house, going over to a pen sitting on the couch.

My eyes whipped around the place. It was tiny, with two doors open. I could see a small bedroom and a half bathroom through the open doorways. I looked back at the open front door and wondered what would happen if I ran. A thick copse of trees hugged close to the cabin outside.

A notebook hit the table in front of me and I jumped up in surprise. Mothman stood on the other side of the table, his hands up, a pen hanging between two clawed fingers. I looked down at the notebook.

"*I'm not going to hurt you, Ava,*" he had written. My mouth cracked open. He *could* communicate. He even knew English! Which meant he was as intelligent as me. A being that could be talked to, reasoned with, and understood.

Also, he knew my name. Seeing it scrawled out on the paper in his handwriting felt surreal. I looked up and nodded at him. I believed his words. He'd had plenty of opportunities to hurt me and hadn't. He'd saved me numerous times. In the woods, on the bridge, and even catching me falling out of the sky.

He relaxed as I nodded, his hands going down to his sides and his shoulders evening out. I tried to look at his face but it was just dark. The collar of his jacket was flipped up high and his wide-brimmed hat blotted out any light.

"Thank you for saving me. You're... Mothman?" My eyes slid to his back. The wings were gone. The back of his duster had been modified so that there were two long slits down the entire back. His wings could burst from the openings and then tuck back in that way. I couldn't imagine being capable of flying whenever I wanted. I used to dream of it all the time as a kid, flying over the trees.

Questions began swirling in my head, a hundred all at once.

"Is this your place?" That seemed the easiest way to start.

He nodded in response to my question and I swept my eyes around the place again. This was the home of Mothman, a mythic monster. Honestly, I expected a gruesome cave like the park ranger had talked about. This place was simple—lots of wood, scavenged furniture, and overall a sense of quiet seclusion that felt almost depressive.

"Are those your movies?" I asked, tipping my head at the bookshelf. I was curious how he got electricity for the TV. Clearly, he wasn't hooked up to any electricity grids out here. Mothman nodded again, animatedly, like he was excited I was interested in him.

I started to relax more. This felt oddly normal, or at least not as if I were in a life or death situation. He picked up the notebook and began writing again. He walked around the table and handed it to me this time. I stood there, breathing heavily but took it from him.

"Are you curious about me? I'm curious about you." His hands came up slowly and settled on my shoulders. I dropped the notebook on the table and tensed as I felt the weight of his hands. He slowly massaged his fingers into my muscle before one hand slipped down my arm, trailing the length. He slid his fingers around my wrist, tickling the sensitive skin. I swallowed thickly.

"Have you been around many humans?" I asked. He lifted my hand and traced my fingers delicately. The thick, pointed talon that tipped his finger dragged gently over my palm. The skin tingled where he touched, the hairs on the back of my arm lifting up. He didn't answer me but instead kept exploring like he'd never seen a human up close. Maybe he hadn't. Maybe I was his first.

He dropped my wrist and brought both his hands up to my shoulders again, massaging the muscles slowly, watching to make sure I didn't act too frightened. I wondered what he thought of me, if he thought anything at all. I wondered why he saved me.

His thumbs began rubbing my collar bone, giving a deeper massage. Tension began to leak out of me and I relaxed into his touch. My strained shoulder ached but started to loosen. It felt good after what felt like hours of tension. I eyed the splinter for a moment. It was still there, just a stupid annoyance to worry about later.

His hands moved from my collar bones, going lower. My eyes widened as he trailed his fingers over my breasts. His head tipped to the side as if he didn't understand that part of me.

"Um," I started but then his big, dark hands were gathering up my breasts. He held them, squeezing and feeling while I sputtered on what to say. His thin, long fingers were gentle and appraising as he tested the weight and shape.

His thumbs rubbed over my nipples. I squeaked in shock as they pebbled in response, a prickling thrill I hadn't expected. Every nerve was on fire now. I could still feel the trails his claws left on my palm, the indents of his thumbs from when he massaged my shoulders, and every swipe he stroked against my chest. I stood there stunned by how I was reacting to his explorations.

He noticed my tension so he left my breasts alone. His hands dipped lower, smoothing over my belly and fanning out over my hips. I took a stuttering breath, trying to calm myself down.

"Can I do the same?" I asked, reaching out a hand towards his collar, aiming for where a jaw or neck might be. What was under his coat? What was under his hat? He didn't seem to mind at all as my fingers slid into his collar. Amazingly soft fur threaded between my fingers as I stretched up on my tiptoes to touch him.

"Wow," I sighed, feeling awed. Each thread of fur was so thin but as a whole was amazingly thick. My hand sunk into the texture. Mothman removed his hands from my hips and leaned over for his notebook, picking the pen up. I pulled my hand back and held it in a loose fist at my chest, savoring the soft texture of his body.

"*We have to take the wet clothes off so you can get warm,*" was written on the paper. The slight shiver in my body must have been apparent to him. What he said made sense but I didn't really want to do it.

"Can't we build a fire?" I asked, looking around for a fireplace. There wasn't one and I wondered if he ever felt cold with such thick fur. Instead of writing anything in response to my question, he just began to slide his claws under the bottom edge of my shirt. I felt them gently scratch across my tummy before warm palms pressed against my skin and began sliding up.

I sucked in a breath of shock as I felt his rough, calloused hands climb up my body. My eyes widened and I looked up at him in shock as he pushed my shirt up my ribcage. I was so taken back by the situation that I lifted my arms without complaint so that he could move the shirt higher up. His hands were so large. The fingers wrapped easily around each one of my arms, circling them as he moved the shirt all the way up.

There was a moment when the shirt hit my wrists that I grew concerned he'd suddenly stop, trap my hands, and bind my wrists like they'd been earlier tonight. A cold dread hit my stomach. He didn't though, didn't hesitate at all, just slid the shirt free from my body and draped it over the table's chair.

My arms wrapped around my body. The air wasn't cold but my body still was. I needed warmth. Clawed fingers slid back onto my skin, talons slipped into the top of my shorts, meeting at the middle. He tugged on the material in the center and I gasped as I lurched forward a step. His head tipped to the side, his glowing eyes on my face as his fingers slipped the button loose and tugged the zipper down.

My face must have relayed my quasi panic because he

tapped the notebook on the table where he'd written that my clothes needed to come off. I swallowed and nodded. I didn't feel like I could talk right now. This situation was odd. My body shouldn't have been reacting like it was, as if this were something sexual when it wasn't at all. He was just curious to touch me and trying to help.

With my shorts open, he dipped his fingers between the fabric and my skin. I stilled as I realized he'd slipped his hands into my panties too and was now slowly dragging them down my thighs. He went to his knees before me, his eyes burning at the area between my legs as he helped me step out of my wet clothes.

Mothman stood up and draped my clothes on the table. Which left me only in a bra, shivering in front of a seven-foot Mothman with his western garb and overwhelming presence. His glowing eyes burned into my chest as he began to reach for the bra but I shook my head.

"It's dry," I rasped out, twisting my hands in front of my hips. "Do you have clothes or a blanket or..." Or something? I felt so exposed, the air of his cabin touching nearly every bared inch of me.

He grabbed my hand and walked me over to the couch. I sat down, at least happy my ass wasn't on full display.

Mothman draped a blanket over my shoulders, making sure it covered me as much as possible. He straightened and mimed sipping from a cup. He also gathered all his fingers to a point and patted it above where a mouth could be.

"Oh!" I said, understanding. He was asking if I needed something to drink or eat. Honestly, that just made me think about how long I might be here. I wanted to get back to my car. I wanted to call the police and see Caspian. I wanted to call my mom and go home, stay tucked in with my family for months before leaving the house again.

My eyes felt wet as I started to think about what I'd been through. What Caspian's band had been through. Mothman dropped to the ground on his knees in a rush. He brought his hand up and caught a tear on my cheek, brushing it away. Then he got up and retrieved his notebook, writing something on it.

I tried to hold off the tears but they slowly rolled down my cheek. Sobs wanted to break loose but I couldn't do that now. First I wanted to get home, then I could burst open and deal with all of this.

Mothman handed me the notebook.

"*Don't cry. I can make you feel better. Is that okay?*" A monster was offering to make me feel better. It caused a laugh to burst from my mouth at the absurdity of it.

"Okay, I guess that's fine," I said, smiling at him. With that, he abruptly snatched the notebook from my hands and tossed it behind his shoulder. My eyes bulged at the brusqueness. He pressed his hands into my knees and slowly spread me open. My heart thumped wildly in my chest.

"I'm not sure about this anymore," I said in a rush of panic. His head shot up to me and then he shuffled to his notebook. He flipped it open, thumbing through pages, then he turned it towards me, showing me a drawing.

It was a moth sitting on a flower. Its long, tongue-like proboscis was nestled in the flower, drinking in the nectar. My mouth hung open in awe as I traced the edge of the paper. It was an amazing drawing.

"You drew this?" I asked and he nodded then pointed at the flower then towards my legs. My eyes widened in understanding. He thought I looked like a flower. He dropped the notebook and gently encouraged my legs to open again. I guess I could let him look for a moment. I could understand his intense curiosity.

I stilled in shock as something long and thin began to slide from his mouth in the recesses of his hat. It was pink and fleshy and so very, very long. My mouth dropped open as I watched it grow closer to me. Goosebumps broke out over my skin, my mind started to scream at me to run. *What was that?!*

It slid between my legs. My eyes dipped to the drawing on the floor and I sucked in a breath in shock.

"It's not really a flower!" I gasped. At the same time, his proboscis tongue latched on. It was warm, wet, and circled perfectly around my clit. Then it vibrated and sucked, tugging on the bundle of nerves.

An orgasm immediately barrelled into my chest, seemingly cleaving my soul from my body. I screamed from the intensity of it, the sound still raspy from overuse. My back arched and I lost my vision as I thrashed roughly with the most powerful orgasm I'd ever had.

I writhed, tears popped from my eyes, my insides violently clenched. The pleasure was almost too intense but his tongue kept sucking more pleasure from my body despite that. I suddenly gushed between my legs, warm liquid spilling out and a deep rolling pleasure accompanied the action.

A guttural groan rolled from my lips. I wasn't sure when it had happened, but now I was laying out on the couch, stretched out over its length. Mothman had moved over top of me, looking down at me from above. One knee was pressed between my thighs and his tongue-thing was long enough to stay attached to my clit as he hovered over me.

A wicked, demonic mouth smiled from the shadows of his hat. Wide, white teeth stretched across the entire length of his face. It was terrifying and yet my body kept seizing rhythmically in pleasure. I whimpered and clawed at the couch underneath me, I couldn't seem to find the urge to run from the terrifying creature. My instincts were weighed down by the satisfying pleasure blanketing my body.

"It feels so good," someone mumbled pathetically and I realized it had to have been me. The suctioning ended and all the tension left, leaving me feeling boneless. *Holy. Fuck.* My body gave a tremor in the aftershock of the orgasm. My insides felt tired from how hard they'd clenched.

A thick thwack bashed into the front door. Splinters of wood sprayed into the house as the head of an axe appeared. The axe sucked back out of the hole and then a human Caspian kicked in the door, his angry eyes settling on Mothman and me.

Horror splashed across Caspian's face. Then a deadly calm settled over him, chilling me to the bone. His body rippled back into monster form as his empty eyes settled on Mothman.

"You're fucking dead." The words were pulled through the teeth of his mouth, violent and deadly. A raspy hacking laugh, almost so deep in tone I could barely hear it, came jumping out of Mothman as he swung off the couch and stood in front of me. He faced Caspian with wide-spread legs and shoulders held back like he was proud.

Caspian stomped towards us, raising his axe, but suddenly cried out, dropping the axe and clutching his head. Mothman made that hacking, demonic laugh again.

"I'm going to peel the skin from your body and eat it while you watch," Caspian growled, grabbing his weapon again.

"No!" I gasped. My voice was still breathy, but loud. "He saved me, Caspian." I shook my head. He'd saved me more than once. He wasn't a bad guy. I owed him my life. Caspian looked over at me like I had two heads, his eyes bulging in disbelief. Then a violent shiver ran up his body as a look of hurt and panic flashed in his eyes. He gripped the axe harder, swinging it up and rushing at Mothman.

He yelled out as he rushed towards Mothman swinging the axe. Mothman jumped out of the way and the axe slammed into the small kitchen table. The piece of furniture had already been on its last leg so when the axe splintered its middle, it cleaved in two, collapsing in a mess on the floor.

"Caspian!" I called, grabbing my clothes that had been knocked to the floor and quickly sliding them back on. Caspian cried out in pain, one hand going to his forehead.

"Shut the fuck up," he hissed out as he charged at Mothman again. Mothman sighed and then pulled out his gun.

"No!" I cried out, flinging myself between them. I faced Caspian, cradling his face in my hands. His eyes stayed aimed at the other monster with murderous intent. His entire body was flexed for violence, ready at a moment's notice to take its opening.

He was still a monster as I touched him. His skin's texture felt different, almost rubbery. My fingers tickled the edges of his gills. His strange grass-like hair rested on my knuckles.

"Caspian, look at me." The tension was so thick in the air I could barely breathe, too worried we were a breath away from violence. I slid my hands down his chest then trailed them lower. My hands swept over his lower stomach then I moved to his hands. I touched the webbing between his fingers, rubbed gently on it in curiosity. His eyes rounded in shock and he jerked his attention to me.

God, I'd nearly lost him today. Nearly lost him and all he had wanted was for me to love him.

"I love you," I told him, tears burning my eyes. The axe dropped to the floor loudly as his large eyes darted back and forth between my own.

"What?" He asked, all the violence gone from his tone.

"I love you," I repeated, leaning into him, wrapping my arms around his body until I could feel the sharp dorsal fin at his back. "I love you so much, Caspian." He inhaled sharply and shuddered beneath my touch. His arms wrapped around me and he buried his face into the crown of my head.

"You really love me? You aren't just saying that?" He asked, his voice wavering in desperation. His needle-sharp talons dimpled my skin as he gripped me to him. "Even like this?" He whispered as his cheek pressed into my head.

"Yes," I said, clutching myself to him and never wanting to let him go again. He tugged me away from him and bent down closer to my height, looking me in the eyes. My gaze trailed over his gills, the long points of his ears, the abnormally large eyes with freakishly huge pupils. His lips were puckered slightly, pushed outwards because of all the sharp teeth hiding behind them.

My instincts rattled inside me, bucking for attention. I swallowed them down and held Caspian's gaze. My hand trembled as I reached forward, cupping his cheek in my hand. He leaned into it, his eyes hopeful.

"I love you," I softly said again and twin tears leaked from his eyes. A big breath rushed out of him, his entire body sagging as the tension left him. A small laugh of euphoria burst from his mouth, his hands stroking my cheeks. Then he seemed to remember everything else. His gaze and hands swept over me desperately, looking for any sign of harm or distress.

"Are you okay? Does anything hurt?" He even lifted the hair off of my neck and ran his fingers across the nape of my neck. He brushed his fingers through my hair, touching my scalp delicately.

"I'm fine. My shoulder is strained a little—" I was cut off as he saw the wound on my lip from when the door hit me earlier, in the bathroom when I was found. I pushed the memory away, hating how crisp the terror still felt

"When did this happen?" He snarled. His eyes shot above my head, flaring in hatred at Mothman behind me. "Did he hurt you?" The words fell from his mouth like a threat.

"No—"

"He was doing *things* to you." His eyes flared open wider as if just remembering what he walked in to see.

"Caspian, he didn't understand," I said, feeling awkward and embarrassed about the entire strange situation. Did Mothman even understand what had happened when I orgasmed? Caspian's eyes bugged out of his head then he shot a disgusted look at Mothman as he straightened up.

"He understands," he grumbled, eyes swiveling around the room. He saw the notebook and got it, flipping it open as he brought it to me. Mothman made an annoyed click noise in his mouth before he huffed and crossed his arms.

"He most definitely understands, Ava," Caspian said, showing me a drawing in the notebook. My eyes bugged as I saw a cartoon drawing of me crossed-eyed and drooling with my tongue hanging comically out of my mouth. Mothman gripped me from behind in the drawing, his wide smile drawn in. On the side of the drawing, he had written: "*save a horse, ride a cowboy*".

"Oh," was all I could say because what the heck was I looking at! I didn't even know how to grasp the wildly different perception I'd had in my head. Mothman reached over and pinched the notebook from Caspian's hands and stuffed it in a pocket of his duster.

"But..." I started, trying to find some explanation. Caspian lifted me up in a bridal hold as his body transformed in a mere half-second to look human again. The change rippled over his body in a wave.

He carried me outside of the cabin in his arms without another word. Brandon stood near the porch, his hands shoved in his jean pockets, his shoulders stiff as he looked around at the surrounding woods nervously. His eyes flipped to us as we came out.

"She okay?"

"She's okay," Caspian responded, looking down at me tenderly with a smile. "She loves me," he announced in a daze. Then he bent down and kissed me, a groan of satisfaction rumbling from his mouth into mine. "Ava," he mumbled between kisses. I clung to him, finally feeling completely safe with him here. Finally thinking I might be okay as his soft lips molded to mine. His tongue dragged across the seam of my lips.

"Uh..." Brandon responded awkwardly. The booming steps of Mothman came from the porch as he followed us out. Caspian twisted us to face him and I gripped his shoulders.

"Don't follow us! How many times do I need to tell you she's *mine*?"

"Caspian, I owe him my life," I pleaded. I looked back at Mothman's cabin and was hit with a sense of loneliness. He must always live alone and that felt depressing to me. Clearly, he craved communication and touch.

Caspian's lips slammed shut at my response and his face turned sour. He jerked away from Mothman and began stomping into the woods. He was clearly unhappy but didn't complain when Mothman followed this time. Instead, he just sighed but accepted he was here.

Brandon's eyes were saucers as he stood shocked in place, looking at Mothman. He sucked his lip into his mouth nervously then began to follow us.

"I can walk," I said.

"He'll grab you and fly off again," Caspian mumbled in agitation. Mothman shrugged as if that was a very likely possibility. Brandon shifted away from Mothman, even going so far as to stay close to Caspian despite knowing what he was. Probably hoping the monster he knew was better than the one he didn't.

"You sure he doesn't eat people?" Brandon whispered to Caspian.

24

Ava

The campground was on fire. The flames roared and cackled. Brandon looked haunted because he knew what was burning. The tour bus, our cars, our phones, all of our things... and the bodies of his bandmates.

There was no doubt that Loren was responsible for the fire because of the potent, eye-watering stench of gasoline wafting around us.

The weight of the catastrophe bore down on us as the light of day crawled up over the mountains. We didn't welcome it. The brightening sky felt like a cruel joke. Instead of promising us that things were about to get better, all it did was bring our horrible situation into the light. All it did was promise us that daytime wouldn't save us and that there was still more in store.

This fire meant we were now trapped in the woods, too far away to make it out in a single day. How many miles were between us and the nearest town? The highway? There was a madman on the loose--greedy and angry. We'd suffered through death and trauma but the fire told us it wasn't over yet.

It didn't matter that we were tired, hurt, and raw. *It wasn't over yet.*

"The ranger station," I said, turning to look at the others. Brandon kept looking at the fire as if he expected someone to come walking out. "We saw it when we drove in. Three miles before the campground," I said to Caspian. He was the only one paying attention. Mothman was stomping around, eyes scanning the woods, looking for signs of Loren.

"Good thinking," Caspian said, nodding. His arm slipped around me and he pulled me into him. He looked back into the fire. The flames had a way of pulling our attention, they danced, mesmerizing our worn out minds. Loud cracks echoed out from the fire and the loud bang of a falling tree made my heart race. This was on the verge of becoming a true forest fire. Someone would notice it soon, right?

"Your violin..." I said to Caspian. It had been a family heirloom, something so old they couldn't even be certain the year it was made.

"It was just a violin," he sighed before tentatively reaching for Brandon. His hand hovered over the other man's shoulder before he finally dropped it on to him. Brandon startled, turning to look at Caspian in shock. Caspian squeezed his shoulder then pulled back awkwardly.

I realized I'd never seen Caspian have any close friends. He was popular in school but he was the type that floated from friend group to friend group. There was never any depth to his socialization. Caspian wasn't exactly the charming, socializer with a heart of gold that I had imagined. Was he close to anyone other than me?

"We should go," Caspian said.

Something whizzed by our bodies, a tiny thing speeding

through the air and getting lost to the flames beyond us. A bullet, I realized.

Mothman ran towards us, his leather duster flapping behind him as he pointed off in a direction we should run. His red eyes burned, a static hiss in my mind kicked up before fading away again. I watched him run at us, my mouth cracking open and my heart thumping in my chest.

My shocked reaction was instinctual. He was just so tall and his body a mysterious hulk beneath his worn leather. He had wings, a frightening mouth, and talons on his long, thin fingers. The flames and approaching day lit him up, making it more than apparent he wasn't human. Only the shadows of night could fool someone into thinking that.

The monster won't eat you, I told myself.

Another bullet blazed by, snapping me from my reverie. A burning line seared into my arm. At first I thought the fire had somehow lept out and lashed at me. I looked down to see the skin on my upper arm cut into a straight line. Blood welled up inside the wound then began to trickle down.

"I was shot," I said in shock. Just barely, but I'd been shot. It took me back to that night at the concert. The chaos, the stampede, the blood on my face, the screams. Simon's face. Matthias' dead expression. My knees suddenly went weak, my heart uncomfortably fluttering fast and light in my chest. Caspian snatched me up roughly before I fell and took off behind Brandon.

We darted straight into the woods, heading the way Mothman had pointed out. Bullets bit into the dirt behind our heels like a ravenous animal snapping at our feet. I clutched onto Caspian while Brandon and Mothman ran beside us.

Caspian started to fall behind. Bruises were under his eyes and his arms were beginning to shake as he held me.

He was clearly exhausted from everything he'd been through. I shivered as I thought about the fight next to the river, when that man—dead now—had tried to kill him.

"Put me down," I insisted and he looked at me in concern but there was no choice; It was either put me down, or eventually fall over with me in his arms. He didn't stop as he moved me down and we ran hand in hand. A bullet hit the earth right next to me and a scream tried to burst out of me but my throat was still too ragged.

Ahead of us Mothman stilled at my raspy cry then swiveled around. We ran past him while he stood there, looking behind us towards the threat. I could hear Loren stomping behind us, reminding me of that night in the woods with the raccoons. *Stomp. Stomp Stomp.* Right behind me.

I shuddered in shock, realizing it may have been him that night. Caspian gripped my hand and kept dragging me forward as I paused to encourage Mothman to press forward.

"Mothman!" I yelled at him. What was he doing? He was standing right in the open. Any second a bullet could rip into him. Brandon yelled out in front of us, a vicious snarl of frustrated anger.

"It's a wall of rock!" He cried out, standing in front of a slice of rock that ran upwards a hundred feet and stretched in both directions. He yelled out in a rage and threw a fist into it. I sucked in a breath of shock. He gave an angry hiss of pain as he pulled his bloody hand back, looking no less pissed off.

Mothman pointed to his right, directing us while still facing the threat. We started to move in that direction, our hands brushing over the rock wall as we went. A bullet snapped off in front of us, spitting shards of rock out in an explosion. We jerked to a standstill.

The situation sunk in. We were trapped, standing in a line against a wall like prisoners awaiting execution.

That's when Loren finally came bumbling from behind the trees, a scoped rifle raised up, his eye staring down the long barrel. He still wore his ball cap but now it was drenched in so much blood that it dripped down onto his cheek and rolled into his neck. Despite the deep tan of a man who worked in the sun, he looked pallid. Dark bags were under his eyes and sweat beaded up everywhere on his body.

Something was clearly wrong with him. He staggered when he walked. His face was stretched into a smile that looked both pained but manic. His eyes were wild. The blood slipped from his ball cap again, sliding down his cheek like a tear. He reached up and tugged off the hat so he could swipe at the blood and sweat trailing into his eyes.

When his hat came off, I saw a fresh wound on the side of his head. It was ugly, biting straight through his skull and exposing a wet pink color underneath. A thick chunk of graying hair was missing. I jerked in disgust and my eyes wrenched away from the sight. Loren slammed his ball cap back on and readjusted his rifle to line up the aim.

"Think I'm that easy to kill?" He asked Mothman. A laugh rolled from him. He swayed on his feet then righted himself, taking a wide stance. This man wasn't normal, or at least it felt that way. It felt like he'd never die and instead would keep tormenting us over and over until he finally killed us all. Pick us off, pretend to die, come back and do it again.

"I'm not letting you go," he told Mothman. No one doubted him. Mothman was his white whale, his obsession.

Mothman was also his excuse to be the human monster he'd become. He had a rancid soul that wept putrid from behind his dead gaze. From the moment I first saw him materializing in front of me in that bathroom I could sense the stench of moral decay.

Mothman stood there with one hand near his hip, his fingers wiggling like he was in a showdown. My eyes bugged. Was he going to try and shoot first?

Caspian winced, grabbing his forehead.

"Are you okay?" I asked in a panic. He shook out his head and brushed off whatever pain he had.

"He said keep going. There's a cave."

"What about him?" I asked. Caspian sent a look over my shoulder to Brandon. "I'm not leaving him. He's kept me alive, Caspian. I owe him my life," I rushed out, swallowing down a bitter taste. My eyes kept flitting back and forth between Caspian and Mothman as anxiety began to itch in my gut.

Caspian grabbed my face and planted a quick kiss on my lips. I looked at him, his tired brown eyes, his black hair a matted mess. I just wanted this to be over. I wanted Loren to fall over dead, succumbing to his wounds. I wanted to see my family.

"Yes, he saved you and he wants to save you again." Caspian looked almost thankful, his eyes sweeping out to the other monster with appreciation in his eyes. "He wants you to escape." I shook my head. I didn't want anyone to get hurt or die. Mothman shifted slightly and a bullet bit into the dirt next to his boot.

"Don't move unless I tell you to," Loren grumbled, slowly crawling closer to Mothman. Now they were no more than ten feet apart.

Mothman made a quick grab for the handgun at his

waist as he rushed forward. Loren's rifle went off and I gasped but no one was hurt. Mothman had pushed the rifle barrel towards the sky. Loren dropped his rifle and reached out towards Mothman's gun, snarling. The handgun went off twice, wasted bullets shooting harmlessly skyward.

Caspian grabbed my hand and pulled me roughly in the direction of the cave. Brandon was right behind me, his hands on my shoulders, pushing me forward while Caspian pulled. They worked together to quickly move me forward. I watched as Mothman and Loren struggled with one another, afraid to see what was happening but too concerned to look away.

Mothman swung one leg up and snapped forward in a lunging kick that caught Loren hard between the legs. Loren wheezed and Mothman pulled back and slammed his fist into the side of Loren's head, right near the open wound. Loren's eyes widened and his body jolted like he'd touched an electric eel. He fell to his knees and Mothman kicked dirt in his face before grabbing his gun off the ground and squeezing the trigger.

It clicked, empty of bullets. Loren shook out his head, winced, then laughed as he reached out for his own rifle.

Mothman turned and ran towards us. His wings flung out and his boots lifted slightly from the ground as he whooshed forward, catching up in an instant. He pointed out a place on the rocks and we ran until we got there.

A cave gaped in front of us, cold, moldy air trickling out. It was inky black. A horrible feeling came over me and I gasped and reared back.

"No!" I cried but Caspian kept pulling, Brandon kept pushing, and Mothman grabbed my other hand and dragged me in. The splinter got irritated as Mothman grabbed the hand and my vision went white a moment as I sucked in a breath. Sweat popped up on my forehead from the sharp pain.

Still, my instincts bucked like an unbroken horse. Chills raced over me and I started to shiver again. My intuition was telling me to turn around running and screaming from this cave.

Once we were a few feet inside, my urge to flee settled down. There was no other choice but to move forward. I stopped putting up a fight and we began to walk into the darkness.

25

Ava

Loren could be heard near the entrance, growling and mumbling half-delirious. The red glow of Mothman's eyes were faint as we went in deeper. It was the only light I could see.

We twisted through blackness, walking blindly until Loren's growls and threats were a distant noise. The silence that followed felt eerie. The drip-drop of liquid echoed around us along with the echoing shuffle of our shoes. I was chilled again, unable to warm up. I shivered and closed my eyes. I couldn't see anything anyway.

I wanted to ask if we could stop. If we could go back out now but I was afraid that my voice would alert Loren which way to go.

We continued to walk in a line, each one of us touching and brushing against each other so we wouldn't get lost. Brandon had a strong grip on my forearm and never let go. Caspian clutched my hand to his chest, walking in front of me.

At first I figured he had to be gripping Mothman but then I realized he could probably see in the dark. He had

Run & Hide

those oversized eyes with the big pupils. My mind wandered, probably trying to concentrate on something other than the dark cave. I wondered how Caspian hid what he was for so long. I wasn't angry, I could understand why he did it. It just seemed such a strange life to live, continuously hiding what he was, having no deep connections. I squeezed his hand and he squeezed it back in the dark.

Red, glowing eyes swung around and looked at us. The sound of something scratching hissed in the dark and then a tiny flame ignited. Mothman held a match aloft, guiding it into an oil lantern. He lit it and adjusted a knob on the side.

The place brightened softly around us—still dim but I could see now. We were in a little cave room. There were things inside here—old wooden crates, a metal mining cart, a pick axe. Outside the opening to the room was a long tunnel. Left was towards the way we came and right went deeper in. Under the dirt floor in the tunnel, I could see the glint of buried metal. It appeared to be tracks for a mining cart.

Mothman set the lantern down near the wall and began moving stuff around. He seemed familiar with the place even though it was all coated with a thick layer of dust and dirt. He grabbed a green canvas sleeping bag, shaking it out and then laying it down near the back wall. He then went over to some wooden crates and collected some cans out of them. He grabbed a canteen hanging from a nail in the rock wall and shook it. Water splashed inside. He set it all next to the sleeping bag while I watched him. It was as if he was building himself a nest.

Brandon shuffled around, his eyes taking everything in. Caspian leaned back out of the cave room and peered down the tunnel both ways for a while, his eyes large and black.

A hand slid around my wrist and I startled. I looked up

to see Mothman gently encouraging me towards the sleeping bag. I followed him and he set me down on it. He rushed over to another spot and grabbed a worn blanket. He shook it out and dirt snapped off it. Once he'd cleaned it enough, he draped it over my shoulders.

Then, to my shock, he settled himself behind me. His long legs spread out on either side of my crossed legs. His body bumped against my back. Mothman tentatively brought his arms in closer, setting his hands on my knees. His fingers rolled in slow circles over my skin, playing with the crease where my leg was bent.

His warmth drew me in. My shivering body needed it and he was big and all around me, warming me up.

Caspian came stomping back in with a furious look on his face. Just then Brandon slunk to the floor, pressed his face into the rock wall, and started to cry. Caspian halted, looking like a deer in the headlights as he watched Brandon cry. His wide eyes swiveled around in panic. It was the only part of him that looked inhuman at the moment.

Mothman began to pet my head and made a little chirp noise in his throat, like he was pleased with me settling into him. Caspian shot Mothman a glare but then tentatively shuffled towards Brandon. A look of discomfort was barely contained on Caspian's face. He swallowed and bent down next to Brandon.

"Hey, um..." he started. Brandon suddenly reached out and grasped Caspian, holding him. Caspian crouched in wide-eyed shock, his arms held aloft like he had no idea what to do. Brandon cried against his chest.

"They're dead," he croaked before resuming his sobs.

"Yeah," Caspian commented forlornly. He relaxed and began rubbing the other man's back. My own eyes began to

Run & Hide

water too but then Mothman reached up and removed his hat, setting it on the floor next to me. I looked at it in shock, unsure if I should turn around and look at him. I gulped.

Soft fur began rubbing against the side of my cheek, Mothman rubbing his face against mine. His hands began rubbing up and down my thighs. I turned my head slowly to see the creature beside me.

Black fur was everywhere. I couldn't see a nose or mouth, just lots of fur and two red glowing eyes. At the top of his head two feather-like antennae stuck up. They moved, slowly swirling about. Then they pressed down to the back of his head as I looked at them with wide eyes.

Mothman brought his hand up then his long, thin fingers slid across my face, cupping my jaw as he looked me over. After a moment he made sure the blanket covered my shoulders then opened the canteen for me to take a sip. Caspian watched without expression, saying nothing as he observed Mothman take care of me. Brandon still clung to him but seemed to lack the energy to sob anymore. He slumped down and eventually fell asleep gripping Caspian's arm as if afraid to be left alone.

My head began to fall forward. Now that we could rest a moment, I felt exhausted. We all did.

"When will we leave? What happens next?" I asked with a sluggish voice, trying to stay awake as long as possible.

"Loren is still in the caves, shuffling about near the entrance. There's no way he can find us though. This place is a maze," Caspian said, confirming to me that he *could* see.

"So we're stuck?" I asked as Mothman gently traced his fingers up my arms. His warmth bled into my back and legs, making me even more tired.

"He's hurt badly. He can't stay out there for long,"

Caspian said, watching Mothman touch me. His face twitched and his jaw flexed. "Are you okay, Ava?" Caspian asked.

"I'm fine for now," I answered, then wondered what exactly he meant. Was he asking if Mothman was bothering me? Mothman leaned back against the wall and pulled me to rest on him. I wondered what it would feel like to rest my cheek on his fur. It sounded better than the leather. That didn't really matter when I was this tired though. It didn't take long to fall asleep, my eyes slowly closing as I watched Caspian watching me.

I WOKE UP, having no idea how long I'd been asleep. The lantern was still going. Caspian was asleep, slumped against the wall. Brandon laid on the floor next to him, his face relaxed as he slept. I started to close my eyes again when I heard it. It must have been what woke me.

At first I thought it was Loren and felt dread. The distant voice came again. It didn't sound like Loren at all. I moved off Mothman and he didn't stir. His eyes were closed and he didn't wake up when I shuffled off him and towards the tunnel. I grabbed the lantern and moved out onto the buried track, looking towards where we came. I saw nothing.

"Please, is someone there?" A faint voice came from behind me. Chills lifted on the back of my neck as I turned to look down the tunnel that went deeper into the darkness. "Please, I need help." I looked at the men sleeping and decided not to wake them until I knew something more.

I stepped further down the tunnel, not wanting my voice to accidentally wake them. Little rocks moved as I walked. I didn't go far as I lifted the lantern higher and tried to see anything in the darkness in front of me.

"Hello," I called. My voice whispered down the empty, black tunnel. I waited for a response.

"Hello?" Finally came back, almost an echo of my own voice. I swallowed and took a few more steps. The darkness in front of me was so thick the lantern didn't light up more than a few feet in front of me. It was just more of the same tunnel, nothing to see.

"Is someone there?" I asked.

"I'm stuck," the man's voice came. He sounded drained, beyond tired. "I was climbing... please," he begged. "Are you real?" He finally asked. His voice sounded faint, still far off. It echoed through the tunnel, bouncing off rock.

"I'm real."

"Please, I need help. I'm stuck." He repeated his earlier words almost in eerily perfection of the earlier tone. "Please, can you help me?"

"Yes," I responded, imagining a man wedged between rocks, the space too tight for him to get out. He must be in the dark, all alone. He could have been here for days. "We'll help you. It's okay now," I said, hoping to bring him some comfort.

"We?" He asked, his voice almost too curious as if he were less tired than he originally sounded.

"Yes, I'm here with others. We can help you. Just hold on." I started to shuffle back towards the cave.

"What's your name?" He asked. I stopped and looked back into the blackness.

"Ava."

"Ava," he sighed in relief. I started to shuffle back towards the cave again.

"Please," I heard called out. I stopped and looked

towards the voice. I swallowed, chills on my arms. The dark tunnel stretched blindly in front of me. "Please, I'm stuck. I was climbing..." he repeated his earlier words perfectly. I shuffled backwards slowly, not taking my eyes off the darkness in front of me.

"Please."

The sound of someone running made my heart lurk in my chest. *Stomp, stomp, stomp.* I was so concerned about the voice in front of me that I didn't realize the noise was coming from behind.

Stomping was right behind me and then a body crashed into mine. I went down to the ground roughly, all the air knocked from my chest. The lantern fell from my fingers. My cheek bit into rough gravel and my escaping breath unsettled the dirt. Immediately, I dug my fingers into the ground and pulled, trying to drag myself away from the body half on top of mine.

A threatening groan, more animalistic than human, rasped out behind me. I kicked and pulled, stretching and turning. Hands wrapped around my calves and I was flipped on my back, my shoulder blades sharply nestled into the mine cart tracks.

Loren looked up at me, so much blood dripping down into his face it was slipping into his mouth. His teeth were bared and bloody. His ball cap had fallen off when he crashed into me. I tried to scream but only a rasp came out. No one was coming, at least not fast enough.

The lantern's flame flickered dramatically as he began to crawl up my body. His eyes were wild and bulging. His gun was nowhere to be seen. He tried to fiddle with the knife holder but his fingers kept slipping off the pouch, unable to unbutton it. He grunted roughly in frustration.

I kicked at the ground, pushing my body upwards. He

didn't let me get far, sitting down on my legs and weighing me down. He huffed, his eyes closing. His body swayed and he had to prop himself with one arm as he tried to gain more strength.

His eyes tipped up to me and he snarled, wet blood staining his gums and between his teeth. Unless he fell over dead, I was going to die. Tears streamed down my face, my arms scratched at the dirt floor. My fingers bumped into something, the barest edge of something hard.

I sucked in a breath and tried to strain to grab it. My fingers wrapped around a wooden handle. Loren finally managed to pop the button on his knife holder. He smiled, dragging his tongue over his teeth, then spat blood. He had to swipe at his forehead and eyes to try and clear his vision of the smear of sweat and blood that ran in rivulets down his face.

He settled his fingers around the knife and everything inside me screamed. He lifted off my legs slightly as he pulled the knife above his head, ready to surge downwards towards me. I stretched to grab the wooden handle with both hands and then gave a raspy cry as I swung it like a club with all the strength I had.

My eyes widened as I saw I was holding a pickaxe and that it just sunk into the side of his head. He didn't make any noise at all, just froze up. I slipped backwards, quickly dragging myself from under him.

Finally, he began to make some noise, a hiccuping stilted cough. He staggered to his feet and swayed to the side. The lantern light shone on the pickaxe sticking from the side of his head, where the open wound had been. His back smacked the wall of the tunnel. I looked at him with my mouth agape in horror.

I started to shift back towards the cave on the opposite

side of the tunnel. Loren didn't seem to notice. His vacant eyes were aimed forward and his mouth was strained open as he continued to make that horrible hiccuping croak. His hands finally moved upwards and he touched the handle of the pickaxe.

The breath rushed out of me as I saw him grab it two handed and begin tugging.

"Don't," I begged, my voice a wharbled mess. He either couldn't hear me or didn't care. He pulled the pickaxe from his head in a sickening slurp. It came out almost too easy, confirming it had slipped right into the open wound and buried in as deep as it could go. The pickaxe dropped to the ground and his eyes flipped up to me. His face furrowed in confusion and he stepped towards me, reaching out.

I writhed against the wall, grabbing at the rocky surface as I quickly stepped away. One step, two step--he walked like Frankenstein, barely in control of himself. The croaking noise wouldn't stop either. He'd taken a moment to inhale but then the noise had come right back. I hated the sound. It grated at my nerves. I pressed my hands to my ears but it still wormed in my head.

He took one more step and collapsed. The sound finally stopped. The only noise now was my breath.

"I..." killed him. I swallowed thickly.

"Ava?" The stuck climber called. I swallowed again.

"We're coming," I croaked.

"Hurry," he responded. I grabbed the lantern and ran back to the cave. The guys suddenly jolted awake. Mothman looked at his empty arms in a panic. Caspian jerked away from the wall inhaling sharply. Brandon shot up, sitting upright on the ground. They all turned to me stumbling into the room before I dropped to my hands and knees on the floor.

Run & Hide

"Loren," I whispered. Mothman moved from the room in a blurred rush. Caspian came to me, wrapping me in his arms and squeezing. His hand smoothed down my back.

"What happened?" He murmured in my ear.

"He's dead," I said in a blank voice. My entire body was trembling. Mothman rushed back into the room and crouched down next to me. He must have seen what happened to Loren. Caspian jerked me away from Mothman. Mothman huffed and touched me anyway, petting my hair while Caspian rubbed my back. I allowed myself to briefly revel in the simple bliss of the moment before I sat up straight.

"There's someone trapped in the mine. We have to help him," I blurted. I said it as a settled fact, which in my mind, it was. I tugged myself from Caspian and Mothman's attention, looking around the cave for any helpful supplies.

"Now?" Caspian asked in disbelief. Mothman was still sitting on the ground next to him, looking as if he didn't plan to get up either.

"Yes. He's been stuck for a while. We don't know how bad it is." Caspian gave me an apprehensive look. Brandon got up quickly and started to help me look for anything useful.

"Stop being a selfish asshole. We aren't leaving someone here alone," Brandon commented.

"Wouldn't it be better to get the rangers?" Caspian countered, his large eyes flicking back and forth between Brandon and me. I shook my head. There wasn't time for that. It could take all day to get a ranger here and that was only if they had anyone to spare while dealing with the carnage and fire. We were here now and I wouldn't be able to live with myself if the man died because I wouldn't walk a little deeper into the cave to help.

Brandon and I found a few more canteens. He nodded at me and I took a deep breath, then we headed out into the cave.

"Wait! We're coming," Caspian called.

To be continued...

AFTERWORD

This book is part of the completed Myths & Monsters series.

Run & Hide - Book One

Hide & Seek - Book Two

Seek & Find - Book Three

Find & Destroy - Book Four (Novella)

Myths & Monsters Omnibus
All the books, plus bonus material.

ABOUT THE AUTHOR

Beatrix Hollow survives in a puddle of mud sometimes called East Texas. She writes morally questionable paranormal romance that frequently has horror themes. Sometimes there's even a strange kink and interesting appendage. She finds dark, steamy, and humorous themes fun.

She studied creative writing and psychology at Virginia Tech, used to be a professional ice cream maker, and enjoys looking at artwork of raccoons.

beatrixhollow.com

instagram.com/beatrix_hollow

Printed in Great Britain
by Amazon